Someone was  unbidden to her mind as a chill raced up her spine.

Without warning the river churned to life, bubbling over the wharf like a thick broth over the sides of an iron pot. Athena reared back, her hooves flaying the air. Isabel clung to the saddle as her heart hammered in her chest.

From out of the turbulent waters, a man dressed as a Highland warrior appeared before her.

Isabel's heart pounded as he turned slowly in her direction. She expected the man to transform into a dragon before her eyes. Moonlight spilled over him, holding him in its embrace. He reminded her of the Greek and Roman gods she painted at the artist's studio.

Startled by this creature, her horse reared up on its haunches and fought against its restraints. If it were not for Athena's response, Isabel would believe the man was only an illusion. A character ripped from the world of her fantasies and daydreams.

His eyes met hers and she thought her heart would stop beating.

Praise for Pam Binder

"Pam Binder gracefully weaves elements of humor, magic and romantic tension."

~Publishers Weekly

~*~

"Ms. Binder establishes herself as a powerful and inventive voice in paranormal romance."

~Romantic Times

~*~

"Between the covers, you'll find not only a hero, a heroine, and the villain found in most romances, but a truly delightful and heartwarming romance."

~America Online Romance Fiction Forum

~*~

"Action-packed and filled with romance and danger."

~ParaNormal Romance Reviews

The Immortal

by

Pam Binder

Immortal Warrior, Book 2

The Immortal

Cover Art by *Debbie Taylor*

The Wild Rose Press, Inc.
PO Box 708
Adams Basin, NY 14410-0708
Visit us at www.thewildrosepress.com

Publishing History
First Edition, 2022
Trade Paperback ISBN 978-1-5092-4097-5
Digital ISBN 978-1-5092-4098-2

Immortal Warrior, Book 2
Published in the United States of America

Dedication

To my father, Donald W. Pleier.
A great man who taught me the importance of family.

Prologue

The Present

A wildland forest fire in Montana was not the place to die. Molten-red and amber flames rose like a wall before William MacAlpin. They surrounded him in a smothering heat that promised death. Over an hour ago he'd smoke-jumped into this section to help rescue fellow firefighters, but time was running out. He didn't know how much longer the men and women would survive. He motioned for them to follow him through the inferno. It was their only chance.

William gripped his long-handled ax as he hacked his way through the choking underbrush and channeled his anger toward clearing a path through the flames. Anger pushed him forward, and frustration fueled his temper. As usual, the force of nature resulted in the loss of life.

He intensified his battle through the trees. William relished fighting any force that did not value life as he did. When he'd heard firefighters were stranded, he'd asked only one question: How long would it take for the pilot to drop him over the area?

A sapling fir tree sizzled into flames beside him. With one efficient swing of his ax, he lopped it in two.

William shouted over his shoulder. "Hang on everyone. We're almost home."

Shouts drifted toward him over the roar of the inferno. He saw a flash of yellow jumpsuits. It was a team of firefighters coming to their rescue. They cleared a path toward him.

A tree crashed and sent tremors rippling through the ground. In the next instant William and the firefighters he led broke free of the fire and headed for a clearing. The area was set aside as a temporary command post. So far the blaze was contained with a system of deep trenches. But if the wind changed, it would be a different story.

William slowed his pace as he reached the clearing. Removing his helmet, he wiped the sweat and soot from his forehead. It'd been a long day, but there was still work to be done. He'd take a fifteen-minute break and see where else he was needed.

He heard a dog bark, then saw it bound toward him, dodging and weaving around firefighters who tried to catch the animal. William grinned, pride swelling. His dog, Misfit, only allowed you to catch him if that's what he wanted all along. He and the dog were alike in that regard. Misfit was a mixture of golden retriever, German shepherd, and—William suspected—wolf. The animal had followed him home one day and refused to leave.

William smiled as the dog leaped toward him. "Well, Misfit, you're a welcome sight. I'm glad Murphy let you loose."

He heard his name shouted over the crackling of the fire. It was Murphy, the pilot who'd flown him to the rescue site.

Murphy skidded to a halt. "Hey, pal, don't be blaming me. Misfit just showed up here dragging what remained of his chain behind him." Murphy scratched Misfit behind his ear and changed the subject quicker than you could say wildfire. "That was the last of the stranded ground pounders. Doc said you got them all out in time. Smoke inhalation and a few burns but they'll be as good as new in a couple of days."

William ordered Misfit to settle down even though it was like trying to contain a two-year-old in a toy store. He didn't like the idea that Misfit had pulled loose from his constraints. The dog only did that when there was an intruder. He'd better check out the place he'd rented before returning to the fire. Heat from the flames and the Montana sun cooked the air. William almost missed the rain. Almost.

He reached for the canteen of water Murphy offered and took a long, refreshing drink, pouring some in his hand for Misfit. "That's good news about the firefighters. Any word about the weather?"

"We caught a bit of luck. There's rain on the way, and the Chief says that will help our efforts to contain the fire." He paused and slapped William on the back. "The Chief will want my head on a platter when he finds out I dropped you in that sector by yourself. You're one crazy Scotsman. Why didn't you wait until we could form a rescue team? I know you like to work alone, but you can't put this fire out by yourself."

"There wasn't time. We received word a crew was stranded on the North Slope and the wind was kicking up. If I'd waited, they'd all be dead."

Murphy removed his baseball cap and rubbed his head. "Just be careful. I've lost too many friends to that man-eating beast, and you know how I hate picking out sympathy cards. You may act like you're as bulletproof as a superhero, but when you're dead, you're not coming back." William fought back a smile. He was closer to a mythical character than his friend realized. Both he and the man of steel lived a double life.

Misfit tugged on William's sleeve as though trying to pull him away from the conversation. Dark foreboding curled around him like billowing smoke. His dog acted this way with only one person—his uncle Gavin MacAlpin.

William wiped the sweat from his forehead again and headed toward his Jeep. "Hey, Murphy, I should take Misfit back home. I'll be back to relieve the next shift."

"Take your time. It's under control."

Murphy's words drifted on the roar of the wildfire as William dumped his gear in the back of his Jeep. Misfit bounded into the passenger's seat. The dog seemed eager. William hoped it was because Misfit was anxious to go home, and not because they had an unwelcome visitor.

William started the engine and began the climb up the road leading to his cabin. It was only a couple of miles away, safe from the fire's wrath but not the smoke-and-ash-clogged air. Misfit's tongue lolled on the side of his mouth as he breathed heavily. The animal was uncharacteristically quiet. William resigned himself to the fact that someone was waiting for him.

When William finally turned down the gravel road leading to his cabin, he was not surprised to see a silver sports car parked by the front door. One thing was certain—there was no way he was going to let his uncle draw him in again. William was out of the business. Let the young idealists fight the battles. He'd done his part.

Out of respect for his mother, however, he would hear the man out. She was Gavin's, as well as the legendary Lachlan MacAlpin's, sister. William parked his Jeep in the driveway. Before he'd turned off the ignition, Misfit bounded out the open window and relieved himself on the tire of his uncle's car.

William slid out of the Jeep and smiled. "Good boy. Couldn't have said it better myself."

His uncle Gavin was leaning against the doorframe of the cabin with a scowl on his face. His arms were folded across his chest. The dark suit and gold wristwatch he wore cost more than William's income for a year, maybe two. It was a lifestyle William had rejected long ago. Some said Gavin used to rebel against any type of authority before he took over his position on the Council. William believed it was just propaganda, created to try and breathe life into the well-dressed statue standing before him.

Misfit growled, and the hackles on his neck bristled. Gavin arched an eyebrow. "Your dog doesn't like me."

"What's to like? You send people to their death."

Gavin's scowl deepened. "You know it's against the rules of the Protectors to own a pet."

William clenched his jaw. "So I've been told. You let yourself into the cabin, I see."

"It was unlocked. You shouldn't be so trusting."

"I'm trying something new." William stormed toward his uncle, taking pleasure when the man stepped aside to let him pass. Gavin must be desperate. Good. Then he wouldn't· be disappointed when William turned him down. Misfit followed close behind, a low growl expressing his own opinion of Gavin.

5

Entering the small, one-room cabin, William headed over to the sink and jammed a metal bowl under the faucet and filled it with water. He set it down for Misfit and leaned against the counter, trying to control his growing impatience.

"Montana's a long way from Scotland. I must be your last resort."

Gavin strolled over to him and picked up a long cardboard tube. "You haven't opened your birthday present from Angus."

"I've been around a hundred years, give or take a decade. I don't open birthday presents anymore."

Gavin rested the tube against the wall. "Fair enough. I also noticed you don't have much in the way of food. Your dog eats better than you do. Did you give up food as well?"

"You didn't come here to discuss my eating habits or whether or not I open my gifts."

"As always, you're not much on small talk." Gavin shrugged. "I'll get to the point. Bartholomew's escaped back in time to the sixteenth century. Among other things, our informant tells us that Bartholomew plans to change history."

William whistled through his teeth. "I remember reading the man's file. A real deviate, but Bartholomew usually hires others to do the really dangerous stuff. The man once vowed to seek revenge against Lachlan for killing his brother. You should have let Angus behead him when he had the chance."

"That's not our way."

"The hell it's not." William pushed away from the sink. "Don't give me the company line. Our people are obsessed with death. A doctor would have his work cut

6

out for him trying to psychoanalyze our people. We spend more time obsessing about death than humankind."

Gavin's voice was as bland as his suit. "I can't argue with you on that score, but the fact remains that Bartholomew has escaped, and the Council feels you're the best one for the job."

William's laugh was hollow. "Too bad you've done away with the old custom of forcing a Protector to take an assignment."

"That's not exactly true. There are always special circumstances. You can't hide out here forever, William."

"I'm not hiding. I'm saving lives, making a difference."

Gavin combed his fingers through his hair. "John's death wasn't your fault. He knew the risks."

"I cut off the man's head. How can that not be my fault? This is crazy. I want you to leave."

"You were acquitted by the Council of any wrongdoing. William, you were trained since birth as a Protector to uphold our laws, and you are the best we have. You're also a master at blending into your surroundings. John disobeyed orders, and you did the only thing you could. You followed yours."

"That's why I quit. I was too good at letting you people tell *me* how to think. How to feel."

Gavin's expression darkened. "Your demons are not mine to fight. Besides, this time there's more at stake than just a code violation. I've brought along Bartholomew's file—"

William interrupted. "I read Bartholomew's file when he was first imprisoned. It doesn't matter. You're not listening. I'm not interested."

Misfit padded over to the door and barked. "Need to go outside, boy?"

The dog barked again as though in reply.

William walked over to Misfit, promising himself that as soon as Gavin left, he was going so far undercover that no one would find him. He didn't understand why they wanted him so badly anyway.

William opened the door for his dog and watched as he raced toward the fir trees, no doubt hot on the trail of a fat squirrel.

Gavin had moved to stand beside him. At least part of what William had heard about his uncle was true. Gavin was as silent as a cat, and probably just as unpredictable.

Gavin twisted his gold watch around his wrist. "William, have you heard a word I've said?"

"Yes, unfortunately. Why not let Bartholomew change history? Maybe his version will turn out better."

"The last time something of this magnitude occurred, it resulted in a small ice age in the Middle Ages. We were able to bring things back to normal over a period of a few hundred years, but this time it might not be so simple. If we don't stop Bartholomew, the ripple effect might result in the same catastrophe that sank our Island home."

William wondered what was taking Misfit so long. He left the door open for the dog and crossed over to the kitchen. "Still not interested. I quit the Protector business. Remember?" William filled a pot with water and put it on to boil. "Want dinner?"

Gavin grimaced. "Instant macaroni and cheese? I'll pass. Our informant didn't know who was behind it, but he could tell us that Bartholomew was given instructions to use the Elixir of Life to try and extend the life of Queen Mary the First, preventing her half-sister, Elizabeth, from ascending to the throne."

William dumped dry noodles into the water. "You mean old Bloody Mary? Wasn't she the one who wanted to reinstate Catholicism and liked to burn Protestants at the stake?"

"One and the same."

William tossed the empty box of noodles in the trash under the sink. "Aside from the persecution of innocent people, what is so significant about extending her life?"

"Keeping her alive will unsettle an already unstable Europe, making it easy pickings for the Renegade Immortals. The world will be plunged into chaos, making the Dark Ages look like the Age of Enlightenment."

"I still don't know what that has to do with me." The water came to a rolling boil. "Why don't you or Lachlan take care of this mess?" William took the pot off the burner, splashing hot water over his hand. "Damn."

"Lachlan's not available, and I'm needed to investigate another problem. Besides, lad, this is a job for a Protector."

"You should have saved yourself the trip. I'm not going."

"I was afraid you'd say that."

Gavin crossed over to the open door and waved his arm. William heard footsteps over the gravel driveway and sprang into action, grabbing Gavin and putting a kitchen knife to his throat. "Okay, Uncle, who are your friends?"

"Easy, lad. That knife's cutting into my flesh."

"It will slice clean through your neck if you don't answer my question."

Gavin nodded toward the open door as the men crowded around the entrance. "They're here to persuade you to take the assignment."

"You might as well signal them to start the bloodbath, because you still haven't given me a reason that will convince me to drop everything and travel five hundred plus years into the past."

"Bartholomew's a coward. It's never been his style to take his enemies straight on. He likes someone else to do the dirty work. As an added bonus, and with Bloody Mary in his power, he will systematically have all of Lachlan's relatives murdered. A fitting revenge for Lachlan killing his brother, don't you think?"

William eased the knife away from Gavin's throat. "Okay, so you have my attention. Who are Bartholomew's first victims?"

"Your parents."

Chapter 1

"This time will be different."

Flames from hundreds of candles flickered over the artist's studio where Isabel de Pinze painted. She said the words aloud again, but with more conviction.

"This time I will create a masterpiece."

She was one of the few who remained this late at night. However, unlike the other artists, her dedication had not borne creative fruit. Isabel stepped back from the canvas and proclaimed it a failure. She rubbed her wrist. It ached from long hours of painting. She would welcome the pain if she achieved her goal. But it was not to be. No matter how hard she worked, she found it difficult to breathe life into the image on the canvas.

A likeness of the god Poseidon stood on the ledge of a cliff overlooking the ocean. It was to be part of a collection given to Queen Mary in celebration of her renewed good health. The physical proportions of the mythical god were accurate. The colors of the raging sea and storm-fed sky were realistic. It was the soul of the painting that was missing.

She yanked her splattered smock over her head and tossed it over a chair. The smell of paint assaulted her senses. Normally, it was a fragrance more pleasing to

11

her than the queen's most precious French perfume. But in the lengthening hours of the night, it caused tears to brim in her eyes. At five and twenty she had avoided offers of marriage and a secure life in order to follow a dream she now believed might elude her.

Paulette, her friend and mentor, walked over and picked up a silver-gray cat, stroking the soft fur. Paulette's hair was autumn red, and she wore a formless, sun-bright gown.

She smiled. "It grows late. I have ordered your horse be brought to the front entrance." Paulette nuzzled her face against the cat's head. He purred contentedly in her arms. "Puck is the most affectionate cat I have ever seen. He is still grateful to you for rescuing him from the alleys of London." Puck purred again as though in response, settling in Paulette's arms. She paused. "What troubles you, lass? I have never seen you look so discouraged."

"I lack talent."

Paulette laughed. "Now I know you will succeed. You speak like a true artist, not satisfied until you have created perfection. Mayhaps painting is not where your talents lie."

Isabel sighed. "It was no better when I tried to sculpt." She placed the protective cover over her portrait. "What I seek eludes me. I wish to capture what you and Ossian do so effortlessly. The people you create look as though they could walk off the canvas and speak."

"Ah, but to achieve the level of awareness you seek you must always—"

Isabel interrupted her. "Suffer? Please do not tell me I am too young, or that if I was born ugly I would understand life's mysteries."

Paulette laughed again. "No, that is Jardin's philosophy, not mine. She is a bitter woman, but that is a story for another time. Your talent will awaken you to new levels when you begin to take the time to laugh and enjoy the world around you. You are much too serious, Isabel de Pinze."

Isabel had heard this argument before, but she disagreed with Paulette. There would be time for laughter when she achieved success as an artist. Until then the only path toward her goal was hard work. She turned and put the thick wool cloak around her shoulders.

"I know you mean well, Paulette, but the portrait of Poseidon is lifeless. I may just lack the talent to go further. Thank you for having my horse brought around. It is time I returned home to the manor. Myra will be worried."

Without waiting for a response, Isabel hurried out of the artist's studio and into the cool night air. Her horse, Athena, was waiting for her. She patted the animal's soft, sleek mane and whispered a greeting. Isabel mounted with the ease of someone who had spent her childhood riding horses, and she turned Athena in the direction of the manor.

Her horse's hooves echoed over the deserted streets of London as she sped along the perimeter of the Thames River to the manor house near Hampton Court. The full moon was hidden behind dark clouds, and a light dusting of snow began to fall.

She shivered and drew her cloak tighter around her shoulders as an icy wind blew her hair free of its braid. Isabel could never remember a winter so cold. What was more, there was a stillness in the air, as though the world waited in anticipation.

She brushed the dark foreboding aside. She had little time for such foolish thoughts. Just the same, she rested her hand on the dagger strapped to her waist, feeling the strength of the blade seep through her. In the last four years she had never been without it. And tonight, she was grateful for the gift.

The dagger had been a present from Angus and Myra on her twenty-first birthday. They were two loving people who had raised her as their own when her parents had been killed on a battlefield in Scotland. The blade was meant to keep unwanted suitors at bay. The cold steel gave her comfort. It had worked well. A husband would not understand her desire to become an accomplished artist, a profession dominated by men. Her dream was too important to leave in the hands of someone who might disapprove.

Although it was not unusual for Isabel to ride alone, it was after midnight and Myra would be concerned for her safety. Isabel urged her horse into a faster gait as she turned down a narrow alleyway. Wood buildings stood like silent guards on either side of the road as the street veered closer toward the water. This route was a shorter distance to the manor and would save her time.

Isabel sighed. She tired of her double life. By day she was one of hundreds of servants who attended to the needs of the court of Queen Mary I of England. During the day, as Isabel assisted Myra in the cookroom, Isabel's waist-length black hair was secured at the nape of her neck and her figure was hidden under layers of garments. At Hampton Court her identity and desires were of no consequence. It was only at night, when her duties were accomplished, that Isabel felt really alive and free to explore the world of an artist.

The silence pressed around her on the road leading toward the manor. She was not used to the solitude. Her life on the fringe of court meant people always surrounded her. Her horse, Athena, tossed its head as though reflecting her unease.

Suddenly, Athena came to an abrupt halt near the wharf and pawed the ground. The horse's hooves scraped on the cobblestones and the action vibrated through her. It jangled her frayed nerves. Why had her horse stopped? It was not like Athena to act so skittish. Isabel bent down to comfort the animal, then straightened in her saddle and looked around. All appeared quiet, too quiet.

The moon crept out from behind the clouds and shone on the ebony waters, spreading its silver glow in ever-widening circles. Waves lapped against the wharf and foamed around the pilings. Someone was coming. The thought sprang unbidden to her mind as a chill raced up her spine.

Without warning the river churned to life, bubbling over the wharf like a thick broth over the sides of an iron pot. Athena reared back, her hooves flaying the air. Isabel clung to the saddle as her heart hammered in her chest.

From out of the turbulent waters, a man dressed as a Highland warrior appeared before her.

Isabel's heart pounded as he turned slowly in her direction. She expected the man to transform into a dragon before her eyes. Moonlight spilled over him, holding him in its embrace. He reminded her of the

Greek and Roman gods she painted at the artist's studio.

Startled by this creature, her horse reared up on its haunches and fought against its restraints. If it were not for Athena's response, Isabel would believe the man was only an illusion. A character ripped from the world of her fantasies and daydreams.

His eyes met hers and she thought her heart would stop beating.

He walked toward her. She noted the colors of his plaid were muted by water and shadows. Damp hair grazed his shoulders, and his eyes were dark and intense. The stranger reached the shore and rested a hand on the hilt of his sword, surveying the docks with an air of authority.

Isabel's pulse rate jumped another notch just as Athena became calm. She patted the horse on its neck, more for herself than Athena. The stranger moved silently in her direction, his gaze never leaving hers. Her throat was dry. It was impossible to breathe. Was this how an animal felt when it was being stalked?

Isabel pulled on Athena's reins and dug her heels into the horse's flanks, but Athena did not move. The horse was as bewitched as she was.

Unable to retreat, time seeming to slow, Isabel recalled childhood stories of fire-eating dragons and men and women who lived forever. Shape-shifters that could change their form at will and sorcerers who could paralyze you with a glance. She gripped the dagger, wishing Angus had given her a sword in its stead. She could be dragged to the Otherworld by this creature, never to be seen again. She willed the mad thoughts from her mind. She should dismount and run, but curiosity and something she could not identify prevented her from leaving.

The stranger paused in his advance, drawing his sword from its scabbard in one fluid motion. The blade glistened like molten steel in the moonlight and sent shivers through her.

Now she would die. And still she could not move.

Chapter 2

A battle cry split the air.

Isabel glanced over her shoulder and saw shadows take form and spring to life. Four men descended on the stranger, their swords arched over their heads as they ran past her. The sound of metal striking metal rose above the pounding of her heart. Fire-red sparks flew from the steel of the men's blades as they attacked.

The stranger was outnumbered. From the recesses of her memory a nightmare emerged. She had been too young to remember the details of the night her parents had been ambushed and killed, but two things were forever etched on her soul—she had never driven the thoughts of betrayal nor the smell of death from her mind.

She ignored reason and pulled her dagger from its sheath. It was inadequate to the task that lay before her. It did not matter. She could not stand by and watch a man die.

Isabel dug her heels into her horse's flanks, and this time Athena bolted forward. They leaped into the fray. Athena's hooves echoed over the cobblestones as the horse shortened the distance that separated Isabel from the battle.

Already two of the assailants lay in a pool of blood. A red stain seeped into the porous ground. The attack raged on. Suddenly one of the men turned on her. His eyes mirrored death as he grabbed the reins of her horse. Athena's nostrils flared as she whinnied in protest, trying to pull free from his grasp. Isabel tightened her grip on the hilt of her dagger and stabbed him in the shoulder. The blade sank into flesh. Isabel swallowed the taste of bile in her mouth as she fought to stay on her horse. The shock of what she had done flowed over her. She had never used her weapon before on human flesh.

Her assailant growled in pain and yanked the dagger from her. He held fast the reins of her horse. With his free hand he reached for her arm and dragged her to the ground. His fingers formed an iron grip around her wrist. Panic raced through her as she fought to pull free of his grasp.

In the next instant the man screamed as he was jerked away from her. His arms flapped in the air like those of a puppet on a string. Someone stood behind him with a knife to his throat.

With a flash of steel, the stranger sliced her assailant's throat. The man crumpled to the ground.

Just then, Athena's eyes widened. She reared on her haunches. Isabel tried in vain to bring the frightened horse under control. Athena was not a warhorse, and Isabel suspected the violence and death had unnerved the animal.

The stranger reached over and grabbed the reins. He stroked Athena's neck, quieting the animal.

He turned toward Isabel. Silence lengthened like the shadows over the dock as she gazed into his eyes. This man had conquered his assailants in one moment and tamed her horse in the next. Isabel was right to compare him to the heroes of her childhood.

Her mind raced. She had no idea how he came to appear from the river. It could not be magic. There must be a rational explanation. After all, this was the sixteenth century, not the age of Merlin and King Arthur. Perhaps a boat was anchored beyond her vision and the man had swum to shore. Perhaps he was a thief, or here to meet a woman. Endless possibilities coiled around her in an ever-tightening grip, but one fact remained. She had never seen anyone like him before.

Her voice was whisper soft. "Thank you, sir. You saved my life."

His smile stole her breath away, and she forgot her apprehension.

He smiled again. "And you saved mine. I was outnumbered, and you distracted one of the men long enough for me to gain the advantage." He bowed slightly. "I owe you my life. Most people would have looked the other way." He reached over and touched her face. His eyebrows drew together. "You're bleeding."

His touch sent warm shivers through her. Confused by her response to this total stranger, she backed away. "You must be mistaken. I am sure I was not injured."

He stared down at the smudges on his fingers. "Paint." He smiled. "It's just paint."

"I am an artist." She wished her voice had not sounded so uncertain.

"A woman painter in the sixteenth century? Impressive." His eyes reflected a deep yearning and then, as though by magic, the vulnerability she had seen faded, replaced by a rebuff. "You could've been killed. Wait here until I've finished disposing of the bodies. There could be others, and it's too dangerous for you to be here alone."

He sheathed his sword and began to slip the bodies into the river one by one. She gripped the reins of her horse, not certain why she stayed as he bid. She should fear for her life. He was a skilled killer, dispatching those who attacked him with ease. For some reason she did not fear him. She would be dead now, she reasoned, if he meant her harm.

From his brogue, he was a Scot, although the lilt was not as strong as Angus's and was laced with an accent she did not recognize. Well, knowing he was from Scotland explained his fighting skill. Perhaps he was a spy.

There was an uneasy peace between Scotland and England. The smallest event could ignite a war. Angus was tolerated at Hampton Court only because he was a merchant and brought exotic spices and silks from Asia. The stranger would be a different story.

The man turned from the water's edge and walked toward her. She noticed his unsteady progress as he drew nearer. Something was wrong. His face was contorted in pain as he grasped his side and slumped to the ground. Blood seeped through his fingers, and color drained from his face. For the first time she noticed he was injured and bathed in blood. A deep gash sliced through his shirt to the flesh beneath.

Dropping Athena's reins, she rushed to his side and heard a voice of warning in her mind. *Do not be concerned with this man. You do not know him.* Isabel ignored the words. He was injured. She would not leave him.

His eyelids drooped, and his breathing came in ragged gasps. He seemed aware of her inner turmoil. "I won't hurt you. My name's William." His voice trailed off with the wind. "I need your help."

The tone of his voice made him sound more human.

Her heart softened. "I am Isabel."

He clenched his jaw and shuddered. "I don't know how long I can hang on." He took a shallow breath of air.

His blue eyes were a stark contrast to his dark hair, and their intense gaze jolted her. His features were chiseled, and his muscles clearly defined through his wet clothes. She counted to ten in Italian and tried to bring reason back into play. Just because his appearance robbed her of breath did not mean he was not dangerous. She paused. Or maybe it did.

However, he had asked for her help.

Myra often scolded her for bringing home stray and injured animals, and as a result they had a menagerie of dogs and cats. There were even some at the artist's studio. She wondered how Myra would feel about her bringing home a man.

He tried to stand. The effort caused him to wince in pain once more. Isabel was certain he would not survive alone. He had saved her life. She could not leave him here to die. She strengthened her resolve and wrapped her arm under his shoulder, trying to pull him to his feet. He was heavy. It was like trying to lift a marble statue.

William was a foot taller than she and built as though he were indeed chiseled out of stone. Her legs and arms shook from the effort to help him stand. Warm blood spread over her arms from the wound in his chest. Even if she did manage to hoist him onto her horse, there was no guarantee he would survive the journey ahead.

He slipped out of her grasp to the ground. She paused for half a heartbeat. She had to stop the flow of blood or he would die. She peeled back the hem of her skirts and tore strips of cloth from her linen sheath, winding them tightly around his chest. He moaned as she cinched them in place.

Snow began to fall again. She shivered and turned toward the sky. A storm was brewing. She had to get him to the manor. The pallor of his face had grown as white as the bandages, and he mumbled in a language she did not understand. She sensed it would not be long before he escaped into unconsciousness.

She turned his face toward her. His skin was cold to the touch. Odd that it should happen so quickly. "William, you have to stand. I lack the strength to lift you by myself."

He nodded and raised his head. "Why are you helping me?"

Isabel looked into his intense blue eyes and wished she knew the answer to his question. She whispered, "I am not sure."

His gaze held hers. Isabel's pulse rate increased as her lips parted. He moved closer to her. She could feel his warm breath on her skin. As though in slow motion, he reached for her and drew her toward him, kissing her on the mouth.

Her senses reeled. It was as though she had stepped too close to a blazing fire. Heat poured from him until she felt her skin would ignite into flames. Reason fled. All that remained was the feel of his lips on hers. The kiss deepened, exploring, questioning. A groan escaped from her lips—or was it from his? His hand was at the back of her neck, drawing her to him. She came willingly, wanting to feel him, taste him.

Then as quickly as the kiss began, it ended.

He pulled back from her, taking the warmth with him. She could still feel the imprint of his lips and the passion they'd unlocked. She shivered from the absence of his touch and tried to block out the need to lean back into his embrace. She stole a glance at him. He looked as startled as she felt.

His body shuddered as he leaned against her to push himself to a standing position. "You smell so good." He paused to look at her. "I kissed you. I'm sorry, I don't know why I did that."

Isabel ignored the way her pulse raced when he spoke. "You are injured and not thinking clearly."

His voice was low. "No, that's not it."

"Perhaps in your pain you became delusional and believed I was your wife, or—"

"There's no one in my life."

He leaned more heavily against her. "Why aren't you frightened of me?"

She was surprised by that fact as well. "You do not look so fierce right now. Rather helpless, actually."

He laughed and then winced. "Oh, that hurt." He glanced in the direction of Athena. "Do you think your mare can carry us both? I need to get someplace safe where I'll have time to heal."

Isabel nodded. "She is stronger than she looks."

He pressed a kiss on Isabel's forehead. "Like her owner." They continued the short distance of a few steps to her horse in silence. A part of her welcomed his touch, while another wondered why she felt drawn to him. He needed her help, she reasoned, and she could not turn him away.

Muscles aching from the effort to hold William steady, she guided his hand to the saddle and then helped him place his foot in the stirrup. Athena stood as still as the gargoyles guarding the entrance to Hampton Court. It was as though the horse sensed the importance of the next few moments. If William failed to climb into the saddle, Isabel doubted he would have the strength to try again.

The leather creaked as William took a deep breath and pulled himself onto the horse. He slumped forward.

Isabel scrambled behind him and grabbed the reins. She turned Athena in the direction of the manor. The artist's studio was closer, but she had only begun her apprenticeship with them recently and was not sure she could trust them with William's life. After all, Ossian, the master of the artist's guild, was a friend of the queen. Until Isabel knew William's identity for certain, it was too much of a risk. The only place she knew he would be safe from prying eyes was at the manor.

William's breathing was shallow, and his body temperature had dropped. He was shaking so badly that she feared he would tumble off the horse. She pressed her body against him, adding her warmth to his.

His hand covered hers, and he squeezed gently. "I've decided you're my own personal angel. I didn't think I deserved one."

She heard the sadness in his voice and wondered at the cause. He might recover from the flesh wounds he received tonight, but she sensed there were others far more serious.

Isabel spoke gently. "William, everyone deserves

an angel to watch over them."

His head slipped forward, and his hand loosened his grip on hers. She said a silent prayer, hoping his real angel was listening. She edged Athena through the back streets toward her destination.

The light snow had turned to flurries and swept around her on icy currents. Oil lamps flickered and sputtered on each corner. It was likely their passage would not be noted in this storm, but it would also slow their progress.

Her mind raced with the enormity of what she had done and what lay ahead. She had no idea who William was, but she dismissed the idea that he was a creature from the water's depths. His kiss had been real enough. Logic and reason argued that if he were such a being, he would be immortal, and this man was flesh and blood and bleeding to death.

William swayed in the saddle.

She grabbed his belt. "Hold fast," she ordered. She knew that if he began to slip, she would not have the strength to prevent his fall, nor would she be able to help him mount her horse a second time.

He nodded in response but did not speak.

They had to make it. She needed Myra's help in caring for William.

Time dragged to a standstill as Isabel wove through the streets of London. She concentrated on reaching the manor. Shadows stretched over the cobblestones in skeletal fingers toward her, clutching at her legs. She was shivering so hard her teeth ached, but it was not her own welfare that consumed her but William's. Whoever he was, he had risked his life to save hers. She could do no less for him.

Chapter 3

Before Isabel's bone-chilled body the manor house rose like a beacon of light at the end of a row of ancient oak trees. It stood half way between the frantic life of the city and the intrigues that infected Hampton Court. Angus had named the manor "A Safe Harbor," and the words had never rung so true.

Relief washed over Isabel as she approached. She almost wept with joy as she urged Athena forward down the long road leading to the manor. The bitter cold wind lashed against her skin, and there was a fine layer of ice covering her cloak. She did not know how William had managed to stay on her horse. Isabel could no longer tell if he was alive or merely frozen in place; they'd spoken only briefly since they'd begun their journey from the river. She suspected he was conserving what little strength he had left—if he was still alive.

A warm, welcoming glow shone out of the windows that flanked the door to the manor. Myra was waiting for her.

Isabel's teeth chattered with the effort to speak to William. "We are almost there. You will like Myra. She has far more knowledge than I in the healing arts and is the most skilled cook at the queen's court. Her recipes are finer than even Forsyth's, who claims to be the queen's best chef. If truth be told, he is a better painter than cook."

She paused to move her fingers. They were stiff from the cold. She had an overwhelming desire to pause by the side of the road and rest in the soft snow. She straightened, frightened by the impulse she knew would result in her freezing to death.

She resumed her one-sided conversation with William. This time she spoke in a stronger voice. "I do my best to help Myra, but like Forsyth, I am more skilled with brush and canvas than a skillet. Myra claims I could burn boiled water. If you had to rely on me to prepare your meal, you would starve. Now, you might be wondering what I could offer a man as wife. The answer would be absolutely nothing, which suits me just fine."

Isabel passed under an archway of overhanging oak branches and led Athena beyond the stables to the front door of the manor. She would see to her horse's care later; first she must help William inside.

As she dismounted, he pitched forward in the saddle.

His face was the color of cold ash.

She swallowed back her fear and shouted through the whistling wind, "Are you able to dismount?"

An eternity crept by until he raised his head and spoke. "Yes," he whispered. His voice was a low rasp.

He dismounted, but his legs buckled as soon as his feet touched the ground.

He leaned against her for support. "Where are we?" His jaw clenched as though even the effort to speak caused him pain.

"My home." Her muscles strained to hold his weight as she rapped lightly on the door.

The shadow of a smile touched his lips. "You should worry not about what you could offer a man but about what he could offer you."

Even through the bitter cold, her face felt warm. He had heard every word she had spoken. He must think her a fool.

She knocked on the door again and in the next instance heard a dog bark within the manor. It was Apollo.

Seconds crept by. As she was about to knock once more, she heard muttering and a shuffling sound coming from inside her home.

The door edged open. A warm breeze and the rich aroma of baking bread floated toward her. Roasted almonds, cloves, ginger, cinnamon, and apples all blended together to welcome her.

Myra stood in the doorway. She wore a white starched cap that covered blonde hair laced with gray. It framed a heart-shaped face. She was holding onto the collar of a black wolfhound. Her thick Scottish brogue was sweet music to Isabel's ears.

"There ye are, lass. I was worried half out of my mind. Come in before ye catch your death." Myra opened the door wider. Her eyebrows scrunched together as she frowned. "Who is this creature?"

Isabel stepped into the warmth with William at her side. "He appeared out of the river and we were both attacked. I could not leave him. He saved my life and was injured."

The dog barked again. Myra shook her finger at the animal. "Shush now. Go over to your bed and be still."

The wolfhound hung his head and obediently padded over to the hearth.

Myra's voice was a soft whisper. "What do ye mean he 'appeared' out of the water?" Her face was as white as bleached linen. "Have ye lost your mind? Ye cannot keep him. This is not a stray animal in need of food and shelter, but a grown man. I cannot allow ye to bring him into our home."

Isabel felt tears sting her eyes. Myra was right, but it did not matter. She reached over and squeezed Myra's arm and whispered, "I know. But we have to help him." Isabel took a deep breath. She did not want to try explaining something she did not understand herself. "Please, this man is injured and in need of our help. That should be enough."

Myra nodded slowly. "I know, I know." She sighed. "Well, then, we must work quickly. From the look of his clothes, he has lost a lot of blood."

William moaned and started to pitch forward. Isabel felt herself being pulled down with him. Myra reached for his arm and placed it over her shoulder, helping Isabel stabilize him.

Myra grimaced. "Oh, but he is a big one."

Isabel stole a glance toward Myra. "Is it all right if we use the guest chamber?"

"Aye, of course. Then later ye can explain to me how it is that ye have talked me into helping a perfect stranger."

"Myra, I think it is obvious. You are an angel."

"A fool would be more accurate."

William's feet shuffled across the stone floor as the two women guided him toward the guest chamber at the end of a long hallway. Once inside the room, they eased him down onto the bed gently.

Isabel stood back and rubbed her shoulders. The

muscles ached from exertion. She bent to examine William's injuries. They had started to bleed again. "I did the best I could, but the bandages have come undone."

"We must remove them and clean his wounds. But first I want ye to change out of those garments and into warm ones. I dinna want two sick people on my hands."

Isabel hugged Myra quickly. "First I will tend to Athena. She fought through the storm like a true warrior's horse."

Before Myra could voice a protest, Isabel ran from the room and into the courtyard. She was able to wake the stable boy, Brian, who helped her with Athena. Isabel then hurried back into the manor.

She raced up the winding staircase to her chamber and tore off her clothes, then pulled a wool sheath and tunic over her head. She left her wet clothes folded over a chair and retraced her steps, grabbing a stack of clean linens to use as bandages.

As she reached the chamber, Myra had things well in hand. William's sword rested against the wall, and his clothes were draped over a bench by the hearth.

Myra was cleaning his wounds. She turned toward Isabel and shook her head. "I must tell you, the lad's injuries are grave. So much blood, and if he does recover, he will have many scars. If we are to help him, we must keep our hands as steady as our minds. Tell me again how ye came to rescue this lad."

Isabel's hand trembled as she took the soiled cloth from Myra and handed her a clean one. She willed her body under control. Myra was right. They had to stay focused.

William shuddered and winced in pain, but he did

not open his eyes. From his expression he looked as though he fought a violent battle. She swallowed her tears and wished she could ease his pain. She resigned herself to wiping his brow with linens soaked in clean water.

Myra cleared her throat. "Did ye say he just appeared out of the water without warning?"

"Yes. It was odd. Perhaps he swam from the other side of the river or from a boat anchored out of sight."

Eyes still closed, William arched his back. His arms thrashed about, knocking the water bucket off the nightstand. Water splashed to the floor.

Myra yelled, "Isabel! Help me hold him down."

Isabel jumped onto the bed and held William's shoulder as Myra did the same. It was like trying to control a wild horse. William's body shuddered and then quieted until he was again locked in a deep sleep.

Myra wiped perspiration from her brow. "He is a strong one, all right. He might just survive after all." She reached for a spool of silk thread and a needle. "I fear bandages alone will not stop the bleeding on the largest of his wounds. They will have to be sutured."

As Myra sewed the ragged edges closed, Isabel cleared away the soiled bandages.

Myra nodded toward her. "Ye did the right thing to bring the lad here."

Isabel kissed her on the cheek. "I knew you would understand."

"I dinna say I understood, only that it was the right thing to help an injured man." She smiled. "Ye are probably wondering why I was baking an apple-and-fig pie along with my bread so late at night."

Isabel retrieved the overturned water bucket. "It

makes perfect sense to me. You were worried about me, and you missed Angus."

Myra sighed deeply. "Aye, lass, ye are correct on both accounts." She stepped back and cleared her throat. "It will be up to the lad's own strength to pull him through the night. I'll wash everything of his before I go to bed. There is nothing like clean garments to make a body feel fit and good as new. However, I dinna recognize his plaid. 'Tis a shame, as that might give us a clue to his identity. We will have to invent a story that will explain both his appearance and his condition."

Isabel realized her instincts about Myra had been correct. She would protect William. Isabel walked over to Myra and hugged her. "I love you."

Myra blinked and stared at Isabel. "Well, now, what was that all about, child?"

"You know how dangerous it might be for all of us. The queen does not trust strangers, especially ones from Scotland. Yet you are still willing to help him. You have the kindest heart."

Myra blinked away the tears brimming in her eyes and smiled. "I suppose they can only hang us once for harboring a criminal."

"William is not a criminal."

Myra cocked an eyebrow. "William, is it? And how can ye be so sure he is not a wanted man?"

How could Isabel respond when she was not sure of the answer herself?

Myra did not press her question but nodded toward William. "That is the best my skills can do. If he has not regained consciousness by morning, we will send for a proper physician. I have heard one arrived in the last few days or so and is so well thought of the queen has given him a room within the walls of Hampton Court. It has been a long night for ye. There is nothing more that can be done for William. Ye should try and rest."

"I am not tired, but you must try to sleep. I will watch over William."

Myra yawned and retrieved William's clothes and the soiled linens. "Ye promise?"

Isabel nodded and watched Myra leave. Then she turned toward William.

Sleep.

It was the last thing in her thoughts. And even if she lay down, she doubted she could close her eyes. Her thoughts raced and collided at such a pace that she could not tell where one ended and the other began.

A rational, sane person would wonder who this man was and why he was attacked so viciously. However, that was not what kept her awake. There was only one question burning through her like a white-hot flame.

Why had he kissed her?

****

William MacAlpin knew he'd been betrayed. The ambush was proof that Gavin had been right in asking for help. His mind drifted as he fought to stay conscious just a little while longer in order to assess his situation.

He struggled to remember everything that had happened since his arrival in this century. He remembered the attack, the woman leaping into the fray to save him. What was her name?

He resisted the black void that meant to swallow him whole.

Isabel. Yes, that was it.

He remembered the journey through the streets of London in the mind-numbing cold as she'd pleaded with him to stay conscious. She'd spoken words of hope, as well as things he knew had been meant to keep him alert and awake.

He drifted once more and knew for certain the ambush at the river had not been an accident. He'd survived this long because he didn't believe in coincidences. This theory, and a legendary survival skill, were family traits.

A wave of burning pain rolled over him. William lacked the strength to open his eyes. It was as though his body floated in the dark vastness of space. Another wave of pain crested and shuddered through him.

He recognized the signs. It had occurred countless times before.

He was dying.

But where he lay was soft, fragrant, and warm. The scent conjured a vision of the courageous and beautiful Isabel, who had risked her life to save him. He remembered the need to kiss and embrace her that had overwhelmed him before he could question the reason why. That had never happened to him before. He'd used her shoulder to lean on and had been surprised at the strength in such a small frame. He doubted she would have been so generous with her help had she known who and what he was.

His mind drifted once more as the pain dulled. It wouldn't be long now before he lost consciousness. He clung on as long as he could to this world. He suspected it was a form of self-preservation that harkened back to the human beginnings of his race.

However, that was long ago, and in the twenty-first century, less than three hundred of his kind remained where once roamed thousands. How long would it be before their existence would be only a memory? Even now humankind believed that if his race existed, it was only in legends and myths. Stories, they rationalized, that were exaggerated with the telling. The misconceptions were encouraged. It was safer for both races to foster the lie.

William heard someone walk toward him. Their footfalls crunched over the rush-strewn floor. Instinctively he knew it was a woman and hoped it was the same one who'd brought him to safety. She smelled of lavender and roses. He inhaled the heady fragrance and remembered the intoxicating aroma. It could only be Isabel. Her scent had surrounded her like a spring rain when she'd come to his rescue. Her beauty had stolen his breath, and her courage, his heart. The knowledge hit him like a physical blow.

His first impulse had been to gather her in his arms and kiss her. He'd forsaken his discipline and training and given in to the temptation. Her warm lips had molded against his. The contact had jolted him. He fought against the irrational desire that sped through him like a wildfire through a tinder-dry forest. Why had he kissed her?

Somewhere in the recesses of his mind he remembered a legend. According to ancient records, there were rare instances when members of his race could sense their soul mate upon first meeting and first touch. When this occurred, logic and reason evaporated, replaced with only one desire—to be with that person.

The notion had always intrigued him, but if true,

the timing was lousy. He'd spent his life successfully controlling his emotions. He could only hope the legend was false. Otherwise this would prove to be his most difficult mission to date.

He drifted once more to the moment by the wharf when he'd asked for her help. He didn't know why he'd uttered those words. He'd never done so in the past. Yet he'd known even before she'd helped him mount her horse that she would say yes.

The whole incident was more fantasy than reality. Few of his race ever sought to help him, which was why he seldom asked. It was a direct result of his secret identity. Among his own kind, he was more feared than admired.

Isabel began to hum softly, and her voice eased the pain of his soul, as well as his body. He would like to stay longer in her presence. Maybe she was not real after all but only a dream of perfection thrust upon him in an imperfect world.

He would awaken and she would be gone.

It was just as well. The thought brought renewed pain that had nothing to do with the wound in his side and everything to do with the emptiness in his heart.

She touched his forehead with a damp cloth. The impulse to pull her into his arms overwhelmed him, even knowing he lacked the strength to comply. He fought the need she stirred within him. It was an emotion he thought he'd long ago both banished as well as extinguished from his soul.

He remembered his pilot, Murphy, referring to him as some kind of superhero. Like those fabled characters, William lived two separate lives.

However, instead of living at least one of his lives

as a mild-mannered reporter or in some similar occupation, he lived both his lives on the edge. In reality, being a smoke jumper was the less dangerous of the two. His other identity was as a Protector. It was an elite group, even among his own kind. And it followed a simple rule—to keep your heart as impenetrable as the steel of your sword. It was a concept he must never forget. Especially now. There was too much at stake.

Chapter 4

The gray light of dawn slipped through the cracks in the wood shutters as Isabel stretched her tired muscles. She leaned against the chair and yawned. It had been a long night. William's wound had finally stopped bleeding. She hoped that was a good sign.

A few hours ago, when Isabel leaned over to tuck the blankets around him, she had feared he'd stopped breathing. She had forced the thoughts from her mind. His face had been ashen, and in the last few hours he had not stirred.

Restless, she stood and walked to the hearth to warm her hands. She glanced toward the bed. They had bandaged him as best they could, but Isabel wondered if it had been good enough. "Only time will tell," Myra had said, and the words grated against Isabel's mind.

An orange-and-white cat stretched and padded toward her from its place beside the hearth. It had been out looking for mice when Isabel arrived last night, and it seemed in need of attention. It rubbed against her leg and meowed.

Isabel reached down and lifted the animal in her arms.

"Yes, Zeus, I know. It is time for your breakfast. You must not have had much luck on your hunt last night."

The scruffy wolfhound, Apollo, raised his head and

barked. The sound lifted the somber mood in the chamber.

She smiled. "Are you hungry as well?"

The dog barked again, bounded to its feet, and trotted over to the door of the adjacent chamber. He stood like a guard at the entrance.

The door creaked open slowly, and Myra walked in, tucking strands of hair behind her cap. She leaned down to scratch Apollo behind his ear, then nodded toward William. "Did he awake during the night?"

Isabel shook her head as she rubbed her chin over the top of Zeus's head. He nuzzled under her neck and purred. She too had hoped William would have regained consciousness by now.

Myra shivered and rubbed her arms. She lowered her voice. "What do we really know of William? Those men who attacked him by the river might have just cause."

Isabel had never known Myra to be so cautious. Myra, like Isabel, was always giving whatever spare coin or food they had to those less fortunate. Myra saw the good in people, and her own generous heart shone through in her eyes. The hesitation in her voice concerned Isabel.

Myra wrung her hands together and paced in front of the fire. "Could I have been mistaken? It was so long ago when…" She hesitated and glanced toward the bed. "Did ye notice the strange mark on his wrist? I think I was too tired to comment on it last night. I awoke this morning thinking about it."

Isabel had not. Her focus had been on his loss of blood and that he had not seemed to be breathing. "Why would something like that be important?"

"Aye, perhaps I am wrong." Myra yawned. "It was such a long time ago. The best thing to do is to seek the advice of a physician. The lad is beyond my skill."

Despite Myra's dismissal of the mark, Isabel noticed that Myra grew more agitated by the minute. Even the animals picked up on the increased tension in the air. Zeus squirmed out of Isabel's arms, jumped to the floor, and bounded toward the cookroom. Apollo perked up his ears and was looking in Myra's direction as she wore a path across the stone floor, silently muttering to herself.

Isabel kept a calmness to her voice she did not feel. She did not like the transformation that came over Myra. "I thought you did not trust physicians?"

Myra shrugged. "Perhaps not, but there is no one else to consult. The women healers in London would not come so close to Hampton Court. This is a dangerous time for women to have such a skill. They fear discovery. So many of them have been accused of witchcraft and hanged, or worse."

Isabel pulled the wool blanket over William's shoulders and wondered if there would ever be a time when a woman could explore her talents without fear. She sighed. Perhaps it was not to be and dwelling on it would not change the crisis at hand. She frowned.

"I agree that we cannot ask a healer, but why would one of the queen's physicians concern himself with a request made by one of the servants?"

Myra smoothed the folds of her skirts. "The man I have in mind is named John Campbell. I am told he has already made a good impression on the queen. Anyway, 'tis worth a try."

Isabel watched as Myra wrapped her shawl around

her shoulders and hurried from the room. Her behavior was odd, indeed. But then Angus, the man Myra loved, was gone longer than usual. Mayhap it was Angus's absence that altered Myra's normally calm demeanor. It was a rational assumption, but Isabel had a difficult time convincing herself that was the only explanation. Something else was bothering her, and it was more than having an injured man in their chambers.

****

This could not be happening, not again.

Myra dismounted. She left her horse in the care of a stable boy as she quickened her steps along the misty, snow-drenched path toward the wing reserved for the royal physicians. She knew the older ones would not even consider soiling their hands by tending to someone from her class. Myra hoped the newly arrived physician, John Campbell, would be a different matter. It was important, for more than one reason.

Myra had not lied to Isabel when she'd said the seriousness of William's wounds was beyond her abilities. However, there was another reason she wanted John Campbell's help.

She wanted him to put her suspicions to rest.

There was something odd about William and the mark on his wrist. It was in the form of a sword. She had seen its like once before and then only briefly. The similarities of the two images nibbled at the back of her mind like a mouse at cheese. It must be overwork and lack of sleep that had her imagination running wild.

Or perhaps it was just that she missed her Angus. He was gone longer than was his normal custom, and despite his claim that he was always careful, she was worried about him. She rounded a corner and paused in front of the door she knew was assigned to the new physician.

She knocked, and the sound echoed in the still air. Shivering, she pulled her shawl closer around her shoulders. The physicians made her wary with their potions and surgeries, which often resulted in their patients' becoming more ill than they had been before. These men were a stark difference from the gentle ways of the healers from her village in Inverness.

Myra jumped as the door was jerked open. "Yes? What do you want?"

The rod-thin man was well over a head taller than Myra. His ebony black hair stood stick straight, and his hawklike nose and eyes peered at her like a predator at its prey.

She shivered, and her voice trembled. "I am Myra, sir. My daughter and I are in need of your assistance."

His eyes narrowed. "What female ailment could be so serious it could not wait until a decent hour of the day? Come back later."

He started to shut the door, but Myra wedged her foot in the opening, preventing him from accomplishing his goal. "Please, sir, 'tis not for us that I seek your help but for another."

He sighed deeply. "Out with it. I'm bone tired."

"'Tis…" Myra searched for a way to describe William that would not put them in danger.

"I don't have time for this. Ask someone else."

"Nay." The sharpness and tone of her voice surprised her and renewed her conviction. She needed his help, and she would not leave until she had accomplished her goal. She made up a story she hoped the physician would believe.

"'Tis my daughter's husband that needs your assistance. He was attacked in the streets of London last night, and I fear he is dying. We did the best we could, but…"

He rubbed his eyes. "All right. All right. I'll go. Wait here while I dress."

Myra withdrew her foot, allowing him to slam the door in her face. She stepped back and took a deep breath. Her opinion about physicians had not changed. In fact, her dislike of them only increased. But she had accomplished her goal, and that was all that mattered. She was sure Isabel would understand the necessity for the lie that William was her husband. It seemed the only option.

The lass had an aversion to marriage and commitment that bordered on paranoia. Myra and Angus had thought she would outgrow it as she matured, but it only deepened. Angus did not understand. Myra, however, knew exactly how Isabel felt. She remembered the same fear that had consumed her at one time.

Myra smiled to herself. That was until she had met Angus.

John Campbell shivered in the cold as he rode behind Myra toward the manor house. Mist clung to the morning air like spiderwebs in a neglected corner of a dungeon. Tending to the needs of a wounded man was the last thing on his mind, no matter that the appeal had been made by the intriguing woman who called herself Myra.

When she'd first appeared on his doorstep wearing a mousy brown garment and a starched linen cap, he'd had no interest in helping her. But when she'd prevented him from shutting his door and then demanded he reconsider, he'd taken a second look at her. It was then he'd recognized the banked fire reflected in her eyes. He meant to explore his theory that behind the drab clothes hid a passionate woman. And there was also the question regarding her name. It was unusual and at the same time sounded familiar.

He brushed the notion aside to decipher later, when there was more time. He never forgot a name or a face. It was both a gift and a curse.

When they reached the manor and dismounted, he handed the reins to the stable boy and followed Myra through a shadow-draped archway. During the day he rarely thought of all those he'd known. It was at night, in the black chambers of his dreams, when the faces came to him. In the years he'd lived, he'd known many who'd died cursing his name. He chuckled under his breath. Those were cherished moments and made him feel powerful. However, there was a price to pay. At night, while he slept, his victims returned to haunt him.

It had been during such a nightmare, where the souls he'd killed had been clawing at his mind, that he'd heard the knock on his door. He'd embraced the reprieve, the more so because it had come at the request of an interesting woman. The profession he'd chosen this time was not only the most logical occupation for what he planned but it also gained him the respect he normally paid for.

When he'd arrived in the sixteenth century, he'd introduced himself as a physician to the court of Queen Mary the First and set the plan in motion. No one suspected he was Bartholomew, an escaped renegade from the hidden prison underneath Urquhart Castle.

He smiled, pleased that everything had gone off according to schedule. He had taken the added precaution of hiring a gang of mercenaries to guard the bank of the Thames River near London to make sure no one was sent to bring him back. All was quiet. No doubt his location was still a secret.

The air grew more chilled as he paused at the entrance and cursed London's climate. If not for his thirst for revenge, he would have chosen a warmer environment. He shivered, wishing he'd worn an additional cloak. The weather was colder in London than he'd remembered. He realized the numerous layers of clothing the people of this time period wore were more for warmth than fashion.

Once inside the manor, he followed Myra through the Great Hall and entered what he suspected was the chamber of his patient. A fire blazed in the hearth, and candles added light. He was surprised at the size of the room, as well as the rich furnishings. A black lacquered cabinet with red and gold dragons entwined over the front panels stood beside a massive four-poster bed whose thick red velvet curtains were drawn around the perimeter. Hanging from the walls were vibrant purple-and-green tapestries depicting Helen of Troy and the Trojan Wars. Two ladderback chairs faced each other in front of the fire. It was a chamber meant for someone who was both educated and well-traveled. Or the mistress of such a person.

Myra claimed to be a simple cook in the queen's employ, but her furnishings suggested another source of income.

His interest in her increased tenfold. Perhaps she'd at one time had a generous benefactor at court. King

Henry the Eighth was known not only for his many wives but for his numerous mistresses, as well.

Although Myra's blonde hair was laced with gray, it shone with warmth in the firelight. The shape of her face and figure was also pleasing. She was still attractive, and it was easy to see that she'd once been a great beauty. Further, her gentle smile and the laugh lines around her eyes spoke of a life devoid of the debauchery common to those who lived at court. He'd learned to identify such people to use their vices, as well as their vulnerability, to his gain. In return, they were drawn to him like an insect to a deadly web.

For a woman to have survived in sixteenth-century England for so long spoke of the depth of her skills. He was intrigued. Perhaps there would be time for pleasure if the plan went ahead of schedule. A woman of her age would welcome the attention of a man who appeared ten years her junior. He suppressed a smile, wondering what her reaction would be if she knew his true age to number in the hundreds.

Myra tapped him on the shoulder, interrupting his thoughts as to how best entice her to his chamber.

"Sir, the man I spoke of earlier lies on the bed. My daughter, Isabel, is concerned that he does not appear to be breathing."

Her voice was youthful and gentle, and he doubted she'd ever raised it in anger. However, there was a secret that floated around her. He could smell it.

John Campbell crossed to the place indicated. He would feign interest in this man and thus gain the woman's confidence. Already the prospect of a diversion warmed his blood. He concentrated on the role he would play.

He drew back the draperies framing the bed. Indeed, there was a man lying there who appeared as still and motionless as the standing stones that sprang from the Highlands. A younger woman came to stand by his side. This must be the daughter Myra had spoken of earlier.

His blood surged anew. Her beauty was stunning. Thick black hair framed a flawless complexion, and dark eyes stared, unblinking, in his direction. Although he could not detect any family resemblance, the same air of independence surrounded them both. This day held more promise than he'd first thought. It had been a long time since he'd been interested in bedding both mother and daughter. And from the state of the daughter's husband, the man would be in no condition to object.

He turned to the daughter and plastered on his most sympathetic smile. "I fear, lady, that your husband does not look well. But I shall do all in my power to see to his recovery." It was a lie, but they couldn't read what was in his heart. That was most fortunate, since he'd long ago sold his soul.

The young woman's eyes widened, and her voice cracked. "Husband? He is not my—"

Myra squeezed her daughter's arm. "'Tis no use denying who he is, Isabel. I told the physician everything."

John Campbell didn't miss the exchange between mother and daughter. He knew when someone was lying. After all, he'd done it enough times himself to recognize the signs. He doubted the couple was wed. The injured man was no doubt a lover she wanted to keep a secret. Maybe it was not the mother who lived a sordid life but the daughter. Yes, this day was progressing nicely.

Myra was speaking to him. "As I told ye, sir. Isabel's husband was attacked. We fear he may not recover from his wounds."

He could not have agreed more. It didn't take a physician to determine that the man's heart had stopped. He reached for his patient's wrist to continue the farce. As he suspected, there was no pulse.

Isabel moved closer to him and held a candle. The light flickered over the man on the bed. "Will he live?"

John Campbell laughed, but he hastily covered his involuntary outburst with a cough. He ignored the desire to tell Isabel that nothing would breathe life into this corpse, save magic. Instead, he concentrated on the illusion of examining his patient.

He took the candle from her and brought it closer. It illuminated the man's face. There was something about his features that was familiar, but it eluded him. He shook the unease that shuddered through him as he fought to reclaim his composure.

As impossible as it seemed, the man resembled his mortal enemy, Lachlan MacAlpin. John Campbell took a calming breath. Maybe the light was playing tricks on his mind. These women would not bring him here to examine an immortal. Unless, of course, they didn't know. He focused once more and turned the man's wrist over.

He sucked in his breath. What he saw sent shudders rippling through his body. The flame wavered in his grip. He tried to swallow. The walls of the chamber seemed to edge closer toward him.

A birthmark, the length of a man's index finger and

in the shape of a sword, was visible.

His hand shook and his mind screamed, "Impossible!" But there was no mistake. It was the mark of a Protector. This man was not dead but locked in the Healing Sleep of the Immortals.

The two women were speaking to him at the same time. He couldn't distinguish one from the other. The air in the chamber was suffocating him. He had to leave. Somehow they unwittingly were thrown into his path. He didn't like it when his plans were complicated. The women would have to be eliminated. He shoved the candle toward Myra. The flame quivered as she grabbed it.

She frowned. "What is it, sir?"

He shook his head. There was still a chance he could turn this to his advantage, but he must move quickly. He had only two days.

"How long has this man been in this condition?"

Myra looked toward her daughter and then the physician. "He has been unconscious for a few hours only."

His heart beat rapidly in his chest. Time. There was still time.

John Campbell's voice was shrill in his ears as he barked out commands. "This man is dead. There is nothing I can do. Do not move him. I will send someone to take him from you before his corpse begins to rot."

He ignored their collective gasps and protests as he rushed out of the chamber and into the courtyard. When he was safely outside, he yanked the reins of his horse from the bewildered stable boy and turned his animal toward Hampton Court. He tried to bring his erratic breathing under control.

He'd been followed. Were these women innocent bystanders, or were his instincts correct and they were hiding something from him?

John Campbell gripped his riding crop and slashed it across the rump of his horse. He was impatient to return to Hampton Court. He would not believe that it was a coincidence a Protector was so close at hand and acting the part of husband, even to so delicious a woman as Isabel. The Protectors were a solitary lot, all emotion trained out of them since birth. It was clear. The mercenaries he'd sent to guard the Thames River had failed. His only hope was to make sure the man in Myra's room never regained consciousness. Then he could learn how much the women knew and deal with them at his leisure.

His normal breathing returned. Yes, there was no need to panic. He had more than enough time to dispose of the Protector. But he must be vigilant. If there was one Immortal in his midst, there might be more.

Chapter 5

Angus's long journey was nearing its end. The afternoon mist wove through the hunting park and gardens leading to the entrance of Hampton Court. His manor house was just beyond the queen's grounds.

A light snow had begun to fall. It was as though an angry river sprite had blown freezing air toward London. It clung to the branches of the trees like the secrets that dogged Angus's mind. But it mattered not. He was almost home. He spurred his horse forward, anxious to hold Myra in his arms again.

Angus guided his horse, Wolf, past the main entrance to Hampton Court, which was guarded by stone gargoyles. He could swear they followed him with their eyes. They had outlived their previous masters, from Cardinal Wolsey, through the reign of King Henry the Eighth, his son Edward the Sixth, and now Mary Tudor. He and the gargoyles shared a bond. They were immortal and would endure as he had. He wondered if they ever tired of outlasting those they came to know and cherish.

As he grew near, one of the queen's guards waved and shouted his name in greeting.

Clouds swallowed the light and cast the day in shades of gray. But even in the shadows he was recognized. It filled him with an odd mixture of pleasure and concern. His features, he often believed, were as indistinguishable from other men's as the gargoyles were from each other.

His survival depended on his ability to appear and disappear unnoticed. He blended into a crowd and was considered just another Scot down from the wilds of the north.

He hid his features under a bushy red beard and shoulder-length hair that was braided at the temples. It effectively disguised his appearance, as well as the fact that he did not age. His height was impossible to disguise, but his bulk he hid under layers of earth- and forest-colored plaid fabric that wound around him in the fashion of the Highlanders. His clothing covered not soft flesh but hard muscle.

Angus passed by the pond gardens stocked with trout for the queen's table and through the oak-lined road that led to his manor. He bent down and patted his horse on the neck.

"Won't be too long now, lad."

A dilemma faced him. He was becoming too well known in London. It could jeopardize whatever new assignments might come his way. In the Beginning Time, the first Council of Seven had outlined his role. He was to act as a mentor to those destined to be leaders. It was a position for which he felt well suited. But to be effective, he must be able to come and go without detection. When the guards recognized him, Angus knew he had overstayed his time here.

Angus rubbed his tired muscles, knowing all he needed to recover fully, in both mind and spirit, was to pause for a time in Myra's embrace. Just to be in her presence caused his mind to be at peace. He smiled, remembering the reason he'd named the horse as he had—wolves mated for life.

The day the colt was born was right after he'd first met the gentle Myra. It had been outside the Merry Widow Tavern. He'd still been celebrating a victory in a battle against a neighboring clan over the theft of cattle. In truth, he had celebrated overmuch.

Angus remembered he had staggered out of the tavern, still holding a tankard of ale. He had spent the night and most of the morning there and had been so preoccupied with retelling his feats of valor to a fellow celebrant that he had slammed into Myra.

He still remembered the incident as though it were yesterday.

Myra had been carrying a basket filled to the brim with fresh-baked bread and fruit tarts. She'd stumbled backward, lost her footing, and landed in a mud puddle in the center of the rut-lined street.

He had stood there, like the dolt he was, staring in silence and disbelief.

Angus smiled again.

He remembered it was her eyes he'd noticed first. As blue as a summer sky and as clear as a mountain spring. Her hair had been as gold as a field of wheat and her features capable of turning a man into a poet.

She'd struggled to regain her feet in the puddle, surrounded by waterlogged baked goods. He, however, had stood as though rooted to the ground.

Angus never knew why he had not assisted her sooner.

Perhaps it had been the lingering effects of the ale that had addled his brain, or perhaps it had been her beauty. All he'd known was that he could not move. In the next instant, she'd flashed those incredible eyes toward him. A mixture of anger and attraction had glittered in their depths.

Her expression had unbalanced him. When she'd stood, she'd been covered in mud from head to toe. She had put her hands on her hips and told him he was a great clumsy oaf. He had not disagreed with her. But no one, man or woman, had ever made him accountable for his behavior. He'd listened in shock and then had been hypnotized by the sound of her lyrical voice.

Two things changed for him that day. The first was he never again let his drinking consume his life, and the second was that he knew he had found a woman he could love with his whole heart.

He smiled and shook free of the pleasant memories as he hurried on his way.

Angus reached the stables and dismounted. He led Wolf inside, removing his horse's saddle and the bundles of gifts he'd brought with him from Italy. He'd built an identity as a successful merchant. It was a profession easy to prove, as his duties took him to exotic lands. However, it was time to move on. He decided he would have to tell Myra they would be leaving London soon. He hoped she would understand.

Angus filled a bucket with oats and fed Wolf. As the horse was munching contentedly on his supper, the stable boy rushed forward from around the corner. The gangly youth sputtered his apologies for neglecting his post.

"Sorry, yer lordship. Good to see ye again, sir. Was talking to one of the queen's stable hands about the newest physician at court. It won't happen again, sir."

Angus smiled. "No harm done, Brian."

Angus rubbed Wolf on his cold nose. He really did

not mind the lad talking to others. It must be lonely for him. Usually, on a manor of this size, there would be more servants, but Angus guarded his privacy. The less people who knew about him, the safer for all concerned.

The youth reached for a brush for Wolf. "The physician's not like ye, sir." Brian's eyes darted to the left and right as though expecting to see the man appear from behind a thorn bush. Brian whispered, "I seen the look in his eyes. That one is ready with the whip."

Angus did not abide mistreatment of either man or beast. He had traveled to the Mediterranean to help defuse injustice, while it still festered and flourished at home.

He put his hand on Brian's shoulder. "Did this physician harm your friend?"

Brian shook his head. "It's the horses we're most concerned for. We kept thinking what kind of a healer could John Campbell be if he liked setting a whip to his animal?"

"You make a good point. Keep me informed of the man's behavior."

Angus was a collector of information. He learned there was never such a thing as too much knowledge, especially in his line of work. And Brian had proved to be helpful. Angus learned more about the inner workings of the palace's inhabitants from the boy than by attending a week's worth of events at court. However, it concerned him that someone might be mistreating the animals. He would make sure he met this John Campbell personally.

Angus retrieved the bundles of gifts and the red leather-bound book he always kept with him and headed toward the entrance of the manor. Once inside, he shouted a greeting. A quiet permeated the torchlit rooms. He scratched his beard. At the very least, Apollo should be barking a greeting. Something was wrong.

In the next instant, the door to the guest quarters flew open.

Isabel's face was tearstained as she rushed into his arms. "Father, we are so glad you are home."

As always, it warmed his heart when Isabel called him Father. Before he could ask the cause for her distress, she reached for his hand and pulled him into the Great Hall.

"Father, the physician told us William is dead, but it is so hard to believe. It is more like he is caught in a deep sleep." He set the bundles down, keeping the book tucked under his arm. "Why is it ye have a dead man in the house? And who is William?"

At that moment Myra entered from the direction of the cookroom, carrying a large container of water. She dropped the bowl. It crashed to the floor, breaking into chunks and spilling the contents. Her hands rose to her face to cover her screams of delight.

She ignored the mess and flung herself into Angus's arms, covering his face in warm kisses. He pulled her closer as his heart filled with love.

She tugged on his beard. "Ye were gone too long this time, my love. I almost forgot what a great smelly bear ye are."

Angus laughed and kissed her hard on the mouth. He whispered against her ear, "That proves my love is greater, for I never forgot that you smell like a spring day in the Highlands. I brought presents for all."

Myra smiled against his mouth and whispered, "Ye

beside me is all the gift I need."

Isabel fumbled with the shards of the pottery bowl Myra had dropped to the ground.

Angus realized he had forgotten Isabel was in the room. Myra had that effect on him. The burdens of responsibility fell from his shoulders when Myra smiled at him. He put his arm around her waist and nodded toward Isabel.

"Well, daughter." He paused, liking the way the word sounded. Although Isabel was not his and Myra's by blood, they could not have loved her more. "What is this about a dead man by the name of William?"

Isabel set the shards of the bowl on the table and motioned for Angus to follow her.

Once inside the guest quarters, Isabel pulled back the velvet curtains that framed the four-poster bed. A man lay there as still as death.

Myra touched Angus's shoulder. "He was attacked along the wharf last night, and Isabel brought him here for us to tend." She sighed. "But I fear we were too late to save him. The physician declared him dead."

Angus suppressed the urge to remind them both of the dangers of bringing a stranger into their home. But the deed was done, and he knew the fault for their disregard for safety was in part his own. In the Immortal race, men and women were equals. It was a practice that harkened back to ancient times and was one of their greatest strengths. It was not a philosophy widely shared among humans.

For that reason Angus encouraged and praised Myra and Isabel for their thirst for knowledge and their independence. He'd raised Isabel the way he had because she was of mixed blood, having an Immortal mother and a father from the race of humankind. One day he would tell her. But not now. There was still time.

Myra squeezed his arm. "Angus, your thoughts are far from us. Come, I will fix you a warm meal. There is nothing more that can be done for this poor soul."

He rubbed his forehead as though trying to block out his thoughts and stared again at the man. There was something odd about the pallor of his skin. It was not the color of death. He could understand why Isabel questioned the physician's diagnosis.

"Are you sure the wounds he suffered appeared fatal?"

He did not wait for an answer but moved closer until he stood directly over the bed. Despite the warmth from the fire, a chill shuddered through him.

Myra nodded. "Aye. His wounds were deep. We cleaned and sutured them as best we could, but he has not stirred since last night."

Isabel's voice was low and strained as though the words were dragged from her. "There was so much blood." Her voice trembled. "It was difficult to stop its flow. When at last it subsided, it seemed as though he stopped breathing as well. That was when Myra sought the advice of the queen's physician, John Campbell."

Angus arched an eyebrow. "And the physician agreed to come?"

It was Angus's experience that the physicians who tended to the needs of the nobility did not sully their hands with servants.

Myra nodded. "John Campbell is only newly appointed to court. I believe he wanted to make a good impression on the queen. However, he told us what we already suspected and declared the man dead. I was about to prepare him for burial." She sighed. "It is the least we can do."

Angus reached for a candle from the table beside the bed. Something was not right. "When did the physician examine this man?"

Myra tucked a strand of hair behind her ear. "He was here just a short time ago. Why do ye ask?"

Although there were no visible signs the man was breathing, he looked peaceful, as though sleeping. Angus paused. Or gathering strength. He had not heard that any Immortals would be passing through London, but still, he had been gone a long time.

He had stood watch over many in similar circumstances. This was how an Immortal appeared when they were recovering from a wound that killed the body but not the essence.

Angus did not recognize this man, but then there were thousands of his kind. Although not as numerous as in the Beginning Time, more Immortals were born each year. They owed the gift of their existence, as well as its curse, to the scientists of Atlantis. Knowing their world would soon be destroyed and the lands they would travel to barbaric, an elixir was devised that would help them heal from their wounds and unknown diseases. However, it worked too well. Once in the bloodstream, it not only healed but it also prolonged life.

But the prize for some was too high. A side effect caused many to go insane. It was a bloodlust that turned a man into a killing animal. There was no way to predict who would be infected and no cure save death.

Angus brought the candle closer to the stranger. It

was impossible to distinguish humankind from an Immortal, save when they were in the Healing Sleep. During this time, three dark, cobalt blue lines encircled each wrist. His kind believed these marks held the healing energy of the potion that was now an inherited trait. Those who studied palmistry referred to them as a "magic bracelet" and considered them a sign of good luck. In an Immortal, that belief was an understatement.

Angus held his breath in anticipation. In the low light, circles of blue were visible around the man's wrists.

"Father, what is wrong?"

He ignored Isabel's question as he reached for the man's wrist, hoping the marks were not a trick of light and shadow. Instead of easing his rapid heart rate, his pulse increased. He did not imagine the circles. But there was more.

Angus let out his breath slowly. There was also the birthmark of a Protector. His excitement at discovering another Immortal evaporated.

He felt as though all the air had been sucked out of the room. He whispered the word, "Protector."

Myra touched his arm gently. "What did ye say?"

He turned abruptly to Myra. "This man will live."

Myra stepped back, her eyes wide. Angus could read in her expression the moment when awareness took hold of her.

She gnawed at her lower lip. "What can we do? Soon someone will be here to take him for burial."

Isabel stood between them. "I do not understand. How can you say William will live? John Campbell was most insistent he was dead."

Angus gripped the candle. He did not like the

sound of Isabel's voice as she said the Protector's name. "Tell me, how is it you know his name?"

"He told me before he lost consciousness."

Angus willed himself to remain calm. "Was there anything else?"

She hesitated a fraction of a second before shaking her head. "There was nothing more."

She was keeping something from him, he was certain. He set the candle on the table. Maybe he was just imagining her hesitation. It was a long time since he'd had a warm meal and a good night's sleep. Finding an Immortal who was also a Protector had set his nerves on edge.

He also hated keeping the truth from his only child. But it was necessary. When had it become so easy for him to lie? Perhaps he was born with the skill. Still, he despised the ease with which the words tripped so lightly from his lips. He kept reminding himself it was for her own safety that he kept the truth from her of not only his identity but hers as well.

"Isabel, I have seen this type of ailment before. William will live." That fact, at least, was not a lie.

Angus shuddered, remembering an incident when, had he not recovered in time, he would have been buried alive. No matter what he felt about Protectors, he could not allow that to happen to anyone.

He put his hand on Isabel's shoulder. "If John Campbell's men come for William, please inform me at once."

Isabel nodded slowly. She turned toward the bed and gently brushed strands of William's hair from his forehead. The gesture troubled Angus. Isabel was by nature a compassionate woman, but something in her expression suggested she felt more for this man than a mere concern he would recover. The prospect of romance had always been pushed aside in her quest to paint.

At Myra's advice, Angus had not pressed for Isabel to marry, although seeing her in a loving relationship that would bear children was a secret wish of his. However, it would not be wise for her to fall in love with an Immortal. Their lives were not easy. Isabel need only ask Myra. He had told Myra his love for her would never falter. But as she grew older and he remained the same as when they first met, he could see the pain in her eyes, and the doubt. It cut him deeper than any wound he had ever experienced.

He placed his arm around Myra's waist and leaned toward her. "I have to put some things away in my study first, and then we will have the evening together." He smiled. "I hope you like the gifts I brought home."

"I need no gift, only you." She kissed him lightly. "I will make sure the lad is comfortable and then meet you in the study."

He was warmed by her comment and her kiss, but he noticed she also stared in Isabel's direction. Had Myra also noticed their daughter's uncharacteristic interest in William? Myra, above all others, knew the price for loving an Immortal.

If his heart were made of stone, like that of the gargoyles guarding the entrance to Hampton Court, he would not feel pain. But although an Immortal, his heart beat as strong as any man's. And now it ached.

He left Myra's side, taking the stairs to his chamber two at a time. When he reached the landing, he looked down at the leather-bound book he carried before locking it in a cabinet. It held many secrets within its covers. The most precious to him was the identity of Isabel's parents.

Chapter 6

Satisfied that William was resting comfortably, Myra retreated to the Solar. Angus was already there, coaxing the dying embers in the hearth back to life. It was a room on the south side of the manor, where Isabel painted. Hugging the far wall was a long trestle table. Arranged neatly over its polished surface were clay containers of oil, water, bowls of powdered colors, and a pestle and mortar for mixing the paint. Normally, it lifted Myra's spirits just being here. But that was not the case today. The events of the past evening were taking their toll. She had recognized the expression on Isabel's face. How could she tell Isabel there was no future for her with William?

She allowed herself the luxury of watching Angus. Even after so many years together, her heart beat more rapidly when he was near. She had been looking forward to his return, and now it was spoiled by the intrusion of the stranger. She felt a pang of guilt at the selfish thought.

Nonetheless, she was unable to shake the feeling that the sudden appearance of William did not bode well and might change their quiet existence. She knew the majority of her anxiety was a result of Isabel's interest in the stranger. Myra did not want her daughter to share her fate and hoped her suspicions were unfounded. Loving an Immortal was not an easy path.

Angus stood and dusted off his hands as he reached into the folds of his shirt. He pulled out a small box wrapped in red silk and handed it to her. "I had it made for you in Italy."

Myra forced a smile on her face. Angus was always bringing her gifts on his return trips. She knew it was his way of telling her she was always in his thoughts. She would have preferred his presence to gifts.

She sat down next to the hearth and opened the box. Nestled in a bed of black velvet was a gold ring. Red rubies were encrusted in the band, forming the letter M. She slipped the ring on her finger and whispered, "It is wondrous, my love, and so beautiful."

Angus knelt by her side, taking both her hands in his. He kissed the tips of her fingers. "It pales in beauty beside your own."

She laughed. "Ah, what a silver tongue ye have, my great bear of a man."

He winked. "Ye inspire me." Angus pulled her to her feet, and his expression grew serious. "As much as I want to avoid the topic, I know the appearance of the stranger lies as heavy on your mind as it does on mine. What do you know of him?"

"Only that Isabel witnessed his attack along the Thames River and sought to help him. When he was injured in a fight to save her, she felt compelled to bring him to the manor."

Myra said aloud the question she could not utter in Isabel's presence. She did not want there to be any doubt. "Do ye believe William is one of your kind?" It was difficult for her to say the word "immortal" out loud, he knew.

A shadow crossed Angus's features as he walked over to the fire. He stirred the embers until the flames rolled in controlled fury over the wood. "Aye. He has all the signs. You say Isabel brought him here last night?"

Myra nodded as a shudder racked through her. She crossed her arms over her chest and gripped them to help stop the trembling that shivered through her body.

He heaved a sigh and rose to his feet. "It willna be long until William recovers. One more day, at most. As a Protector, 'tis said they heal in half the time as other Immortals. 'Tis only one of the many things that sets them apart."

She nodded again, knowing there was more. "What else troubles ye, my love?"

Angus hesitated. "Even amongst a clan like the Immortals, the Protectors are a strange breed."

Myra heard the concern reflected in his voice. She remembered the day Angus had brought the infant Isabel to her and told her the babe's parents had died on a battlefield in Scotland. The child had been an answer to Myra's prayers. She had not questioned how Isabel had come to be entrusted in her care, only that it fulfilled a dream she had abandoned when she had pledged her love and life to Angus.

Angus had told Myra they must keep the identity of Isabel's parents a secret. Isabel's mother was an Immortal, but her father was not. Their union was against the laws of the Immortals, and if discovered, it could be dangerous for Isabel. Angus and Myra had lied to Isabel, telling her they did not know the identity of her parents. It was the hardest thing Myra had ever done. At the time, she had not questioned Angus, but now she was not so sure.

Despite the cozy warmth of the fire, Myra shivered as she walked over to Angus and wove her arms around him.

He held her close. "We must be very careful. Protectors are only dangerous to those who disobey the codes of the Immortals. Once they are assigned to track down an offender, they cannot be stopped. And they always work alone. They are ruthless and without emotion."

Myra shuddered as once more she thought of Isabel. Her parents had disobeyed the Immortals' codes. Myra thought it inconceivable that Isabel should be judged for their crimes. However, she knew she would never understand all the rules of the Immortals.

"Do ye know who William hunts?"

Angus shook his head slowly. "Nay, but I know what is in your thoughts. It cannot be Isabel. No one knew of the union between her parents."

Myra felt the resolve of a lioness protecting her cub. "But how can ye be so sure?"

"As you know, Immortals are infertile unless they take the Elixir of Life, which, if successful, reverses their gift of immortality, giving them the ability to produce children. However, the elixir is guarded and given only after sanction by the Council of Seven. I never fully understood how Isabel's mother was able to steal the elixir without detection."

Myra would not voice her secret frustration that the Council of Seven had refused Angus's request for this elixir. They claimed his role as mentor to young Immortals in need of leadership training was too valuable to be lost in a union with a mortal woman.

When the Council refused his request, he did not press them further. When she was younger, she had asked Angus to defy the Council. She'd come to realize his sense of duty was stronger than his love for her.

She swallowed down the tears that, even now, after all this time, threatened to choke her. After a while, she'd stopped asking and resigned herself. She knew Angus's first loyalty was to his own kind. More than once she'd thought to leave Angus, but her love for him was too strong. She could not bear a life without him.

However, she did not want the same heartache for her daughter. Isabel deserved to be with a man who could give her all of his love, as well as a stable home and children.

Angus was talking again. Myra concentrated on his words, although she had heard this story many times before. It was as though he never understood what had motivated Isabel's mother to defy the Council. Myra did. It was love.

Angus took a deep breath. "Isabel's mother, Marguerite, stole the Elixir of Life from the Chamber of Knowledge at Urquhart Castle. It was an extreme violation of our laws, and the penalty was death. She took the name of the person who helped her to her grave." Angus kissed Myra lightly on the lips. "But enough of such talk. There is little we can do now. We must wait until the Protector awakens."

Myra's lips trembled. "We could run."

"Nay. If indeed the Protector has learned of Isabel's parentage and tracked us this far, there would be no escape. Besides, there is a chance Isabel will be spared. 'Tis not her crime but that of her parents."

"And what of our crime for protecting her and

keeping knowledge of her existence from the Council of Seven?"

"Again, to run now would seal our fate. 'Tis well known that if a Protector is required to chase his prey, he prefers to bring them back dead. Our only hope for survival is to keep silent. After all, so far Isabel has proven that the Council's theory regarding children born from mixed blood was correct. They believe that a child from a mixed union will not inherit the gift of lmmortality. It is the reason marriages between an Immortal and a member of the humankind race was forbidden in the first place. Our numbers are small enough as it is."

Myra hoped he was right. It would be so much easier for Isabel if she was a mortal woman. While Isabel was growing up, Myra was always alert for any signs the child had inherited her mother's traits and was an Immortal. Thankfully, there were none. To the contrary, Isabel still bore little white scars on her knees and elbows from falling while riding her horse.

He smiled. "Now, my love, let us make the most of our time together."

As always, Myra struggled to block out the fact that Angus was different. For her it was a battle she could never escape. She would age while he would remain the same as on the day they'd first met—a man in his early thirties. In her heart, she was confident of his love. It was only when they were separated that her mind fed her deepest fear. One day he would tire of the old woman she would become, and leave her. But today was not the time to dwell on such things. She would try to live in the present. Angus was with her now, and that should be all that mattered.

Myra put her arms around his neck. "I love ye, my big bear of a man, and we have been apart far too long. Do ye know what are my thoughts?"

He laughed. "Aye, lass, and they are the same as mine."

Angus picked her up in his arms and spun her around as though she were as light as sunbeams. For a time she would forget that she would continue to grow old while Angus would stay as he was now. She closed her eyes as he leaned down to kiss her, transporting her to a time when they were both forever young. His kiss was warm and filled with love. She lost herself in his embrace. Her heart swelled and, as with each time before, she fell in love with him all over again.

****

Isabel sat beside the window in William's chamber. It was almost dawn. A little over a full day had passed since she'd brought him to the manor. Time slowed as though fighting its way through a violent storm as she waited for any sign William would recover.

The only diversion was when John Campbell sent men to collect William for burial. Angus blocked their path, informing them that their services were no longer needed. The physician's men left, but with the promise to return. Angus did not appear worried, saying William would regain consciousness long before the physician gathered enough courage to try again.

But William did not recover and lay as still as death. She pressed her forehead against the cool panes of leaded glass. She wanted to believe Angus, but it grew more difficult with each hour that passed.

She remembered when she first saw William. He'd

appeared out of the churning river like a valiant knight from legends of ancient times, like those heroes of old who battled and single-handedly vanquished his foes. When he'd rescued her, the fantasy had been complete. She was like the fair damsel who was saved from the dragon by a dark warrior. Further, he'd kissed her with such passion that it took her breath away. Her face warmed from the memory.

Why had he kissed her?

She opened the window, welcoming the icy breeze to cool her skin. It had snowed relentlessly since William arrived, and now it clung to the trees and settled in drifts against the walls. Myra said the servants at Hampton Court worked around the clock to keep the garden paths clear for the queen and nobles. It was a backbreaking job, and so far Mother Nature was winning the battle. It reminded her of the one William fought.

Isabel breathed deeply of the cool air and touched her lips with her fingers. She could remember the touch of his mouth on hers. Last night she awoke from a dream in which William held her in his arms, covering her body with warm kisses.

What was happening to her?

Isabel pressed her hand against her stomach to quiet the giant butterflies that fluttered inside. It was to no avail. She glanced outside. Night still held the day in its grasp, reluctant to release it to the sun. Light from the torches glistened over the snow like crushed diamonds, turning the gardens into an enchanted wonderland. It was a time when all should be content to stay abed a while longer. But Isabel was restless.

She turned from the window and stepped toward

the hearth. Picking up her sketchpad, she opened it and sat down near the fire. Angus and Myra, not deterred by the cold, had taken the opportunity to indulge in a carriage ride through the snow to bring little Elaenor MacAlpin home from her visit to Elizabeth, the queen's half-sister.

Elaenor was the sister of Lachlan MacAlpin, a friend of Angus's, and she was staying with them while Lachlan was away. Although Elaenor was only eight years old, she and Elizabeth were friends. But Myra missed her and felt it was time for Elaenor to return to the manor. Angus and Myra promised they would all be back in time to see William awaken from his deep sleep. Isabel wished she could feel as confident.

Isabel returned to her sketching and tried to concentrate. But today, patience was not her best virtue. She forced herself to the task at hand and soon became lost in her work. Myra often said that while Isabel was drawing, time ceased to exist. Her newest project took life as she added depth and shadows to the sketch.

She was trying something new. In the past she had concentrated on bowls of fruit, landscapes, animals, or portraits. Those were acceptable subjects for a woman. To go further and paint the naked human body was not permitted for her gender. However, it was a risk she was willing to take.

She'd talked Ossian into allowing her to help him on his commissioned work for the queen. Mary Tudor wanted a costume ball to take place in her husband's honor, and Ossian had given her the ideal theme.

The artists would re-create a mythical city resembling the ones in Greece and the Roman Empire during the height of their power, complete with replicas of their gods. Isabel had warmed to the idea as well and convinced Ossian she could contribute.

She knew not all of the artists at the Painters' Guild were as agreeable. Forsyth was vocal in his disapproval. He did not feel it was proper for a woman to paint the male form. In the end, his opinions were ignored. He reacted by behaving as though she did not exist. His attitude only reinforced her desire to do as she pleased. No one had the right to tell her who or what she could paint.

Brushing aside her negative thoughts, she focused on the sketch before her.

William was the perfect model. His shoulders and upper body were chiseled and clearly defined. It was an ideal situation—not only was this portion of his anatomy uncovered, but he never stirred. A perfect model, indeed.

The rushes on the floor made a crunching sound, as though something or someone had disturbed them. Startled, Isabel dropped her pencil and looked over toward the bed. A pillow had fallen from the bed to the ground. Isabel was poised on the edge of her chair. Had she seen William's fingers twitch or only imagined it?

She relaxed against her chair. Nay, William still lay in that frozen pose. It reminded her of something she had once seen in St. Paul's Cathedral in London. On top of a coffin lay a life-size stone likeness of a knight who had died in the twelfth century. She shivered at the memory. The man had looked so real she'd thought he would open his eyes at any moment.

She shivered again as she retrieved her pencil. The artists at the studio often said a vivid imagination and a mind open to all possibilities were essential for the creative process. She smiled, remembering her fantasy about William, and she decided she did indeed have all the mental qualifications needed.

Once more she turned her attention to her drawing while she waited for Angus and Myra to return. Lost in her work, she remembered the knight in the cathedral. The sculptor had succeeded in creating a lifelike image.

Isabel longed to have that same ability. She looked toward William, wanting to capture his essence on canvas. If only she knew more details of his life. His passions, his strengths, and his weaknesses. These elements were reflected in a man's face.

In the all-too-brief moments when their eyes had met, Isabel had caught a glimpse of all these things. Perhaps that was the reason she had not fled. Instead of frightening her, his intense gaze had only made her want to know more.

Chapter 7

William was awake. The sensation was like traveling in a train as it emerged from a dark tunnel into the light of day.

He fought to remember where he was. London, England. 1558.

His assignment: Capture or kill the Renegade Immortal known only as Bartholomew.

As always, it was simpler to kill. Less paperwork. Gavin liked it that way. So did William.

He sucked in a breath of cool air and heard the bed creak. Years of discipline kept him rigid and alert. His breathing was shallow, his body as quiet as stone. Experience had also taught him to assess his surroundings before taking action. If he opened his eyes too soon, he would lose the advantage of surprise.

After all, an unconscious man would not pose a threat. He could then disappear and be about his assignment before involving any more civilians. He'd already lost a full day, waiting for his body to heal.

William scanned through his last conscious memory. He'd succeeded in eliminating the men who ambushed him. No doubt the work of Bartholomew.

He remembered a woman. Isabel.

William permitted himself another shallow breath of air.

Instinctively he knew she would be a distraction.

With his eyes still closed, he turned his attention to assessing his surroundings through his senses. He was lying on a soft mattress, most likely made of goose down. There was a comfortable warmth that permeated the air and a fresh, clean scent of lavender. A fire cracked against stone.

William opened his eyes and looked around the room. He recognized the person sitting by the fireplace. It was Isabel.

Damn.

He'd never before felt such a strong pull toward a woman as he had when he'd seen her rush to his defense. Kissing her had seemed as natural as breathing. He dismissed the whole soul-mate theory. He'd just been working too hard without a break. When this was over, he'd remedy that problem. In the meantime, he reminded himself of the training mantra. Distractions caused mistakes and failures.

He tamped down his reaction of pleasure at seeing her and of the overpowering need to rush over and pull her into his arms. She was lovelier than his memory.

She sat before the fireplace, sketching. He remembered the paint on her face that he'd thought was blood. She was an artist. William's knowledge of this time period was extensive, and he knew only well-educated or rebellious women explored the arts. For some reason the knowledge pleased him.

Her hair floated over her shoulders in soft dark waves, begging to be touched. Her profile, and the long line of her neck, made him wonder what it would be like to kiss her bare skin. He wanted the taste of her in his mouth.

Isabel paused in her drawing as though aware of

his gaze on her body. She looked up from her sketchpad and turned in his direction. Her eyes. He had forgotten her eyes. Dark brown. They promised warmth, comfort…passion. He clenched his fists at his side.

This was going to be a test of his will and strength of purpose. He knew how to handle the situation. No matter how intelligent, beautiful, and courageous she might be, she was first and foremost a distraction.

His traitorous mind asked what was so bad about that scenario.

William would be all business. A hard, emotionless being incapable of forming attachments. If only he'd not kissed her. It would be simpler if he didn't know what he was missing.

She stood. The long dress she wore clung to full breasts and a slender waist.

God save him.

He swallowed, determined to gain control of the situation. William slid out of bed. His bare feet touched the icy stone floor. Thankfully the section he stood on was bare of rushes or carpet. He relished the cold and hoped it would cool his thoughts as well as the heat of his body.

He cleared his throat. "Where am I?"

William saw her flinch. Perfect. His voice was harsh, and his words demanding. That should make her want to run from him. Or at least keep her distance.

Her face blushed a soft rose pink that reminded him of spring. He thought she was the most beautiful woman he'd ever seen.

Isabel lifted her chin. "You are in my home. It is located on the Thames River near Hampton Court."

Her voice was strong and steady. If she feared him,

she possessed the strength to hide it well. His admiration grew. And his luck was holding. Not only had he survived the ambush but he was also close to his destination.

She clutched the fabric of her gown. "Your full name, sir? I know you only by William." How had she learned his name?

He scanned his memory and recalled he'd given her that information. He probably felt he'd had to after she'd risked her life to come to his aid. Or the need to kiss her had addled his brain. That was no doubt the real reason.

However, he could not give her more. Many in this century knew the MacAlpin clan. It was too much of a risk.

He kept the tone of his voice intense. She needed to be aware who was in control.

"William is the only name I can give you." He narrowed his eyes. "Who else knows I'm here?"

She smoothed the fabric over her waist. He noted a slight trembling in her fingers and an increase of color in her cheeks. "Only my parents. And of course the queen's physician, John Campbell." She paused. "Sir?"

Counting Isabel, four people knew he was here. He amended his calculation. Bartholomew must know. This could compromise the assignment. He would have to work quickly. He combed his fingers through his hair. "Don't tell anyone else I was here. I'll need to purchase a horse."

"Sir?"

"What is it?" He snapped out the words. Didn't she understand his request? She was standing as motionless as a statue.

A smile played at the corners of her mouth. "Will you also be needing clothes as well?"

"Clothes?"

He said the word slowly. Time screeched to a halt as he looked down and swore. He grabbed a pillow from the bed and covered himself. He was buck-naked. But that was not the worst of it. His reaction to this woman was as plain as day.

"Damn."

He clenched his jaw and fought back the rise of color spreading over his face. "Thank you, that would be a great idea."

Her smile spread across her face, enhancing her beauty and his embarrassment.

She turned and headed toward the hearth. There seemed to be a spring in her step as she retrieved a neatly folded bundle.

"Myra washed these for you. They were soaked in blood. It would be wise if you would thank her for her trouble." Isabel was walking toward him as though caught in one of those movies where the heroine moved in slow motion. She met his gaze. "That is, sir, if you have the word in your limited vocabulary."

She tossed the clothes toward him. He instinctively dropped the pillow to catch them and managed to snag the items in midair.

"Look, woman, I'm naked here. Or are you in the habit of staring at men without their clothes on?"

"Yes, and I have seen better."

He yanked his shirt over his head. This woman was beginning to get on his nerves. The seams ripped as he tugged the shirt into place too quickly. He then wound the plaid fabric around him to form a kilt.

"Myra could repair your shirt." Her smile could charm a cat into giving up his mouse. "That is, if you thanked her for washing your clothes. Do you need any help getting dressed?"

He glowered at her and was impressed she did not shrink away.

William flipped the end of the fabric over his shoulder and belted the cloth in place around his waist. "No, as you can see, I have things under control."

"Are you always in a bad temper when you awake? I think I liked you better when you were unconscious." She put her hands on her hips. "You have not even thanked me for saving your life. I should have left you by the river to die."

She was closing in on him. The tone of her voice was becoming higher pitched by the second. He hated this part—the "I apologize if I offended you" part. He should order personal stationery with those words in bold print written across the top of each page.

There was a knock on the door so loud it rattled the hinges. It offered a reprieve.

William reached behind him for his sword. "Are you expecting someone?"

"My lover," she said with sarcasm.

The thought of her with a lover made him intensely angry. And then frustrated over his unexpected reaction. He was getting in too deep, and he'd only just met the woman.

In the next instant, the door burst open and two men, with their weapons drawn, strode into the room.

William sprang forward and pulled Isabel instinctively behind him as he held out his sword. "Which one of these men is your lover?"

"You are not funny."

The taller of the two nodded toward the bed. "Daniel and I have come for the corpse. We tried earlier but were sent away. Our orders are from John Campbell, the queen's physician."

Isabel stepped alongside William. "My husband has recovered."

"Husband?" William snapped to attention. "When did that happen?"

She shook her head as though dismissing his question as she addressed the men. "You can see for yourself he is well."

William cocked an eyebrow. "Did I enjoy the honeymoon?"

Her response was as icy as a glacial lake. "You may have, but I most certainly did not."

The tall man chuckled and elbowed his companion in the ribs. He nodded toward Isabel. "Well, now, little lady. We have our orders. And from the way you two lovebirds are behaving, you might thank us for disposing of the bloke for ye. But more importantly, if this here man is supposed to be the body in question, then we means to fetch him for our master." He shrugged. "Dead or alive, makes no difference to us."

"You fools." Isabel tried to move in front of William, but he held her in place.

He could feel the heat rising on her skin. "As you can see, gentlemen, I'm alive. There's no body to 'fetch.' "

The tall man ground out his words. "We have our orders." William noticed that Daniel hung back, as though abdicating control to his friend. They meant to attack him. It also meant that William would have the luxury of fighting the men one at a time.

He saw a change pass over the tall man's eyes, signaling the attack only a half a heartbeat before it occurred.

When the man leaped forward, his sword extended, William was ready. He blocked the tall man's blade with his own, then pressed the attack and forced the sword out of his assailant's grasp. It clattered to the floor and spun to the corner of the room. William doubled up his fist and punched the tall man in the jaw. He dropped like a stone to the ground.

Daniel yelled out his frustration and lunged toward William. His skill was more pathetic than the tall man's. Daniel's sword flailed ineffectively in the air. His eyes were wide and reminded William of an animal caught in the headlight of an oncoming truck.

William knocked the weapon out of Daniel's hand and pointed the tip of his sword at the man's throat. Blood formed on Daniel's neck.

William pressed his blade deeper. "I'm feeling generous today. Take your friend with you before I change my mind. And tell John Campbell not to bother us anymore." William loosened the pressure of his blade and stepped back a fraction of a step. "Have I made myself clear?"

Daniel nodded his head like a Kewpie-doll prize at an old-time penny arcade. He rushed over to the tall man and helped him to his feet. As the two men reached the door, it opened.

A salt-and-pepper wolfhound trotted in as though he owned the place, followed by a powerfully built Scotsman, an attractive middle-aged woman, and a young girl of about eight or nine.

William took a deep breath. Great. This was all he needed. More people. He wondered if he should send out announcements. So much for the idea that this was a top-secret mission.

Chapter 8

William kept a loose grip on the hilt of his sword. He'd recognized the Scotsman. It was Angus. The woman must be Myra. She was the only one Angus had ever said he loved. It was blind luck that he should land in Angus's home. It saved William the time of trying to find him. He needed his help, but there was no telling how the man would react. William knew enough about Angus to know he guarded his privacy. The next few moments were critical.

A young girl, with blonde ringlets bouncing around her heart-shaped face, ran past him as though he were invisible. She skidded to a halt in front of the window, pulled open the shutters, and held out her hand. She giggled with delight as the snowflakes dropped on her bare skin. There was something about her that was familiar, but right now Angus was his focal point.

The wolfhound ambled over to the girl and sat back on his haunches in rapt attention, as though she were the most interesting creature in the world. Isabel, Myra, and Angus, however, stood as though superglued to the floor and stared in his direction.

William broke the silence. ''Angus, I would like to have a word with you.''

It was as though the air lifted and the all-clear bell sounded. Everyone talked at once. Their words drowned out each other's until all that was left was a loud hum.

Isabel's voice rang above the others. She came straight to the point. "How do you know my father's name?"

William straightened. How could Angus have a daughter? Immortals were infertile until they took the Elixir of Life. Maybe Angus had adopted Isabel. Someone hadn't done a very good job updating Angus's file.

Angus put his hand on Isabel's shoulder as though to restrain her. "Isabel, please leave this to me."

Isabel's voice lowered. "Father, are you in danger?"

Angus smiled and patted her cheek. "There is nothing to worry about, lass. I am confident there is a logical explanation." William could tell by the way she glared openly at him that Angus had not convinced her. And Myra paced liked a caged animal in the background. He almost envied Angus at this moment. These two women were ready to do battle if they thought Angus was in trouble.

Angus narrowed his gaze. "My daughter has asked a good question. How is it you know who I am, while I know nothing about you?"

William hesitated. He was willing to talk to Angus, but not with the others present. "I believe you know, if not my name, at least what I am."

Angus nodded slowly and inched his right hand over the hilt of his blade. His fingers twitched as though anxious to draw the sword from its scabbard.

William fought against the instinct to tighten his grip on his own weapon as well. "Drawing your sword wouldn't be wise." He paused and stated what he knew would set them at ease. "I'm not here for you or members of your family. However, there is important business Angus and I need to discuss."

A collective sigh wove through the room like a spring breeze over meadow grass.

Angus's shoulders relaxed visibly. "Very well."

"Father, what are you saying? What concerns you concerns us all. You cannot leave with this man. How can you be certain he can be trusted?"

Angus squeezed her hand gently. "You trusted him enough to bring him into our home."

Tears welled in her eyes as she stepped toward William and turned the full force of her anger and frustration toward him. "My father is correct. I regret my act of kindness." She pointed her finger at him. "You must give me your solemn vow you will not harm my father."

For the first time in quite a while William was at a loss for words. Again, Isabel's courage astounded him.

She put her hands on her hips. "I am waiting for your answer."

Angus seemed to find his voice. "Isabel, I dinna think—"

William interrupted Angus and inclined his head toward Isabel. "I vow I will not harm your father." On impulse, he leaned toward her and brushed his fingers across her cheek. The skin was soft and warm under his touch.

She didn't move away but stood her ground.

At that moment he knew Angus could have been the devil himself and William would have shown mercy.

William pulled back from her. What was

happening to him? Unfortunately, he knew exactly. He was convinced it was a full-blown case of lust with a generous dose of respect thrown in for good measure. Actually, it was the latter emotion that had him worried. Lust he could deal with. It had a shelf life and a way of burning itself out. Mutual respect was another matter altogether. This emotion was often a foundation for something permanent.

Angus nodded toward him. "We will be able to talk more freely outside."

William followed him, welcoming the chance to clear his head. He was also not at all pleased with the puzzle Isabel's family presented. Angus and Myra's reaction to him left an uneasy feeling in the pit of his stomach. Angus must know that William was a Protector, and yet the man's first impulse had been to draw his blade. The reaction was not new to William, as most feared him. However, Angus was known for always abiding by the code of the Immortals. Such a man would have no reason to fear a Protector. Yet it was apparent Angus reacted like a man who was hiding something.

This was a complication William hadn't bargained for. Secrets often bubbled to the surface and jeopardized a person's effectiveness on an assignment. A man whose primary instinct was to protect a secret might not use the best judgment. And William needed Angus to be at the top of his game, both mentally and physically.

William walked in silence beside Angus. They reached the gardens near the stables and headed toward the protection of a grove of trees. Although there was a momentary lull in the snowfall, the wind had picked up, and it cut through to William's skin. It was not the first time he marveled at the intelligence of his ancestors and their accomplishments surrounding the science of time travel. One minute he was in the twenty-first century battling the heat and flames of a forest fire in Montana, and the next he was freezing in the sixteenth. He should have thought to bring a warm jacket.

He turned toward Angus. For a brief moment William saw fear cloud the man's eyes. William's unease returned.

No one knew Angus's chronological age or his origins. The only thing known for certain was that his integrity and loyalty were legendary. Both Lachlan and Gavin had assured William that this was a man who could be trusted, as Angus's life was an open book. Then why was an adopted daughter excluded from the man's file? Many Immortals adopted orphaned humankind children. The practice was not forbidden, but the fact remained that Angus had kept the information from the Council. This was not a good way to start.

William chose his words carefully. The beginning of an assignment was always the most difficult. In most cases, you had to convince your contact of an improbable scenario and then hope they had the intelligence and courage to grasp it. Sometimes it didn't work, which was why he preferred to work alone.

He kept his voice light. "What do you think about the weather?"

Angus's teeth clenched. He looked as though he was fighting back an angry response. "'Tis as cold as a whore's teat."

William's mood lightened. The man had a sense of

humor. He'd forgotten that about Angus. William blew on his hands. "Would you say, from your experience, that it's colder than usual?"

"Aye." Angus let the word drag out as he lifted an eyebrow and tilted his head to the side. "I dinna think you asked me out for a stroll in this bitter wind to discuss the weather."

"Actually, that's exactly what I want to discuss with you. Have you ever seen it this cold?"

The wind whipped around the gardens, and a cold blast of air found its way toward them. Angus shuddered as he peered out toward the thick blanket of clouds covering the sky.

His words were barely audible over the sound of the wind. "England's weather is often cold and mean this time of year."

"But this is unusual, even for England. Don't you agree?"

Angus's gaze narrowed, but he was silent.

William waited. It would be more powerful if Angus reached the right conclusion by himself.

Time crept by as Angus ventured out of the protection of the trees and glanced toward the sky. He bent down to examine the snow that was packed in drifts against the walls of the stable.

William stomped his feet to bring life back in them as he waited for Angus. William might be an Immortal, but his body was still affected by the weather. Extremes of hot and cold couldn't permanently harm or kill him, but it was still no picnic.

When Angus returned, William knew from his expression and the purposeful way he strode toward him that the man had reached a decision.

Angus's voice rose over the wind. "The weather is most unusual. 'Tis not just the fact that we have more snow than normal, but it is the texture of the ice. What is even more disturbing is that the squirrels are gone. They are a hardy lot but are nowhere to be found. Is the weather Mother Nature's idea, or is it something else?"

William was relieved. Angus grasped more than he'd hoped. "This has nothing to do with Mother Nature."

Angus's eyebrows scrunched together. "But there is only one reason it feels as though it is the coming of another ice age." He paused. "Has someone tampered with history again?"

"Yes. That's exactly what the Council suspects has happened." William blew on his hands. "What we know for sure is that a Renegade Immortal escaped from one of our prisons and traveled to this century in order to change history. By the condition of the weather, I'd say his plan is already in motion. Our only hope is to contain the damage, reverse it if possible, and then capture or kill him." William hesitated for only a split second. There was more information Angus needed to know if they were to work together. "I'm from the twenty-first century. I've time-traveled from my century to yours to hunt the escaped Renegade."

The words clung to the air like a cold storm cloud. When Angus spoke, it was with a steady voice. "I know time travel is possible. I have witnessed it myself. But when our ancestors discovered how to control the fabric of time, they warned us against using the knowledge to change history. It was what destroyed our world and one of the reasons the Council of Seven was formed." He glanced toward the dark sky. "It is unfortunate we did not listen to them. This must also mean that the Guardian was part of the Renegade's plot. No one can travel through time without the Guardian's help."

William nodded. "As you must have guessed, the Council of Seven is on the verge of hysteria. There are signs that betrayal has reached every level of the Immortal world, even as high up as the Council itself. The part the Guardian played in this conspiracy concerns us all. But my first task is to find the Renegade. Let the Council deal with the Guardian."

Angus's voice sounded strained. "That is good reasoning. You have me at a disadvantage, since I only know you by your first name."

"And that is all I can give you. I can't even tell you the real name of the Renegade who has jumped through time."

Angus sucked in a deep breath. "The hell you say. Am I not to be trusted?"

William paused. "My instructions come directly from the head of the Council."

"Aye. I understand. However, at times I think they have more rules than sense." Angus blew on his hands. "Blast this cold. Is there anything you can tell me about yourself?"

William could not share all aspects about the future, especially knowledge of people Angus might meet, but there were things William could say that would help build a bond between them.

William stomped his feet again to warm them. "I can tell you that my father was the Immortal Declan Redmond. As you are aware, humankind normally takes their father's last name, whereas Immortals take their mother's."

A frown spread over Angus's features. "I have heard of this Declan Redmond of whom you speak. He professes loyalty only to himself and dances close to the edge of being a Renegade. 'Tis hard to believe that in some future time Declan will change his ways long enough to take a wife. What is even harder to understand is that he will sire a child worthy to be a Protector."

William shrugged. "I've heard of my father's past, but that was before he met my mother."

Angus laughed. "I would doubt any woman would want to take on such a daunting task. It would be easier to move a mountain. Can you tell me her identity?"

"Sorry, that's not possible."

"Rules again, but the story of how your mother tamed Redmond is curious."

William nodded. "I agree. From some of the stories my uncle told me, their courtship was unusual, to say the least." He was glad he'd told Angus as much as he had. It was part of the nature of a man or woman to want to feel as though they could be trusted.

Angus scrunched his eyebrows together. "There is something I must ask, if only to ease my mind. 'Tis well known that Protectors complete their assignment at any price. I have seen them slaughter the innocent who get in their way." He hesitated. "Can you promise me no humankind will die?"

"I know the Protectors had a reputation in the dark times of being unjust, but we have changed, and we honor life whenever possible."

"Not good enough." Angus's voice rose. "Your word."

William knew that if he didn't meet Angus's

demands it might jeopardize the success of this assignment. He admired Angus's strength to demand such a vow from him. He could see where Isabel got her strength.

"I give you my word."

Angus nodded and slapped him on the shoulder. "Then I pledge you my loyalty. When do we begin?"

Chapter 9

Isabel did not like to feel excluded, yet that was exactly what was happening. She peered out the window and saw William and Angus in a serious discussion near the stables. They behaved as though they were long-lost friends instead of perfect strangers.

She pulled away from the window, needing a distraction. She crossed in front of the hearth and headed in the direction of the cookroom.

Myra had finished slicing the apples and was reaching for a bowl filled with pie dough. Isabel paused. Myra's expression was shadowed with concern. No doubt Myra too felt that William and Angus's behavior was odd.

Isabel walked over and gave her a hug. "I love you, Mother."

It was a moniker Isabel seldom used. Yet today it was comforting somehow. When Isabel was a child, Myra had told her she loved her as her own but would not be offended if Isabel did not call her Mother. Today Isabel was overwhelmed with the need to show Myra how much she meant to her.

Myra squeezed Isabel and patted her cheek. "Oh, and I love ye, my daughter. Ye have a troubled expression. Is it the stranger?"

Isabel turned and popped a small slice of apple into her mouth. "You and Paulette understand me so well.

Yes. I cannot seem to drive William from my mind. And Angus is behaving as though the two of them are lifelong friends."

"Oh, I do not think they are friends." Myra flopped the pie dough on a floured surface and began to roll it into thin sheets. She changed the subject. "I received word today that the queen has summoned all who work at Hampton Court to appear before her. It may have something to do with the costume ball she has planned. I want to make sure Elaenor has something warm to eat before we leave. She is playing outside. Could ye bring her inside for me? I think she has ventured down by the river again. The way she loves the water, the child must believe she is half fish."

Isabel grabbed a shawl from the hook near the door and braced herself for the bone-chilling wind. It was clear that Myra did not want to talk about William and Angus at this time. It only made Isabel more suspicious.

As she walked outside, she could see Elaenor's outline against the morning sky. Isabel yelled for her, but Elaenor was too far away to hear her.

Elaenor's back was to Isabel. The young girl cradled Zeus in her arms. It looked as though she was talking to the cat as she stroked his fur.

As Isabel approached, she spoke again, raising her voice to be heard over the wind. "Elaenor, Myra said it is time to come inside and get something to eat."

Elaenor turned, wide-eyed and flushed, and then crooked her finger and gestured for Isabel to come closer. Her voice was soft and low. "You must be very quiet, or you will scare her away."

Isabel smiled and did as she was asked, wondering what new game Elaenor was playing this morning. The child had a vivid imagination. Isabel knelt down beside her.

"Did you find a pretty fish to talk to?"

"Shush," Elaenor ordered and pulled Isabel to eye level. "Rotan is not a fish. And I think she would be most offended if she heard you speak of her as such." Elaenor looked toward the river. "Oh, dear. I think you have frightened her away. She says she doesn't like most big people. They don't believe in her, you see." Elaenor brushed her cheek against the top of Zeus's head. "But Rotan is so nice. You would like her."

Isabel marveled once more at the child's imagination and wondered if hers had ever been as rich when she was young. She heard Myra call to them.

Elaenor's eyes crinkled in a smile. "I will race you to the cookroom."

The child took off, leaping over the low beds of herbs as nimbly as the cat she held protectively in her arms.

Isabel glanced over at the frozen water and dreamed of a time when her life would be as simple and fun as Elaenor's. That was not to be, especially now. With William's appearance, her life had suddenly become more complicated.

****

Isabel arrived at Hampton Court just in time. She dismounted and ignored the guard's disapproving gaze. She was late. At the last minute, Myra and Elaenor had decided not to go. However, Isabel thought she should attend. There might be important information regarding the costume ball that she could relay to Ossian.

A buzz of activity charged the air as Isabel headed inside. She had spent her childhood within these walls.

Only the watchful vigilance of Myra and Angus had kept her separate from the court intrigue, first of King Henry the Eighth, then of his son, Edward the Sixth, and now Henry's daughter, Mary Tudor.

However, the queen's policies in trying to reinstate Catholicism made her an unpopular monarch, and her methods caused fear to run unchecked in her kingdom. The queen was nicknamed Bloody Mary by her enemies for the methods she used to persuade her countrymen to abandon one faith for another.

Isabel reached the gilded corridor leading to the audience chamber. The stark gray walls and stone floors of the cookrooms where she and Myra worked seemed a world away from the marble and gold of the queen's audience chambers. The walls glistened from a fresh coat of whitewash, and gold cherubs smiled down from the ceiling. Paintings on the wall depicted scenes where monarchs of the past fought and killed every imagined beastie from wild boar to mythical dragon.

Isabel remembered that as a young girl she was shown these portraits by Myra. The paintings had entranced her. It was not the tales of valor that had intrigued her but the skill with which the artists had managed to capture the emotions of both man and beast. It was in these hallways that Isabel's dreams of becoming a painter had burst into a strong conviction.

The waiting area was filled with the queen's attendants and servants. Everyone who dealt with the queen's needs was here, from the cooks who made her favorite desserts to the shoemakers who tried to satisfy her ever-changing fashion moods. There was a low hum of conversation that seemed to bounce off the walls. The queen's request to speak to her servants was unusual, and it charged the room with anxiety, as well as fear. Normally, the queen—or any other monarch in Isabel's memory—cared not who their servants were, only that their royal comforts were met.

A trumpet sounded, silencing all in the large room. Like sheep driven to the slaughterhouse, the waiting area emptied into the audience chamber.

The chamber glittered, from the jewel-bedecked noblemen and women to the gold-leaf wall coverings. It seemed as though each of the nobles tried to outdo the other in brilliance. There was a marked difference between the bedazzling nobility and the hard-working class.

Isabel noticed a man who stood apart from the rest, in both dress and isolation. He was rod thin and draped in crimson velvet garments. He wore a black hood and cap that covered his features. Her pulse quickened as she recognized him. It was John Campbell, the physician who'd examined William and declared him dead.

An image of William wove through her mind. She remembered the look on his face when he'd realized he was naked, and she smiled. She wished she could have captured that expression for all time. However, before he realized his state of undress, his features could have been chiseled from stone for all the emotion they reflected. In truth, his body resembled the statues and paintings of the Greek and Roman gods the artists were working on for the costume ball.

Silence gripped the audience as another trumpet blared, bringing Isabel back to the present. The noise sliced through the air. The queen was ill, and her ladies-in-waiting stood on either side of her as they helped escort her to her throne. She claimed that, at age forty-two, her illness was a result of her pregnancy. No one believed her. Instead, it was rumored that she was dying. Many were already speculating on who would rule England after her death. The queen's half-sister, Elizabeth, and their cousin Mary, Queen of Scots, were only two of the names on the long list of candidates.

The queen settled back against her throne and raised her voice. A hush fell over the chamber as people strained to hear her.

"You are the pulse of Hampton Court, and we want you all to be of one mind, one purpose. We are assured we are pregnant, and my newly appointed physician, John Campbell, has confirmed my deepest hopes. What is more, he has restored your queen's health, and come summer, there will be a new prince at court."

The hesitation was more deafening than the silence moments before. Like dominos falling, the cheers of those assembled built until the sound echoed off the walls and marble floors.

The queen raised her hand for silence and continued, "All observe more proof to my physician's limitless skill. John Campbell has cured my precious dog, Snowball."

As though on cue, a brown-and-white terrier scurried into the room. There was a collective intake of breath at the dog's transformation. Isabel remembered this animal had been given to Her Majesty when her father, King Henry the Eighth, was alive. That was over fourteen years ago. During that time, Snowball's hair had fallen out in patches and the dog's joints had stiffened until it walked with a marked limp. This Snowball, however, bounced around the room as though it had found the fabled Fountain of Youth.

The queen smiled. "John Campbell has restored Snowball's youth and assures us he will do the same for your queen."

Another round of applause echoed through the audience chamber. The servants hesitated, but one by one they joined in as well. As Isabel clapped, she wondered if everyone was as uncertain as she about the queen's announcement. True, Snowball had made a remarkable recovery, but even the thick court makeup could not hide the hollow dark rings under Her Majesty's eyes.

The trumpets sounded again, and as all bowed low, the queen left in a flurry of rustling silk and satin. The crowd stared openly at the queen's miracle worker. When the door shut behind the queen, a sigh of relief swept through the chamber, almost as strong as the anticipation moments before. The crowd, save Isabel, melted away like a thick mist, and in their place stood John Campbell.

Isabel clenched her hands at her sides. He had pro- claimed William dead when he was not. She was not impressed. In fact, she fought to control her anger. She did not trust him. The man made the hair on the nape of her neck stand on end. His dark, close-set eyes reminded her of the rats that peered out of the back alleyways on the London streets. She swallowed her revulsion.

With a sweeping gesture of his arm, John Campbell bowed low. His features were lost in the shadows of his deep hood. "I was informed your father refused permission to remove your husband's body." He examined his fingernails. "It is well known the dead harbor diseases. You and your lovely mother must convince your father of the dangers."

Isabel felt a small amount of satisfaction knowing Angus, and not this arrogant fool, had been correct about William's condition. It was also obvious that the men John Campbell had sent this morning had been too afraid to report that William was very much alive.

She was glad to be the one to tell him. "My husband has recovered fully."

His voice was a shrill whisper. "How can that be?" His body seemed to tremble with the exertion to bring it under control. Moments crept by as he gained an icy composure. His words flowed out like thick syrup. "I had not heard. Perhaps you will allow me to visit your husband. He may still need my assistance to assure a complete recovery."

Despite the smoothness of his words, she detected anger and frustration under the surface. Isabel did not believe his concern for William's welfare for a second. She felt protective of William, even if the man clearly believed he did not need anyone's help.

She smiled. "It is odd your men did not inform you of my husband's recovery."

He ground out his words. All pretense had vanished. "I agree. Most odd, indeed. But I must insist you allow me to examine your husband. What did you say his name was?"

She plastered a smile on her face, curious as to John Campbell's interest in William. "I did not say his name. He is a very private man." She diverted the topic away from William. "The queen is well pleased at Snowball's health and claims hers is much improved as well. You must be a gifted healer. What is your secret?"

He gripped the vial strung on a silver chain around his neck. "Some say my medicine is powerful enough to change the course of history." He laughed. "Perhaps that is an over-exaggeration. We physicians are often too zealous in recommending our potions. But it is effective, nonetheless, despite the bitter taste. The queen complains of it burning her tongue. Now, if you will excuse me, I must ready the queen for another treatment."

Isabel waited until John Campbell disappeared through the door leading to Her Majesty's chambers. Unease swirled around Isabel, smothering her in its grip. She was more suspicious than ever of the man and of the strange influence he had over the queen.

Isabel turned and headed toward the courtyard. She wanted to return to the safety of the manor. What went on in Hampton Court was none of her concern. It was a lesson instilled in her at a tender age. She quickened her steps. Thoughts of the queen's physician were replaced with those of William. Her mood lightened. Now there was a mystery she wanted to unravel. Asking direct questions regarding his identity had not gained her a clear understanding of who he was or how he had appeared so suddenly. Myra had told her that a question sweetened with honey was easier to answer. Isabel decided to test Myra's theory on William, but first she would visit her secret hideaway, the one place where she could paint in complete privacy.

Chapter 10

The shutters in William's room rattled against the window, and the wind howled outside. Inactivity was making him as restless as the weather. He closed the window against the night air.

He'd lost track of the time. Trying to figure out Bartholomew's next move was a slow process of elimination. He'd used up the last few hours talking to Angus and Myra about life around London; it might give him a clue as to where to start looking for the man. It was too bad there wasn't a way for a Protector to set his arrival time before the criminal's and catch him as he emerged from the water. But, unfortunately, the Council didn't have that technology yet.

Time travel was not an exact science, even to the advanced race of Immortals. It was not possible to duplicate a jump to the exact day. The most they could have hoped for was to have sent William back to within a two-week time period of Bartholomew's initial arrival.

William paced before the hearth. The weather was turning worse by the day. It meant Bartholomew's plan was in motion. He bent down and retrieved a sketchpad he'd seen Isabel working on when he'd first woken from the Healing Sleep. It reminded him she'd not returned, and he wondered what was keeping her.

Both Angus and Myra had decided not to wait for

her, and they had retired to their chamber. They reminded him that just because he was wide awake didn't mean everyone else in the world wanted to be as well.

He flipped open the pad. There were pencil sketches of arms and hands, much in the style of da Vinci. "Not bad."

Once William had been a serious collector. He was fascinated by not only the masters, such as Leonardo da Vinci or Michelangelo, but also by the students they trained. He might no longer be interested in the arts, but the world would be a cold and dismal place without them. William set the sketchpad down on a nearby chair. If William didn't find Bartholomew soon, the world he knew would be forever changed. This evening, Angus had expressed concern that in a large city such as London, it would be difficult to find one man. But William had a plan.

It wasn't by accident that he was one of the most successful Protectors. Before beginning any assignment, he studied the person he hunted until he knew the man as well as he knew himself. Bartholomew was no exception. As with most sociopaths, there was a pattern of behavior. Whenever the man entered a city, even before searching for food and lodging, he would check out two things. The first was to find out who owned the largest collection of books, and the second was to locate the most depraved brothels. In the sixteenth century, books were not plentiful, but brothels were. At first light William intended to search for clues that could lead him to Bartholomew. He would be looking for a recent increase in the number of deaths or disappearances of prostitutes. These occurrences were not that uncommon in London of the sixteenth century. However, Bartholomew's method was unique. In addition to poisoning those he slept with, he pinned to their dead bodies a poem he'd written about them. It was this element William felt would make the man easier to trace.

William stared at the flames in the stone hearth until their glow blurred his vision. He wondered for the hundredth time why this monster had roamed free for so long. Maybe it was because there were so many more who were worse than Bartholomew.

William's stomach growled. He'd not eaten in over a day and a half. The Healing Sleep might enable you to wake refreshed, but it did nothing to stave off hunger. He grabbed a candle from the nightstand and inched his way in the pitch black toward the Great Hall in search of food.

As he approached, he noted the only light came from the glowing embers in the fireplace along the wall. William went about the room lighting whatever candles he could find until a soft yellow haze of light fell over the room. Oriental rugs in vibrant shades of crimson red and cobalt blue covered the stone floor. A pair of Asian vases stood on a gray-marble-topped sideboard, and intricately carved chairs ringed a matching oak table.

A carved chair, upholstered with green silk, sat before the fire. The walls were whitewashed, and stencils of ivy and violets wove around the perimeter of the ceiling in a chain. William could see the benefits to Angus's profession as a merchant, but no doubt it was Myra who made it a loving home. But where was the kitchen?

He heard a loud meow and saw Isabel's cat peek around the carved wooden arm of the chair. The animal leveled his green eyes toward him. As William drew nearer, he saw the cat was not alone.

The child he'd seen earlier today was curled up in a chair before the fire. A book lay in her lap. She must have fallen asleep while reading. The child stretched her arms and yawned loudly.

Again he was struck with how familiar she appeared to him, and then the realization hit him like a body blow. The age was about right, as was the coloring. He also knew she liked to come to London to visit her friend, Elizabeth. And her smile. He knew if he looked in a mirror his expression would resemble the child's. He need only ask one question to confirm his suspicions. Her name.

If she was who he suspected she was, he didn't want to destroy a chance to get to know her better. It would also be easier to protect her from Bartholomew. He squelched his excitement by reaching for the long-handled iron fire tongs and stirring the embers to life. He knew how he must appear to the young girl. He was unshaved and armed with a knife and sword, a man ready for battle. Not a very friendly image for a first meeting.

He searched his memory for common ground. One of seven children, his destiny had been determined by the time he was two years old. He'd spent what was left of his childhood in training to become a Protector. On those rare occasions when he'd returned home for family reunions, he'd been more a stranger than a brother or son.

The child leaped to the ground as though her legs

were made from springs. Her wool nightgown dragged on the floor, and her cap flopped over the side of her face. She flipped it back and stared unblinking in his direction. The strength of will she would display as an adult was already evident. But she appeared wary.

The cat, however, was not as shy. He stretched in a leisurely manner, bounded silently to the floor, and headed straight for him. The creature rubbed against William's leg and purred. He looked down at the animal and remembered his home in Inverness, Scotland.

There had always been an assortment of pets in the MacAlpin household. Although as a child he'd never seen the benefit of having such dependent creatures, his brothers and sisters had seemed to cherish them. And the first thing his mother had always done when he'd come for a visit was thrust one of the little furballs in his direction. She would say an animal had a way of reaching through even the barriers of a Protector's heart and making them human. She'd never given up, even when his siblings had. It had probably been the reason he'd kept Misfit when the animal had appeared at the cabin hungry and alone.

However, he hoped his mother was right. Maybe if he showed the child he was more than just a warrior, she would talk to him.

William bent down next to the animal. He remembered when one of his mother's cats had had a litter. His brothers and sisters had picked up the kittens by the scruff of their necks. He reached over and did the same.

It meowed in protest, swiped William's hand with his claws, and ran toward the girl. He winced at the pain in his thumb and stuck it into his mouth. It looked as if he hadn't lost his touch. That was exactly how his family's animals had reacted to him.

She giggled, reached down, and scratched the skittish animal under his chin and smiled. "Zeus doesn't like to be handled so roughly." The animal leaned his head into her hand.

William cleared his throat. "I'm not very good with animals." He wanted to add people to that statement.

She sank down on the floor next to the cat. Zeus padded into her lap and curled into a ball. She kissed him on the head. "You just have to let them know you mean them no harm."

William squatted on his haunches so he could be closer to eye level. "Do you think that's something I could learn?"

She cocked her head and gazed in his direction. "Humm, I do not know. You are very old to learn, but my father…" It was as though a cloud had passed over her clear blue eyes. A smile quivered around the corner of her mouth. "My father used to tell us, before he got sick and had to go away, that as long as a person was open to change, change was possible. Many in my family no longer believe his words, but I do. Do you think it is possible for a person to change?"

"I hope so."

And for the first time in a very long while, he hoped she was right. It was a complex concept for someone so young, but if she was who he thought she was, it went a long way in explaining her thought process. William suspected that if he was correct, he also knew why the child hesitated when she talked about her father. The man had gone insane.

William forced a smile he hoped was convincing. "Do you think I could try to hold Zeus again?"

She looked over in his direction and held his gaze. She then bent down and whispered to Zeus. She leaned her head toward the cat as though listening to his response.

She smiled. "He agrees. You shall have your second chance, but he would like to know your name."

"William."

She gently gathered the cat in her arms, stood, and walked over to William, where she sat down. "I have decided I like your name."

He grinned. "Really? Are there some names you don't like?"

Her eyebrows scrunched together. "Oh, yes. But I will not know if l like the name until I meet the person."

"Very sensible." She had charmed him to the core.

He wished he didn't know so much about her life. The next few years would be filled with tragedy and loss.

The cat meowed loudly.

"Oh, no, you are petting Zeus all wrong. You must first scratch him behind his right ear. That is his favorite side." She wagged her small chubby finger in his direction. "Remember, you must be gentle."

He laughed. "Yes, milady."

She giggled in response.

He did as she instructed, and, to his surprise, the cat leaned his head toward him instead of taking a chunk out of his hand.

She smiled. "Do you want to know my name? I

think you will like it."

He returned the smile. "I know I will."

William felt all the muscles in his hand tense, and he held the cat tighter. This was the question he'd been afraid to ask. The one he felt he already knew the answer to.

The cat let out a loud meow and arched his back in protest to William's tight grip.

She retrieved Zeus and cradled him in her arms. Her voice held the quality of a teacher patiently talking to one of her students who had misbehaved. "You frightened Zeus." She shook her head and sighed. "You will need a lot more practice." The child nuzzled her head against the cat's. "Are you any better at playing chess?"

He grinned, suspecting that the innocent-looking child was a master of the game. "I'd love to play a game of chess with you."

He heard a slight movement from the direction behind him. Instinctively he reached for his sword. It was in his room. Silently cursing his neglect, he turned toward the sound.

Isabel stood in the doorway. She cleared her throat and smiled. "Elaenor, you are up late. You should be in bed."

He wondered how long she had been standing nearby. What was more, there was a change in her expression that he couldn't define.

But what was most important was the fact that Isabel had just confirmed his suspicions about the young girl. A shiver ran through him as fast as a fire over a stream of gasoline. Suspecting the identity of the child who sat beside him and confirming it were polar opposites. He set his jumbled emotions aside. This was a situation where Elaenor, as well as anyone else, for that matter, must not know of his connection to her.

With the wolfhound on her heels, Isabel set a tray laden with food down on the sideboard.

Elaenor jumped to her feet as Isabel removed a cloth from a platter of steaming food. Hard-boiled eggs, brown-crusted bread, fried tomatoes, and cod steaks dripping with butter all vied for a space on the platter. A pitcher of buttermilk and horn glasses hugged the corner of the tray.

Isabel smiled in his direction. "I thought you would be hungry."

Again the unease returned. Why was she being so nice to him? But at the mention of food, William's stomach growled in appreciation, and he set his questions aside. He knew the English reputation for bland food was almost as legendary as the tales of the Loch Ness monster, but this looked like a feast fit for a king. His normal breakfast consisted of black coffee and a bowl of instant oatmeal—if he had time to boil the water.

He followed Elaenor over to the table. The wolfhound had beaten him there and now stood at eye level with the food, his tongue lolling dangerously close to the platter.

Isabel broke off a generous chunk of bread and set it on the floor. Apollo inhaled it without chewing, sat back on his haunches, and waited for another handout.

William's mouth watered as Isabel dished up generous portions of tomato, codfish, and bread. He used his fingers and stuffed the fish in his mouth. It had a strong, salty taste, but otherwise tasted good.

With a mouthful of food he muttered, "Thank you. I was starving."

Elaenor tugged on his sleeve. Her teacher's voice had returned. "Your mother should have told you that it is not polite to chew with your mouth open."

He swallowed the fish quickly and almost choked. He wanted to say, *You just did.*

William pushed away the warm feelings and turned to Isabel. "This is delicious. I thought you didn't cook."

Elaenor answered for her. "Isabel can cook, but not as well as Myra. She's the best. Even the queen thinks so."

Isabel hugged Elaenor around the shoulders. "You are just flattering me so I will forget to send you off to your bed." Elaenor finished her buttermilk and licked her lips. "But I am so wide awake," she pleaded, "and William promised to play a game of chess."

William finished off the last of the cod and faked a yawn. "Chess is a game played best when both people have had a good night's sleep. As soon as I finish my meal, I plan to go to bed. I want to be alert when we play. I sense you will be a formidable opponent."

Eleanor giggled in response, and the yawn he had faked proved to be infectious. Elaenor mirrored his and rubbed her eyes. "Perhaps I could sleep for just a little while."

Elaenor kissed Isabel on the cheek and smiled toward William. "Do not forget."

William shook his head. "I'm looking forward to it."

He turned to see Isabel staring in his direction. Her expression was hooded, but he saw a flicker of uncertainty spread across her eyes.

Isabel had lost her apprehension. William was a confusing paradox. She had been watching the exchange between him and Elaenor when they had not known she was in the cookroom, and again just now. He talked to Elaenor not as though she was a mere child but as though she was a person worthy of respect.

She pushed her plate aside, suddenly ashamed that she meant to trick such a man into sharing information about himself that he wished to be kept a secret.

He leaned back in his chair. "What's wrong?"

"There is nothing wrong. I am just tired, and there is much for Myra and me to do before I am able to go to the artist's studio tomorrow."

It was a lie. There was something very wrong. She did not want William to be a man of many sides. It would be easier if he were like the men at court. Their intentions were as transparent as glass. They showed attention to others only if it resulted in material gain and power.

He rubbed the back of his neck. "I don't think it's a good idea for you to be going back to your studio in London. It's a dangerous area. Remember, we were attacked."

She decided to take all her warm thoughts about him back. "There was no 'we.' Those men attacked you first. They only turned on me when I tried to help." Isabel gathered the plates and the tray and headed toward the cookroom, confident she had put him in his place. "Good night."

She heard him stand. As far as she was concerned, the subject was closed. She had no intention of letting him dictate to her what she could or could not do. Isabel smiled to herself, knowing he would really be angry if

114

he knew she was in London earlier today without an escort. He might be in danger, but she was perfectly safe.

Chapter 11

Secrets. Isabel was drowning in them. She awoke the next morning anxious to be on her way to the artist's studio. She had dressed in a hurry and checked the weather. Cold and crisp, but so far it was not snowing. The only problem was that William and Angus forbade her to go. Their only reasoning was that William was looking for someone dangerous who might be dwelling in London. Well, that was not her concern.

Isabel entered the Great Hall only to find William warming his hands over the fireplace and Angus stacking wood. She did not care if William had a wonderful way with Elaenor. Right now he was being as hardheaded as the slabs of marble her artist friend, Paulette, worked on in the studio.

Isabel walked past them and paused. She tapped her fingers on a day vase that rested on a side table. "William, I will not remain at the manor like a child who has neglected her studies."

"It's for your own safety." He ducked as the vase sailed past his head and shattered on the stone floor. He stood. "Myra and Elaenor are staying close to the manor."

"Myra had to go to Hampton Court to cook that spoiled queen her favorite dessert, and Elaenor is building a snow castle. They both believe you are exaggerating the danger, and I agree. Perhaps if you told us more about what is so important, we would be more inclined to believe you."

William massaged his temples as a headache the size of the state of Texas burned behind his eyes. That was another thing Immortals were not immune to: migraines. His parents would say it was meant to remind them of their humankind roots. He'd settle for an aspirin.

He turned to Angus. "Reason with her. She's your daughter."

Angus only beamed with pride.

"Wonderful." William was losing the battle. "I can't see the humor."

Angus chuckled. "Can you not? Myra and I learned long ago Isabel's mind was her own, and glad we were of her independence."

Isabel's hands were on her hips and her foot was tapping as though sending out a message in Morse code. She reached for her cape, which was draped over a chair, swung it over her shoulders, and headed for the door.

William leaped into action and blocked her exit. "Where're you going?"

"No one will forbid me to go into the city if I choose to do so. I do not need your permission or your protection."

"Angus and I already explained to you why you should stay close to the manor. There's a killer on the loose."

She frowned. "Just tell me his name and what he looks like, and I shall avoid him."

"I can't do that, but I've already told you the type

of person we're dealing with."

She folded her arms across her chest. "And how do you propose to find this man? Do you intend to go knocking on every door asking questions? 'Excuse me, sir or madam, but I wonder if you could help me? I am looking for someone but cannot describe him or give you his name.' " She glowered at William.

He tried not to get swept up in her ridicule. Isabel had no idea that on other assignments he'd found his target with far less information than he had now.

"This is not your concern. Angus and I plan to divide the city between the two of us."

Angus interrupted. "Isabel. As much as I regret saying this, I agree with William. Please trust me."

Angus's soft-spoken words had an effect. Isabel seemed to be weighing her options. An eternity seemed to pass by before she spoke.

She fastened the clasp of her cloak and turned to William. "Asking questions at the local inns and taverns is only a small part of the puzzle that is London. I know a group of people who travel as though invisible, and you need me to ensure their cooperation. I shall make you a bargain. I will help you find this person you speak of if you agree to take me as far as the Blue Goose Inn. There is something I need there before I go to the artist's studio."

"You're being foolish."

Angus laughed and walked over to stand beside Isabel. "You have done it now, lad."

How had he allowed himself to be backed into a corner?

He was doing this for Isabel's own good. Bartholomew was unpredictable. William didn't want him knowing of her existence. The man was too dangerous.

Her eyes narrowed and seemed to burn through him. It was too late to take back his words. He was used to Immortal women, and to women from the twenty-first century, but this was the sixteenth century, and Isabel was from a race of humankind. She was not used to taking care of herself. It didn't make any sense. She should be grateful he wanted to protect her, but he decided telling her might not be the wisest idea right now. However, the fact still remained that she was wrong and he was right.

"You will stay here."

Isabel reached for Angus's sword and pulled it from its scabbard. "Step aside, William, or I will run you through."

Angus smiled. "I warned you."

William spread his arms toward the ceiling, wanting to strangle the Scot. He frowned. "Why'd you let her take your weapon?"

Angus grinned and shrugged.

William realized he wouldn't be getting any help from Angus. He concentrated on his armed assailant. Why couldn't she just do as he asked?

However, behaving as a tyrant had failed. He realized the only way she'd stay behind was if he tied her to a chair. And that wouldn't work because Angus or Myra—or Elaenor, for that matter—would free her. His only option would be to agree to the compromise she offered. A compromise was offensive to him. It meant he had to take a few steps back instead of driving forward at any cost. He ground his teeth, knowing he had no other choice.

"If you're determined to leave the safety of the manor, you can accompany me into London in a few days."

She edged closer. "I do not intend to wait until you have swept the city clean for my benefit. I intend to leave right now, with or without your permission."

Great. He was losing on the diplomatic front as well. "Isabel, be reasonable—"

She interrupted. "It is you who are not being reasonable. You need my help."

Angus slapped his thigh and nodded. "She is right. Why dinna I think of it sooner?" He shook his head. "She may be on to something."

"Are you crazy?"

"Lad, just listen to reason. Her solution might be the wisest course of action. It is at least worth a try."

William recited the Celtic alphabet backwards. Surprisingly, it helped. He glanced over at Angus, sensing the tide of the battle had turned, but not in his favor. Even among Immortal women he seldom witnessed any as strong willed. She returned Angus's sword. "Of course my idea will work. The people I was talking about live in the artist's community where I paint. Nothing escapes their notice."

William folded his arms over his chest. "If I agree, you'll have to do exactly as I say. No questions asked."

Victory shone in her eyes. "Your wish is my command." He muttered under his breath. "Somehow I doubt that." William opened the door and Isabel breezed past him, heading toward the stables. He braced himself against the stiff wind and wished she were a sensible woman who didn't have an iron will. He spread the cloak over his shoulders and knew he was kidding himself. He wouldn't want her any other way.

Angus walked beside him, grinning from ear to ear. "A bonnie lass with the grit of ten men. With a woman such as that to guard your back, as in the days of the Celtic warrior queens, a man would need little else to sustain him."

"You've raised her well, Angus," William conceded. "However, how do I persuade her to follow orders? Her safety may depend on it."

Angus scratched his beard. "A serious dilemma, but one you must overcome if you are to succeed in not only this mission but those to come. Where Isabel is concerned, I would offer this advice—Respect her intelligence and abilities. She's confident enough about herself to tell you when she is unsure about a situation. Isabel is a reasonable woman. Show her your respect, and she will come to trust you. If she has a fault, it is that she cannot decide which path to take to accomplish her goal." He chuckled. "But I sense you always have a plan."

William reached the stables. Snow dusted the trees like powdered sugar. He tried to absorb the words and treat them as advice and not a lecture. The truth was that he wouldn't be here long enough to really spend time with Isabel. He was surprised at the regret tugging on his heart.

William muttered, "I'll consider what you've said. Where's the artist's studio?"

Angus opened the stable door. The smell of fresh-cut hay and the pungent odor of animals wafted on the air. Isabel was already mounted and waiting for them as Brian handed them the reins of their horses.

Angus accepted his and mounted. "The studio is on

the east side of the river."

William nodded as he climbed into the saddle. "We'll stick with the plan we discussed earlier and try to discover if a well-educated man has appeared in London within the last fortnight. You check out the inn and taverns on the west side, and I'll go with Isabel to those along the east. That way I can follow your advice while protecting her at the same time."

Angus grinned. "Wise choice, lad. There might be hope for you yet. We will find the man you hunt if we have to turn over every rock in the city."

William nodded. "And that's exactly where he'll be hiding."

William looked at the sky as they rode toward London. Even this early in the day, it was growing darker by the hour. It would make their search more difficult, but that was not what concerned him. He was worried about how rapidly the weather was changing. William had thought he would have a few weeks to find Bartholomew. Now he knew it would only be a matter of days before history was altered.

****

In his well-lit chamber, Bartholomew doubled up his fist and struck the stone wall. Pain spiked through him as bones crunched and blood oozed over the injured knuckles. The Protector had survived. The words grated through his mind until he thought he would go mad. He poured a goblet of dark red wine and downed it in a single gulp. He'd not slept since he'd encountered Myra's daughter and learned the Protector had recovered. He slammed the goblet down on the dresser next to the wine bottle. It rattled and threatened to topple over.

He'd been a fool, thinking he had time to deal with the man. He'd forgotten that Protectors did not need as much time to heal as ordinary Immortals. He hoped it would not prove to be a fatal error on his part. He should have cut off the man's head when he'd had the chance and dealt with the women then and there.

Now it was too late.

Bartholomew paced back and forth beside his bed. He did not think he was an evil man. He just felt people were expendable, especially if they stood in his way. Was that so wrong?

He paused to stare at his reflection in the tin mirror on the wall. The plan was supposed to have been so simple. And in the beginning, it had been. He'd skillfully pulled off the charade as the queen's physician, only to encounter a possible obstacle to his success. The Protector. But he would find a way to evade him.

Bartholomew knew his limitations, and the last thing he wanted was to engage the man in a test of skill with the sword. He did not believe in leaving things to chance. And in a fight there were too many variables beyond his control. Outwitting the Protector would be a safer path to take. He smiled. It would make his victory taste all that much sweeter.

He flexed his throbbing hand, noting absently that only two of the knuckles were broken. No matter how many times it occurred, he was fascinated with how rapidly his body healed.

He leaned closer to the mirror in order to gaze at himself. The inferior mirror distorted his image. He pulled back and frowned. He missed the inventions of the twenty-first century.

He blamed his enemy, Lachlan MacAlpin, for his present predicament. The man was a fool. Lachlan had grown to admire humankind, thinking they were equal to the Immortals and even going so far as to fall in love with one of them. Well, it just proved it was time for the Renegades to take back what should have been theirs from the Beginning Time. In order to accomplish this goal, the events of history would be changed, returning the world to a vulnerable time.

All that was needed was to make sure the current queen, the inept Queen Mary of England, stayed healthy. Keeping her alive would prevent her half-sister Elizabeth from taking the throne. It was Elizabeth who would help usher in a new strength and purpose to Europe. The domino effect she would set in motion would enable humankind to flourish and expand their power. In contrast, the effect of keeping Mary alive would be to plunge the world into a deep void of religious chaos.

A takeover by the Immortal Renegades would be inevitable in that chaos. The move was long overdue. And, as an added bonus, Bartholomew would have his revenge against the MacAlpin clan. Lachlan was out of reach right now, but his sister, Elaenor, was living nearby.

When he'd been imprisoned at Urquhart Castle in the twenty-first century, he at first had rejected this assignment. The Renegades had appealed to his sense of family. They'd claimed it would be his chance to avenge his brother Subedei. Bartholomew shrugged, remembering the conversation and his response. He had gone down this path once before and failed. Besides, Subedei's fate had been sealed even before he'd met

Lachlan. The mark of insanity had been on his brother, and bloodlust had clouded his reasoning. Bartholomew had refused the assignment, saying he had no intention of risking his own life.

The Renegades' next comment had chilled him to the bone. In the end he'd had little choice. It was either travel back in time or spend an eternity rotting in chains. When they'd explained it in those terms, the choice had been simple. The added bonus had been causing Lachlan pain from which there was no cure—the total annihilation of his family.

However, his short stay in the twenty-first century before his capture had been more dream than reality. Unlike his insane brother, Bartholomew chose the path of learning instead of the life of a warrior. When he lived in the sixteenth century, he felt it was an era of enlightenment.

He laughed. It was primitive compared to the twenty-first. If it were not for his capture, he would be content to spend his life reading every volume ever written in the quest for knowledge. He shook his head slowly. He missed bookstores.

Bartholomew clenched his fists at the injustice of being forced to do the Renegades' bidding. The throbbing in his hand took on a new level of pain that was hard to ignore. The painkillers of this century were inadequate. That was another thing he missed about the future. The drugs. He reached for a bottle of red wine.

He heard a chair crash to the floor. Bartholomew whirled toward the sound.

The tall man who had failed to bring the Protector to him swayed on unsteady legs. A gash parted the matted hair on his head, and blood streamed down the side of his face.

Bartholomew withdrew a knife from the folds of his long tunic. "I thought I killed you."

Blood sputtered from the tall man's mouth. "Why did you do this to me?"

With one fluid motion Bartholomew drove his blade through the man's heart. He crumpled to the ground like a rag doll and rolled against a dead body.

Bartholomew wiped off his weapon with the man's shirt and placed it beside the bottle of wine. "The reason should be obvious." He chuckled as he addressed the dead man. "I killed you and your ignorant friend because you failed me. Now, where was I before I was interrupted? Oh yes. I was about to get drunk."

Bartholomew lifted the bottle to his lips. He downed a healthy mouthful of the robust liquid and felt its numbing effects flow through his veins. It combined with the exhilaration he experienced from the fresh kill. But like so many times before, the feeling evaporated almost as quickly as it surfaced, leaving an emptiness in its place. Some might say the sensation mirrored Bloodlust. But he was not like his brother. He could control its effects.

He took another long drink, savoring the taste. It was an Italian red, lifted from the cellars of the queen. He doubted she'd miss it. She had no respect for such delicacies. Her only weakness these days seemed to be for food and the warm beverage she had each afternoon.

Bartholomew turned his head, examining his profile in the mirror. He remembered the book *The Picture of Dorian Gray*. The story fascinated him. Through magic, the image of Dorian Gray aged on canvas while the man retained his youth. The portrait also reflected the man's corrupt excesses. When Dorian Gray died, the spell was broken, and his face reflected his black soul while the painting showed the man he was before his fall.

Before reading the story, the concept that a person's soul could be reflected in their eyes had never occurred to Bartholomew.

He focused once more on the plan to change history, as an idea formed in his mind. The Renegade leader's proposal was flawless, but if the Protector and Angus recognized him, all would be lost. He would need a disguise.

Bartholomew picked up his knife, knowing what he had to do next. The Protector would never think to question a man who was scarred. If injured, no matter how severely, an Immortal's wounds would heal without leaving a scar.

He shuddered as the story of Dorian Gray scrolled once more through his mind. He pushed the dark thoughts away. Instead of a portrait reflecting the deeds of Dorian Gray, Bartholomew was using his face to create the image of what lay inside his soul. He would cut his face with his blade, causing ugly marks, knowing he would have to repeat the process often.

Bartholomew took another drink. He clenched his teeth and gripped the blade with his good hand. He smiled, pleased with his creativity. Before he could change his mind, he made the first incision with the knife across the smooth contours of his face.

Chapter 12

It had been a long cold day, and William felt they were no closer to discovering Bartholomew's location than they had been when they'd started out this morning. What was more, he suspected London held some kind of world record for the number of pubs, inns, and brothels that could be jammed into one city.

He dismounted in front of what was to be their last stop, the Blue Goose Inn. It was crammed next to others along the London Bridge. A thick cloud cover smothered the light of the sun until the city looked as though it were painted in shades of gray. Now, as the sun was setting, the colors only deepened. The river was deathly quiet and shimmered as smooth as glass in the torchlight.

The narrow, multi-floor wood building seemed to grow out of the ground. Its dark, weathered planks and smoke-blackened chimneys were indistinguishable from those of its neighbors. Bolted above the entrance of the inn was a wooden sign with the figure of a blue goose painted on the surface.

William tied his horse to a metal hitching post ring and turned to assist Isabel off hers. He had to admit that her company had brightened even this dreary day. When he reached her side, she'd already dismounted and was heading toward the inn.

She shouted to him over her shoulder, "There is

something I must attend to before we go to the artist's studio. I shall not be gone long."

William headed toward the inn. As she'd promised, she'd been a big help to him. Isabel had not so much as flinched when she'd walked into the seedy brothels. In addition, the women there had been more inclined to talk to another woman than they had been to him. At first he'd thought coins would buy him the information he needed, but as Isabel had said, fear was at an all-time high. So far, however, not one person had heard of a man fitting Bartholomew's description. Nor had there been any mysterious deaths.

But the word was on the streets, and in this type of investigation, if something unusual occurred, it would filter back to him. It always did.

William walked up the half-dozen narrow steps into the dark, close quarters of the inn. There was a small room to his left and one to his right. A staircase divided the two. The walls were coated with years of smoke and soot from the fireplace. William guessed the majority of the rooms here were rented by the hour.

In the area to his left, a potbellied bartender served ale and wiped down tables. The room on his right was also stuffed with people, and a low hum of conversation buzzed through the air like bees around a hive. In the corner, two men played chess. At a center table, men arm-wrestled while an assortment of women with faded gowns and breasts that spilled out of their lowcut blouses cheered them on. William headed toward the counter.

When one of the men slammed the other's arm down on the table, a loud cheer rolled, increasing in volume until it seemed to crash against the walls and bounce from the ceiling. William scanned the room. Isabel, however, was nowhere in sight. He wondered how long she'd be gone. He was beginning to worry.

William combed his fingers through his hair. She could take care of herself, he reasoned. After all, she'd told him that often enough. But the thought didn't reassure him. He was becoming very protective of her. He noted his choice of words was both ironic and annoying. He was a Protector of the laws of the Immortals, not of people in general.

One of the women came over to him. She reminded William of the old sepia photographs taken before color was invented. Her face, hair, and clothes all blended together in the same shade of beige.

The woman put her hands on her hips and smiled. Two of her front teeth were missing. "Ye are a fine-looking lad. Are ye interested in a game of hide-and-seek?"

The bartender raised his voice over the din of conversation as he pushed his way toward William. "Zoe, leave the man alone unless he asks. Them's the rules."

Zoe stuck out her chest until her breasts looked as though they would pop through the thin fabric of her dress. "And how does he know to ask, if he don't know what I'm willin' to do?"

William ignored Zoe's offer and looked around. Still no Isabel.

The bartender scratched his belly. "Name's Liam. Can I get ye a drink?"

"I'm looking for a woman."

Low, muffled laughter rolled through the crowd.

Liam grinned, exposing gaps in his crooked teeth.

"Aren't we all, lad? If Zoe is not to yer liking, there are a few juicy morsels upstairs that might be free within the hour."

Zoe let out a *humph* sound. "Liam, what would he want with those tired, dried-out old hags?" She winked and poked William in the ribs. "What the lad needs is a wild toss that'll get his young blood pumping."

Liam snapped the rag playfully in Zoe's direction. "Let it be, lass. Can't ye see the gentleman's not interested? Now, what's this lady of yours look like?"

Zoe lifted her chin and turned to leave. Her hips swayed in an exaggerated motion from left to right and back again. She took a long backward glance in William's direction and headed toward the group of arm wrestlers. "If ye change yer mind, ye know where to find me."

The hum of conversation died as the crowd lost interest in William and continued with their own concerns.

William lowered his voice. "The woman I'm looking for has dark hair and eyes. She was wearing an emerald green dress and came in here just a few minutes before I arrived. Have you seen her?"

Liam looped his rag under his wide leather belt. "Could be I have, could be not. I don't want no trouble here. There's many a lady comes here for a taste of something she can't get at home."

The man was evasive, as though he knew Isabel. From Angus's description of this area, the inn was very close to the artist's studio. For a brief moment William wondered if Isabel was living a double life. Not the one she claimed, that of being an aspiring artist, but something else. But that theory didn't make any sense.

If she had something to hide, she wouldn't come here with him and take the chance he'd find out.

He pressed a handful of coins in Liam's palm. Money hadn't worked so far, but it was still worth a try. It loosened most tongues.

"It's important I find this woman."

The man hesitated for only a matter of seconds before pocketing the coins. "Ye her husband?"

It seemed to always come back to that particular charade. "We quarreled."

Liam smiled and punched William on the arm. "Catch ye with a little sweetmeat, did she?"

The idea sounded unrealistic. How could any man think of another woman if Isabel loved him?

William played the part of a man caught in an indiscretion and hoped it held just the right amount of guilt to convince Liam. He decided Protectors would be best suited for the stage or movies. They were great actors. He leaned against the counter and added color to the deception.

"Aye, that she did. Burst in on the woman and me while we were riding at a fever's pace. Hard to deny what her eyes saw as fact."

Liam shook his head slowly. "Not my business why your wife is here, but if truth be told, I never knew the lass was married."

William didn't like the sound of Liam's explanation. It sounded as though Isabel was a regular visitor at the inn. He kept his voice level. "Where is she?"

"Not sure she'd want to see ye. Ye being such a rake and all. That one is as generous as they come. Good heart, too. If I had such as she, I'd never so much as smile in the direction of another woman."

William couldn't have agreed more. He assumed the role of a penitent husband. He was going to wring Isabel's neck when he found her. He should be tracking down Bartholomew; instead he was discovering that Isabel was living the life of a courtesan. He forced the tone of his voice to reflect regret instead of anger.

"I need to talk to her, beg her to come back to me."

Liam slapped him on the shoulder. "That's the spirit. This here is no place for a fine lady."

Liam motioned for William to follow him up the stairs to the second floor.

William alternated between wanting to strangle Isabel and trying to find a reason to understand the double life she led. A vision of Zoe came to his mind. The woman could be anywhere between twenty and forty. It wasn't a life a person normally chose, but one that chose them. He wondered what drove Isabel down this road, but he vowed to keep it from Myra.

Liam reached the landing of the second floor and headed down a long corridor. He knocked on a door near the end. "Milady, you have a visitor."

William didn't know what made him angrier, the fact she'd lied to him about the secret life she was living or the idea it included other men. He clenched his jaw as an image of her naked and in the arms of another man played across his mind.

Okay, so he knew which scenario tore at him the most. But what could he do? Did she need the money? If that was the problem, he'd enough at his disposal to satisfy a harem full of women. Of course, it was locked in a vault in the Highlands of Scotland in the twenty-first century, but that was beside the point.

The door opened a few inches, and Isabel appeared. "Liam, I do not want to be disturbed."

Liam shrugged his shoulders. "But milady, 'tis your husband. He's here to apologize for ye catching him with another woman. He seems most contrite to me."

Isabel flung the door open. Her mouth puckered as though she had bitten into a lemon. "Oh, he is, is he?"

Liam's head bobbed in agreement as he pleaded William's virtues, as well as assuring Isabel of his contrition, placing him somewhere between King Arthur of Camelot and Alexander the Great. William wasn't sure he liked either comparison. The former had lost the woman he loved to another man, and the latter was power hungry.

William smiled to himself as he watched the interchange between Isabel and Liam. There was something universal about a man coming to the aid of another. It transcended time and place. Men understood the unwritten law that no matter how fierce a warrior, or how skilled at ruling an empire, all men were vulnerable when it involved a woman.

Of course, what Liam didn't know was that he didn't need defending. But the plan gained him entrance to Isabel's secret life, and that's what mattered.

Liam clapped William on the shoulder. "Isabel, can't ye see the man is lost without ye?"

Isabel put her hands on her hips. "On that I will agree with you."

William swallowed the impulse to respond. Instead he lowered his voice and hoped it held the right amount of humility to convince Liam. The other option, of course, would be to demand an explanation. He chose the saner path.

"Isabel, there's something important we need to discuss."

Her smile would have melted an iceberg. "Of course." She reached over and kissed Liam on the cheek. "Thank you. I am not sure I shall forgive him, but you are most kind to play the part of Cupid." She turned toward William. "Come inside"—she paused and flashed him a brilliant smile—"husband dear." Now he was in trouble.

Chapter 13

When the door closed behind William, he cast a quick glance around the small room and was relieved. There was no man in sight. Maybe he'd not arrived as yet. William let out all his pent-up frustration.

"What do you mean by running away from me? I had no idea where you'd gone."

Her hands were on her hips as she tapped her foot on the wood floor. The sound echoed like a drum roll. Evidently his outburst had little effect on her. What was new?

"In the first place, I did not run from you, you arrogant pile of wind. I told you where I was going. All you needed to do was wait. There is something here I need. Besides, if I remember correctly, you said you did not need my help finding this scourge on humanity because you were the best in the world at finding your prey. A man among men, or at least words to that effect."

He winced as his words came back like a physical blow. "But you *have* helped me, and I'm grateful."

"You have a strange way of expressing yourself."

William leaned forward, fighting between wanting to shake her and, God help him, kiss her. He'd never met a woman like her. She wasn't impressed with him—to the contrary, she thought he was an idiot. And who was she to criticize him?

"Isabel, you're evading the real issue. I've discovered you're living a double life. Don't worry, I have no intention of telling Myra or Angus, but I want you to stop."

"I will not."

William's patience was growing thin. "Be reasonable. Maybe it's for the money, or pleasure, but whatever the reason, I can offer another solution."

"I like things the way they are."

William put his hands on her shoulders. "You can't mean that. Look at the women downstairs. Their hard lives have aged them."

Isabel narrowed her gaze. "What exactly are you talking about?"

"I want you to stop sleeping with other men."

She stepped back, stared at him for a split second, and then broke into laughter. "So you would save me from a life of sin? How generous you are."

William calmed his voice. Now was not the time to lose his temper. Maybe she didn't understand his generous offer. "I'm not one to judge. Most people have done things in their life they regret. I only meant I'm willing to help."

"And I suppose you have never done anything you regret?"

"I always do what is expected."

She folded her hands across her chest. "It must be a real burden to be so perfect."

He ignored her slam.

A smile played at the corners of her mouth as she changed the subject. "You would offer yourself as a substitute to satisfy my needs?"

He was on dangerous ground. He sensed he should

pull back. Retreat. A little voice within him kept screaming, *Danger, Danger.* However, it was too late. He'd gone too far to back down now.

The prospect of her naked body made his hands sweat. "Sure, I could. I mean, I would be willing to satisfy you."

She tapped her foot again. "How many times would you"—she paused and hissed out the words—"satisfy me?"

He swallowed, surprised by her openness. "In a week?"

She arched an eyebrow. "In a day."

"Well, I suppose I could…"

She turned and reached for the pitcher on the table.

He ducked as it flew past him and crashed on the floor beside him.

William straightened. He should have listened to the warning voice inside him. Something was not right. "Why are you always throwing things at me?"

"Why are you always making me angry?"

"It's not my intent to make you angry. I'll do whatever it takes to get you out of this life. If you need to have sex several times a day, or if it's the money you need, I'll take care of it for you."

"How generous." Her expression darkened. Isabel picked up the bowl and wound back. "How could you think such a thing of me? I have never slept with a man. And now I know why. You are all arrogant, mindless cave dwellers, with only one thought in that small brain of yours—how quickly you can get a woman in bed."

She hurled the bowl toward him.

It hit him in the chest. William hadn't ducked. He ignored the dull pain. It was overshadowed by what she'd said. Her words kept washing over him like the tide over the sand. She said she'd never slept with anyone. He believed her. He was so relieved he felt like laughing. And then he felt like a fool. She was right. He was stupid. How could he have thought it of her? He struggled with what he could say to her.

The door creaked open, and Liam stuck his head inside. "Is everything all right, milady?"

Isabel stared in William's direction. "I have decided to file for divorce."

Liam shook his head and closed the door silently behind him.

Silence crept slowly over the room so completely that William could hear the sound of his own breathing. He searched for the words to try and explain the misunderstanding.

"Isabel, Liam knew who you were and said many ladies come here looking for something they can't get at home. What was I to think?"

She crossed her arms over her chest. "To start with, I would advise you not to always think the worst. You could have asked me the reason I have a room at this inn. Like all men, you have a one-track mind and believe the only life we could want involves a man. Liam knows I have never had a man in my room."

William bent to pick up the shards of pottery at his feet, to keep his hands occupied. The play of light from the waning sun was casting a rosy glow over Isabel's creamy skin. He longed to touch it, and to beg her to forgive him.

"Liam wouldn't tell me where you'd gone, so I made up this story that you ran out on me because you caught me with another woman."

She knelt down to help him clean up the mess. "You actually told him I found you with someone else?"

Unease tossed around in his stomach. He didn't think he wanted to go over this ground again. It just seemed to confirm his guilt at accusing her of something she didn't do.

She smiled. "So, Liam was trying to make you jealous."

His hand brushed against her. It was like discovering a warm current in a frozen river. It made you want to find the source of the heat. He leaned closer to her.

"Well, I don't know if you could say that, exactly."

"Yes, I could, and what was more, he succeeded."

She stood and placed the broken pottery on a dresser. She wore that infuriating smile women have when they know they're right. There was only one thing left for him to do. Throw himself on her mercy.

"Maybe I was jealous, but there was still no excuse for my jumping to the wrong conclusion. I'm sorry."

Her expression softened. God help him, he wanted to kiss her.

She took a deep breath and seemed to shimmer from head to toe in the glow of the lamplight. "I like you so much better when you are acting human."

But he wasn't human, no matter that he looked the part. He was an Immortal, and a Protector who should know better than to let a woman into his heart.

"Can we change the subject?"

He felt like he was caught in a whirlpool. The perfect thing would be if the ground opened up and swallowed him whole. However, fate never seemed to be on his side. Instead, it worked against him. Isabel was right. He was jealous. At least he'd had the courage to admit it. He hadn't recognized it at first, maybe because it was the first time it had ever occurred. He'd never cared about a woman enough, until now.

William needed a distraction. He looked around the room for the first time. Paintings in various stages of completion hung from the walls or were positioned on easels. There was realism and depth of shadows in the images, which brought the paintings to life. Here was clear evidence of her work.

He said the obvious. "You're using this room as a private studio. Why?"

She nodded. "The laws in England are clear and governed by guilds. Women have to be very careful. Perhaps if I were married to a painter, or a sister or the daughter of one, I would be allowed to work under their protection. Angus has let it be known that he is teaching me that skill. And as long as I agree to paint subjects deemed suitable for a woman, no one questions my work. But I want more. Here I am able to paint whatever I choose. That is the reason I have this room at the inn."

Isabel reached for his hand. "Come, I want to show you something."

Her touch was like an electric shock that unsettled him to the core.

Her eyes widened slightly.

Isabel pulled him over to a cupboard and opened the doors, withdrawing a linen-wrapped frame. She removed the protective covering. She gently touched the signature of the painting.

"This portrait was painted by a woman by the name

of Claricia in about twelve hundred. She was called a miniaturist and illustrated books and manuscripts. Her slender figure, her long, loose hair, and her elegant, wide-sleeved dress were incorporated into the tail of the letter Q This was her signature, as well as a self-portrait. I have done the same with my initial."

The tone of Isabel's voice was laced with passion. She spoke of ambition and dedication and hard work. He was fascinated by her and the touch of her hand in his as she shared her dreams. He had never been a good listener, but with Isabel all he wanted to do was hear the sound of her voice. She wanted him to be human, and for this precious moment in time, so did he.

He again remembered the ancient legend where members of his race could sense their soul mates upon first meeting, and first touch. It was said that on those occasions logic and reason evaporated. And now it was happening to him.

The candles flickered in the room, and a peace settled around him as he leaned toward her. She lifted her chin, her eyes reflecting the warmth of the light. His mouth touched hers. A sensation of heat, and fire, and new beginnings. She molded her body against his, and the need to forget his identity was never stronger. Her arms were around his neck. Her fingers entwined in his hair. Forget. Just this once. Just this once.

The kiss was featherlight at first. It deepened as he pulled her against his body. He was lost in her embrace and in the smell and taste of her. The thought that he did not deserve this happiness interrupted his fantasy of things beyond his reach.

He willed strength into his voice, hoping Isabel would understand. "It's time for us to leave."

Chapter 14

Isabel and William walked the short distance from the Blue Goose Inn to the studio in silence. She was glad they had left their horses behind. It would give her the chance to sort out her feelings toward William. A full range of emotions wove around her. He was becoming important to her. Furthermore, she'd enjoyed his kiss entirely too much.

She slowed her pace along the river's edge to gaze at the night sky. The moon fought a losing battle as gossamer clouds blocked its view of the earth. She tried to determine how she could duplicate the range of hues from slate gray to linen white on canvas.

She glanced toward William. He was carrying the sketches she had wanted brought from her room at the inn. He looked as though he were locked in his own thoughts. William was a hard man to understand and about as responsive as a stone statue. However, it was when he asked for her help, or when they spent time together, that she saw glimpses of the man beneath the impenetrable surface. There was a side to him she very much wanted to know. During those times, his vulnerability, as well as his strength, shone through. It was the man who made her skin warm at a mere glance.

But he was not right for her. The words echoed in her thoughts like a Gregorian chant. He was here on some mysterious mission that Angus and Myra seemed aware of, but like so many times in her life, its true nature was kept from her.

This fact alone should urge her to keep her distance. But it only made her more curious, like the poor ill-fated moth drawn to the flame.

An icy breeze chilled her to the bone. She inhaled deeply and looked toward the sky, hoping the cold would clear her mind. But instead, her imagination took over. If she squinted her eyes and tilted her head, she could imagine the clouds taking the form of a mighty warrior embracing his lady as they rode across the heavens.

Isabel shook free of the irrational fantasy and paused at the staircase leading down to the artist's studio. A carved wooden placard swung on metal hinges that creaked in the cool breeze, the image of a pot of yellow paint and crossed brushes sketched on its surface—the entrance to the Painters' Guild.

William stood beside her underneath the sign. She turned to face him and was jolted by the color of his eyes. In the torchlight they were a deep velvet blue surrounded by lush, thick lashes. She tried to hide the growing heat within her.

The quiet moments they'd spent at the inn, as she'd poured out her love for art, had seemed woven from an enchanted story. He had listened to every word she'd spoken. And when he'd leaned forward and captured her lips with his own, she'd felt her dreams had turned to reality. But the kiss had ended. How could he be so tender one moment and so distant the next?

So here they were at the entrance to the artist's studio. Dual possibilities warred within her. She wanted to be alone with him, and at the same time she sought to be surrounded by a crowd. She knew it was her growing attraction to him that fueled her uncertainties.

"Isabel, what are we waiting for?"

What indeed? her heart responded. "I was taking the time to enjoy this extraordinary night." She needed to break the spell before she was lost. "But you would not understand that concept. All that concerns you is your mission."

Her words sounded harsh to her ears. She knew they were not true and regretted her rebuff. Whatever was troubling her was not his doing. If he did not feel as deeply, that was not his fault.

He cocked an eyebrow. "I can appreciate beauty the same as any man." He paused as a shadow crept over his face and dulled the light in his eyes. "But there isn't time for it in my life."

His statement made it clear. There was no place for her in his world. She had caught a glimpse of sadness in his expression and fought the temptation to hold him. To kiss him again. Instead, she picked up her skirts and concentrated on descending the narrow, icy stairs. She could hear William's footsteps as he followed close behind her. They were steady and sure and irritating. She felt as though she were venturing into forbidden territory. She put her hand out to steady her descent.

She cringed. The wall was cold and slippery. She curled her fingers and withdrew her hand. Maybe it was time she took a few chances.

Isabel reached the bottom steps. The alcove was draped in shadows. William was beside her. She could feel his warm breath on her skin. She closed her eyes and fought against the desire to lean against him. Would he reach out to her and enfold her in his arms?

Or push her away? More likely he would believe she was ill and thus the reason for her colliding into him.

She took a deep breath and knocked on the door. The spell was broken.

The door opened, and a warm golden light streamed into the dark alcove where she huddled beside William. It lifted her spirits. Here was solid ground.

A man whose clothes were splattered with paint—sunflower yellow, powder blue, and meadow green—greeted her. It was Ossian.

Ossian was about the same age as Angus, and he'd always been vague about where he came from. In the end, she'd given up trying to find out. After all, everyone had secrets.

Ossian grinned and reached toward her, pulling her into the room. "Isabel. We were beginning to believe you had forsaken your painting."

She shook her head and smiled. "Never."

The cavernous chamber smelled of oil, paint, and plaster. It was charged with the air of expectancy. A scaffold lined the far wall, where a floor-to-ceiling mural of the war of the gods was in progress. It, along with other works of art, had been commissioned by the queen for the costume ball that was to take place in a matter of days. Blocks of snow-white marble stood on the floor or rested on a long table, awaiting the inspiration of an artist to transform them into a masterpiece. Finished statues re-creating Greek and Roman gods stood on the opposite sides of the mural.

Isabel took a deep, calming breath. She was home. "I would have been here sooner, but I was helping someone with a problem."

Ossian nodded. "And is this man one of the

problems?"

Isabel felt color rise to her face. Had Ossian read her mind? She hoped not. She tried to focus. She was letting her imagination get carried away.

William put his hand on Isabel's shoulder. She warmed under his touch but kept her breathing under control.

He extended his other hand toward Ossian. "Just call me William. I'm a problem-solver."

She clenched her hands at her sides, willing her body not to react to his touch, but she was losing the battle.

Ossian's eyes widened as he looked toward William. "Ah, then you have heard of our emergency. But come in out of the cold. Paulette will be pleased to see you, especially, when she learns you have solved our dilemma."

William followed Isabel into the studio and whispered, "Do you know what they're talking about?"

She shook her head.

Paulette rushed toward her and pulled Isabel into a tight embrace. "We are pleased to see you at last."

Standing along the scaffolding were Forsyth and his assistant, Jardin. She excelled at creating lifelike animals. Her other trademark was that she was never without her sword. Isabel noted that it leaned against a support post next to her. Like Ossian, she had never revealed her past. So many secrets. Isabel was drowning in them.

Paulette handed Isabel a smock. "There is not a moment to lose. We are behind schedule, but the queen will not postpone the costume ball." Paulette winked. "And you know how volatile she can be when she does not get her way. Fortunately, Ossian has a way of soothing her tantrums."

Isabel slipped the protective garment over her gown and smiled to herself. She knew better than to try to get a word in while Paulette was talking. It was one of the things she loved about the woman. Paulette could carry on an elaborate conversation while sculpting.

Paulette grew serious. "You already have started the preliminary sketches of Poseidon."

Isabel nodded.

Paulette glanced toward William. "That is too bad. You will have to make a few adjustments. That one looks taller than Finn, and his shoulders are broader, but he will do. Yes, yes, he will do nicely."

Isabel belted her smock in place and reached for a slender brush from the well at the base of the easel. "I am not sure I understand. Finn is the model I am using for Poseidon, not William."

Paulette shook her head. "I thought you knew and that was the reason you brought William to us. We received word from Finn that he no longer will model for us. We assume he has the offer of a better-paying job." She shrugged. "We wish him well, but that left us without a subject. Although there are many who would pose for us, there are few who have the physical attributes and muscular definition of the sea god. We had almost given up hope, but then you arrived with the perfect specimen." She motioned toward William. "Instruct him to take off his clothes. There is not a moment to lose."

The walls closed in on Isabel as she went over to William. The paint smells she had relished moments before made her stomach lurch. Why had she insisted she was ready for nudes? She should have stayed with fruits and vegetables. She felt her face warm at the prospect of seeing William naked again. But on the heels of this thought came a realization that she did not want anyone else to see him, either. Maybe there was a way out of this dilemma. She calmed a little, thinking she was overreacting. William would never agree to pose naked. He was too serious. For once she was thankful. He would no doubt want to be on his way, searching for the mysterious criminal.

Isabel paused when she reached his side. She took a deep breath. "Did you hear that they expect you to be the model for Poseidon?"

His eyes seemed to twinkle with mischief. "Really?"

She wet her lips. This was not the reaction she'd expected. She pointed the brush at him, punctuating each word she spoke as she jabbed the air in his direction. "It is, of course, out of the question. As you can see, all the gods and goddesses in the murals are nude. Ossian and Paulette will have to find someone else."

He shrugged. "Why? Besides, you told me I don't take enough time to enjoy the beauty around me. Maybe I can change your mind by actually being a part of it."

She folded her arms across her chest. "This is impossible."

A smile tugged at the corner of his mouth. "You think my appearance will ruin your portrait?"

"No, of course not. You have the perfect physique for Poseidon." She hesitated. "That is to say…"

A smile bloomed as he removed his sword and

pulled his shirt over his head.

She wiped her palms on her paint smock and whispered, "What do you think you are doing?"

"Isn't it obvious? I'm taking off my clothes. It seems I'm to be a model." He grinned. "This will be a first."

She averted her eyes and concentrated on a beam above his head, wondering if she could will it to fall on him. "You are not making any sense."

"Actually, it makes perfect sense. I have no talent as a painter, so what better way to blend in here than as a model? I can listen in to conversations and ask questions. No one will take me seriously. We struck out when we interviewed people at the brothels and inns. I'm willing to try something new. It's the perfect cover and an opportunity to find out if they know anything about the man I'm after."

She pulled on the bristles of the brush she held. "Do you understand what is expected?"

"Pretty much. I have attended a few museums in my lifetime." William dropped his shirt over a nearby chair and leaned his sword against it.

Isabel cleared her throat. His muscles rippled under naked flesh. It was one thing to paint Finn. It meant nothing. But this was different, very different. She swallowed. This was William.

He undid his belt. The tartan dropped to his feet in a pool of green-and-blue plaid fabric, exposing narrow hips, muscular thighs...

The brush's bristles came loose in her fingers. Her face burned as though she stood over a blazing fire. Her breath caught in her throat. "You are enjoying this."

He winked. "Aren't you?"

She clenched her hands into fists and turned toward the canvas. The infuriating man was right. The thought of gazing at him as intently as she wanted, for as long as she desired, heated her blood. Her only hope was that she could keep her hands from shaking long enough to hold a brush.

As she walked back to her easel, she froze in place. She turned abruptly to gaze at William again. This time it was not out of desire but something else. William held Poseidon's forked staff and stood on a platform. The light of the wall sconces and candles illuminated him. Paulette was right. He did resemble all the ancient descriptions of the sea god. But that was not the reason Isabel was trembling.

The brush slipped from her fingers to the ground. William stood before her, naked. Absent were not only his clothes but also the linen bandages Myra had woven around him. His chest muscles rippled. He was the perfect male. Too perfect. When Myra bandaged him, there were deep sword wounds slashed over his chest. He should have been scarred for life, but nothing marred his smooth skin.

Isabel held onto the easel to steady her shaking limbs. Her first impression of William when she'd seen him in the river swept over her like a tidal wave. She'd thought him a creature from her fantasies, and she'd recalled the stories told to her as a child about fire-eating dragons, shape-shifters who could change their form at will, and immortals whose wounds healed without leaving scars.

There must be a logical explanation. She tried to dismiss her fears as the product of an overactive imagination. She reached for a new brush. William was real, her mind reasoned. He was flesh and blood.

She glanced toward him again. His skin was flawless. He had sustained life-threatening wounds. Not only had they healed almost overnight, but it was as though they had never been there in the first place.

He smiled at her, and a shiver ran through her that had no connection to the temperature in the room. She dipped her trembling brush in a sea-green paint. Wavy lines appeared on the white canvas.

What type of creature was he?

Chapter 15

The rose shades of dawn seeped through the windows of the studio. It had been a long night. William reached for his clothes, remembering Isabel's reaction to him when he'd disrobed. He smiled. At first he'd hesitated because he knew all his wounds had healed. It was not an easy thing to explain, but knowing Angus's reputation for honesty, he was sure the man had told Isabel he was an Immortal. She'd not commented on the mark of the Protectors. Perhaps she felt it was of no concern to her.

And then he forgot about it, pleased he had the sense to follow Isabel's advice about asking the artists questions. Although they hadn't seen anyone fitting Bartholomew's description, Isabel was right. The artists knew everything that went on in the city. William felt it would be only a matter of time before Bartholomew was captured.

William pulled the linen shirt over his head. The evening had not been a total loss. He was here with Isabel, and he'd had an opportunity to see her paint. He wondered if she realized how talented she was.

William had rarely seen the focus and dedication to art as he had witnessed it during the last few hours. But he understood the work ethic. Although a Protector's destiny was preordained since birth, he was well acquainted with the single-mindedness and discipline needed to accomplish his duties. Perhaps that was the reason he was drawn to fire-fighting. The men and women in that profession also never lost their purpose to protect those in their charge.

Time had ceased to exist for the artists. They'd lost all sense of place as they'd worked tirelessly to create a masterpiece. But now exhaustion had set in. Ossian was cleaning his workstation. Forsyth and Paulette lay curled on a long bench, and Jardin sat on the floor asleep, a paintbrush in her hand.

William wound his plaid around his waist, draping the end over his shoulder and belting it in place. He glanced toward Isabel. She arched her back and closed her eyes. He saw the same fire reflected within her that he'd seen in the others. He could well understand the reason she risked so much.

He remembered listening to his mother tell stories of her life in the Middle Ages. Each century the boundaries inhibiting a woman's freedoms lessened, but it was hard work. According to his mother, it had taken over two thousand years to reclaim the respect they enjoyed as Celts. Although a great majority of the world celebrated a woman's desire to attain her dreams, even in the twenty-first century there were societies in the world that still fought to keep women suppressed, chaining their minds. He found it ironic that women had to fight their way back to equality.

His mother's words haunted him. She felt it was a result of ignorance. He wondered if it was something more. There was fear laced with his mother's hope for humankind. A nation's power and strength lay not only in its ability to wage war but also in its knowledge and acceptance of diversity.

He understood the meaning behind his mother's words. She'd wanted the Protectors to take a more active role in humankind, and she had fought long and hard toward that end. He agreed with her, but the Council of Seven was slow to change their ways. However, change was indeed on the wind. His uncle, Lachlan, had proved that theory once and for all, but now even the Immortals' way of life was threatened.

William remembered his mother's words. *We only fail if we have never tried.*

He wondered if the Renegades' fear of the influence she would have on others had resulted in their agreeing to let Bartholomew seek his revenge on Lachlan's family.

Ossian walked over and clasped him on the shoulder, interrupting his thoughts. "You are not what I expected."

William doubted Ossian was referring to his talents as an artist's model, and he turned his attention to the man with renewed interest. His training taught him that everyone had something to hide.

Before William could respond to Ossian, Isabel appeared. Red and yellow paint smudged her cheeks. Her hair had come loose from its tight braid and lay in a wild tangle over her shoulders. She had never looked more appealing to him.

She stretched her back again, avoiding his gaze. "We should return to the manor before Myra becomes worried. It will take me only moments to be ready to leave."

Isabel removed her paint smock. She draped it over a chair and turned toward her supplies, placing brushes and small jars away in a long wooden box.

She'd been distant to him the whole evening. It couldn't be his nakedness—she'd seen him before without clothes. Maybe it was his imagination and she was just tired.

Ossian motioned for William to follow him. There was something in the man's expression that made William wary. When they were a short distance from Isabel, Ossian spoke.

"We are all grateful to you for acting as Isabel's protector. Angus's duties keep him from London too long."

"She doesn't need my protection."

His words spilled out in Isabel's defense. He didn't like the idea that this man thought Isabel couldn't take care of herself. And then the word Ossian had said took on another meaning. Especially his emphasis on the word "protector." Was it possible Ossian knew who he was?

William rubbed the mark of a sword on his wrist. He had always made it a practice to not hide the sign. Few outside the scope of the Immortals knew of its significance, and for those that did, it served as a warning.

Ossian glanced over his shoulder in Isabel's direction, and William followed his gaze. She was still cleaning her brushes and clearing away her work area. The hair on the nape of William's neck prickled. The artist's studio might be more than it appeared. If his suspicions were true, Isabel might be in danger.

Ossian turned back toward him. "We have little time. I realize your desire for caution, but you need not worry. I know who you are, but I did not want to be overheard by the others." He nodded toward William's wrist. "You wear the mark of the Protector."

William took his time responding. His suspicions were confirmed. He also noticed the man's furtive glances around the room. Ossian was afraid. When William had disrobed he'd realized his mark might be noticed. However, most people thought it was a tattoo instead of a birthmark. It was an unwritten rule that a Protector never denied who he was.

William leveled his gaze. "Yes. You are correct. I am a Protector. What do you know of us?"

Ossian lowered his voice. "That your kind never fails." He swallowed. "You must keep what I am about to tell you from Isabel. It is Angus's wish." He glanced over his shoulder again. "Did you not think it odd that we defy the laws of the queen and allow women to paint whatever they please?"

William didn't think Isabel liked secrets any better than he did, but he kept his voice level. "I felt it was admirable."

"Well spoken. Again you surprise me. I believed Protectors were not concerned with the inequalities of this world."

"Not all. However, I am more concerned with how you recognized the mark."

Ossian strengthened. "If I tell you who we are, it will explain the rest. The artists of this studio are more than we seem on the surface." He paused and lowered his voice. "We are also Immortals."

William's suspicions were confirmed, but he wondered why Angus wanted it kept from Isabel. Something didn't feel right.

"Continue."

"Angus knew this would be the only place in all of

London where Isabel would be safe to paint as she pleased. That Angus also sent you to us tells me he trusts you as well. You are searching for someone?"

William felt the steel barriers rising around him. It was not the first time he was thankful for his training. It had taught him the discipline to bury any emotional reaction. Angus had not told him these artists were Immortals. What was more, he wanted to keep it from Isabel. What else was he hiding?

That Angus allowed his adopted daughter to interact with these Immortals must indicate they were people he felt could be trusted. But William had not survived longer than any other Protector by accident. He trusted no one. The faction of Immortals known as Renegades had functioned since the Beginning Time. It was a reality of the world that where there was good, there would always be evil. And often it was difficult to distinguish one from the other.

He kept his voice and his mind devoid of emotion. It was a place of safety that enabled him to complete his missions with speed and efficiency.

"That you're an Immortal explains why you know who I am. If you know that, you're also aware that only the gravest of circumstances would bring me to your century."

Ossian picked on the threads dangling from the cuff of his sleeve. "You mentioned earlier that you were searching for someone." He paused, and the muscles over his eyelid twitched. "It must be a grievous act against our race for the Council to send a Protector. What crime has the person committed?"

William let the question hang in the air. It was clear that Ossian was afraid. No doubt he too had a secret. But unless it was connected to Bartholomew, Ossian was free to keep his secrets. Let someone else dig into Ossian's life. It was not William's concern on this assignment.

"You know I can't tell you the reason I'm here, but if you learn any information that could be helpful, you can get word to me through Isabel or Angus."

Ossian's eyes brightened. "A favor for a favor, then?"

"Unfortunately, it's not our way." William drew his words out carefully. "I'm here for one assignment and one man only."

Ossian's breathing slowed, and he nodded a silent thank you. "I will see what I can find out about the man you hunt."

Isabel's laughter floated through the charged air, interrupting their serious conversation. She seemed fine now. Her change in attitude toward him must just be his imagination. She was playing with a silver-and-white cat. The animal had grabbed one of the paint rags, and Isabel was trying to retrieve it. There was a stark contrast between the playful activity with the cat and the potential evil that moved in on her from all sides.

He prayed Angus hadn't placed Isabel in a den of lions. He watched as she picked up the cat and settled down in a chair, unaware of the danger that surrounded her. At the moment, the Immortals were amused with her, but if any of them were sympathizers of the Renegade branch, she would be eliminated as easily as they disposed of their empty jars of paint.

The gift of immortality did not come without a price. Some would go insane, turning their love of peace and respect for life into madness, called

Bloodlust. A person infected would kill anyone that crossed his or her path. It had happened to Elaenor's father. He'd killed one of his own sons before he was stopped.

By the twenty-first century the Council of Seven had developed both a test to detect Bloodlust and treatments to keep it under control. But it was not a perfect antidote. Many escaped the net, and for many more, the treatment didn't work. However, in the sixteenth century, there was not even this imperfect solution.

Bartholomew had escaped notice for many centuries. Maybe it was because he didn't fit the profile of an Immortal possessed by the madness of Bloodlust like his brother, Subedei. The Council had thought Bartholomew was merely a sociopath in a world that seemed to breed them. Their opinion had changed.

William walked toward Isabel. His need to protect her was stronger than ever. She was leaning against the back of the chair, asleep, her arms cradling the purring cat. Again her quiet beauty wove around him. He felt a protectiveness surge through him. It took him by surprise. He wanted her out of this place. Despite the objections he knew she would raise, he wanted to keep her safe. He would take her back to the manor and continue this investigation without her. This time he would not listen to her arguments. It was too dangerous for her.

He bent over her and touched her shoulder. "Isabel?"

Her eyelids fluttered. The cat, startled, jumped silently to the floor and padded into the shadows of the studio. Isabel took a deep breath and stretched. The effort caused her breasts to strain against the fabric of her bodice. William felt his blood heat. It was as though he'd walked into a wall of flames. A vision of her waking up beside him flashed through his thoughts. It took all his willpower to keep from caressing her luxuriant hair. William visualized the strong, unyielding power of a sword. It had never failed to pull up the barriers around his heart, providing an emotionless response. Until now, that is.

He shook his head, as though trying to drive the vision of Isabel in his arms from his mind. It wouldn't go away. Keeping his mind and body occupied would help, he reasoned. William reached for her hand.

He drew her to him. "I need to take you home."

Isabel nodded sleepily as her eyes opened and then widened. She grabbed her cloak from a nearby wooden peg and wound it over her shoulders. She appeared nervous around him. He dismissed the idea. She was probably just exhausted.

Her voice was barely above a whisper. "I wish I could stay here."

So did he. If it meant it would only be the two of them.

Alone. He wondered if she could hear the pounding of his heart. All of his training cautioned—no, forbade—emotional involvement during an assignment. He just hoped he had the strength to adhere to it.

Ossian watched as William and Isabel rode in the direction of the manor. He glanced toward the sky and sensed another snowstorm on its way. He bolted the door in place, wishing he could shut out the world as easily as he had the chill night air. Ossian had a premonition that soon all he held dear would be taken from him. He shuddered.

Paulette slipped her hand in his. "Do you believe William suspects?"

She echoed the words that were in his thoughts. It was a habit of hers. "I am not certain. There was an undercurrent to William's probing questions, but then it passed."

Paulette stepped away from him and fidgeted with the tight curls that hugged her shoulders. "And?"

"William made it clear he is after only one man and has no desire to widen his circle." Ossian shook his head. "We walk a dangerous line between the light and the dark, my sweet."

Paulette frowned. "Do not sink into the role of a poet. You did not have the talent for it in the time of Plato, and if it was true then, it is more so now. We must keep a level head if we are to survive. You were always the dreamer." She sighed. "Sometimes I wonder why we were together for so long."

Ossian reached for her hand and kissed her fingertips. The last few months had been difficult for them both. More so for Paulette, he realized. Their bickering was just a reaction to the secret they guarded with their lives—the secret that he and Paulette had a child without the Council of Seven's knowledge.

"Please, let us not argue. I am as worried as you about the appearance of a Protector."

He looked past her. Forsyth was slumped in a chair on the opposite side of the room and was asleep, but Jardin was nowhere in sight.

Ossian turned to Paulette and whispered. He did not want to risk being overheard, even by Forsyth, whom he trusted. "We need to be more watchful now that the Protector has arrived. He is no fool and eventually will track down his prey. Let us not give him an excuse to seek another."

Footsteps echoed through the cavernous studio as Jardin appeared from the shadows and glanced in their direction. Slim and fluid, her movements were smooth and catlike as she walked down the stairs. Ossian kept his gaze steady. Her past was more steeped in shadows than his own. Some said she was a Warrior Queen in the Nile Valley, others claimed she was new to this century. She had asked for a safe place to stay and pursue her love of the arts. Ossian had agreed. He was in no position to judge.

He held his breath as Jardin smiled briefly and left through the back door. It slammed shut, rattling his frayed nerves.

Paulette was fidgeting again with her hair. Her whispers were like a shout in his ears. "I do not trust that woman. She is always watching me when she thinks I am not looking. I am sorry we told her about the babe."

"We had little choice. She guessed you were with child." Ossian's heart hammered against his chest. "But I do not trust her either. Asking her to leave now would draw too much suspicion. We cannot risk it."

He felt, as well as heard, Paulette's sigh. Jardin was a talented sculptress, but he regretted the day he and Paulette had taken her into the studio. It was true he did not trust Jardin. However, his own life was built on a mountain of missed opportunities, regrets, and compromises. As a result, he had a difficult time finding fault in others.

At the time, he had wanted to give Jardin the

chance to prove her loyalty. However, that was before he and Paulette had given birth to the child, Marduk. That blessed event had changed everything.

He put his arm around Paulette and drew her into a tender embrace. Ossian knew her fear for their child caused the bite in her words. He was afraid as well. They had defied the rules of the Council of Seven. If discovered, they would lose their child and their lives. To flee now would be to draw too much attention. It would be especially dangerous with a Protector in their midst. A natural time for them to leave would be after the queen's costume ball.

Ossian kissed Paulette and felt her calm in his embrace. In just a short time they would be safe. All they had to do was wait. He must be confident that no harm would come to them if they were watchful.

Chapter 16

Isabel gripped the reins of her horse. Her hands felt numb. The long ride from the artist's studio to the manor seemed to take a lifetime. Blinding flurries of white snow transformed the crisp, ebony night sky. She glanced over toward William. He rode beside her and appeared unaffected by the weather.

It should not surprise her. Enduring the chilling cold would be a small accomplishment for a man whose life-threatening wounds had healed without leaving scars. Thankfully the wind and snowstorm made it difficult to carry on a conversation. It was just as well. She had no idea what to say to him. She alternated between fear and being more intrigued than ever.

The road leading to the manor was covered with a fresh blanket of snow. Isabel nudged her horse forward, ahead of William's. She was anxious to reach the warmth and security of her home.

As they drew closer, Isabel reined in her horse. Instead of the warm welcome of a well-lit home, it was pitch black. She tried to remember if Angus or Myra had told her they would be away when she returned, but she knew they had not.

William guided his horse alongside hers. He dismounted and walked through the deep snow toward her. His voice rose above the whistling wind, and he glanced in the direction of the manor.

"Something's wrong."

She nodded. "I feel it as well."

He held out his arms toward her, to help her dismount. She knew they would be warm and inviting. The temptation was too great. She swallowed her apprehension and slid into his embrace. He did not release her but kept his arms protectively around her.

His lips grazed her forehead. "You're as cold as ice."

She wanted to tell him that it was her heart that was in danger, not her body. She pulled away from him. "I will be all right as soon as I am out of the storm."

The wind blew the snow in drifts against the sides of the buildings as they walked toward the stables. It was noticeably deeper than when they had left. She looked toward the manor. It was shrouded in shadows. If not for the white snow, it would have disappeared altogether from view. She shivered and patted Athena's warm neck for comfort.

Her mare's eyes were wide, as though she, too, sensed danger.

When they reached the stables, William brushed the entrance clear. He yanked open the door and helped Isabel lead the horses inside and secure them. The thick walls of the stables were an effective barrier against the biting wind and snow, but the air smelled stale and musty.

William moved somewhere ahead of her in the direction of the horses' stalls, but she could not see him. It was too dark. It was as though he was looking for something. Isabel hoped it was an oil lamp.

She heard a crash, followed by the sound of clinking metal as something hit the ground.

William muttered under his breath. "Damn. Why didn't I bring a flashlight into this blasted century?"

Isabel moved toward the sound of his voice. "Flashlight?"

"Too hard to explain. I just overturned a table of iron horseshoes. One landed on my foot."

She smiled. Isabel suspected being clumsy was a new experience for William. "It is odd that Brian is not here to greet us." Her eyes were beginning to focus, and she could make out William's shadow moving a short distance from her. "I think Brian keeps a lantern close to the table you just overturned. Or if we could find a candle—"

"I don't think we should risk being seen."

He moved to stand in front of her, so close she could feel his warm breath on her skin. She heard the warning in his voice.

He wove his arms around her and pulled her closer. "Isabel, Brian is dead."

Her pulse jumped and her legs buckled. If William had not held her, she would have crumpled to the ground. She clung to him. "But who would have done such a monstrous thing? The boy did not have an enemy in the world."

"He had at least one. Brian might not be the main target. I think whoever did this just wanted him out of the way."

Blood pounded in her ears as the meaning of what he was saying took hold. "Do you think someone is here to harm my family?"

"It's possible. I want you to stay here while I check the manor. I don't want anything happening to you."

She stepped back from him. "I will not stay behind.

I am going with you." She clenched her hands at her sides to keep them from trembling. "Do not pretend you care what happens to me. *I* mean nothing to you. How could I? You are not even human."

Isabel walked around William and headed toward the door. She pulled it open.

He was beside her in a matter of seconds and reached for her arm. He turned her toward him. Snow swirled around them in angry flurries.

"What do you mean? I'm not human?"

Standing at the threshold, she stood her ground, refusing to be afraid of him. "Your wounds healed without leaving scars. That, William, is not human."

His expression was lost in the shadows. "What are you talking about?"

A child's scream raced through the snow-laced air. They both said the name aloud at the same time. "Elaenor!"

The screams were coming from the direction of the river. Isabel froze. She had never heard Elaenor scream before. The child was fearless. Where were Angus and Myra? Both would risk their own lives to keep Elaenor safe. It could only mean…

Isabel turned slowly toward William.

His face was a mask, devoid of emotion. A steel-like calm surrounded him. He withdrew his sword slowly and deliberately from its scabbard. The blade glinted like molten steel against the stark white backdrop of snow.

William gazed toward Isabel. How had she become so important to him in such a short span of time? "Stay here, Isabel. I'll bring Elaenor back safely."

With one arm, William pulled Isabel in a tight

embrace and kissed her. It was not in farewell, he reasoned, but out of his need to show her he was human. He knew what lay ahead, and he wanted her to remember that he was flesh and blood. Her face was covered with small, lacy snowflakes, and her lips were parted, still moist from their kiss. He drew back and pushed her gently inside the stable and safety.

William raced to the rear of the manor. It was the place he calculated he'd heard Elaenor scream. More than her young life hung in the balance. The lives of the children she would have in the future were also in jeopardy. His own life was in jeopardy. He could almost feel the presence of his brothers and sisters as he neared the first dead body. No doubt a casualty of Angus's sword, but where was the Immortal?

William leaped over the body, noting the blood staining the white snow. A few yards past the body he found Angus, face down. Two more bodies lay scattered nearby. Angus had put up a valiant fight. William effectively blocked any emotional reaction. His training held.

·William knelt down and felt Angus for a pulse. He was still alive, but there was a thin line of blood across his throat, as though someone had tried to cut off his head. William rose slowly. The attack on Angus confirmed Brian was not the primary target. Whoever was behind this assault had someone else in mind. What was more, they knew the only way to kill Angus was decapitation. William reasoned that Bartholomew was behind this latest attack. It meant William was too close.

He scanned the shore by the river. Shadows moved through the snow flurries in the moonlight. He could make out three men and a small child. Elaenor. They were trying to chase her down, but she was not making it easy for them. Even from this distance, however, he could tell she was tiring. It would not be long before she was caught, or worse.

On a dead run, William arched his sword over his head and raced toward the nearest assailant.

The man hesitated and turned toward him. Fear spread over his face as he raised his sword in defense.

William was in no mood to take his time. With one efficient blow of his sword he knocked the weapon out of the man's grip, and with another he drove his blade into the man's heart.

One of the two remaining assailants grabbed Elaenor and pressed a knife to her neck. "Stay back or I'll cut her throat."

A man standing beside him barked out a response. "Jimmy, are you mad? We can't be bargaining with him. We only gets paid if we bag the girl's head."

Jimmy snarled, "Shut up, you halfwit, and let me do the talking."

William closed in on the man who held Elaenor. His words were deadly calm. "I want you both to listen carefully. The only chance you have of surviving the next few minutes is to release the child. You draw so much as a drop of her blood, and I'll strip the flesh off your bones. It's that simple."

Jimmy cocked a smile. "Finn's right. There's no need to be bargaining with the likes of you. As I sees it, there are two of us and only one of you. I'm thinking you should be the one backing down." He nodded to Finn. "Take him, lad, and be quick about it."

Finn leaped forward, but William was ready. His

blade made a swishing sound through the crisp air as he brought it back and then around, driving the sword into the man's chest. Finn clutched at the gaping hole over his stomach before crumpling to the ground.

William stepped over Finn's body and advanced on Jimmy. "You're next."

Fear rose to the man's eyes. His hands trembled.

Elaenor slid a furtive glance toward William. He saw the courage reflected in her eyes and the determination to survive. William nodded slightly. He knew what she planned to do.

In the next instant, Elaenor bit down on her captor's hand. He yelped in pain and dropped the blade into the deep snow.

William seized the opportunity and attacked. Before Jimmy could react, he lay dead beside his comrade.

Elaenor moved toward William. Now that the danger was past, her tears flowed in a steady stream.

He smiled and hugged her. "You're safe now, Elaenor. No one can harm you."

****

Several hours had passed since Isabel had watched William rescue Elaenor. She had been unable to stay in the stable. Her family's safety had hung in the balance. However, William had not needed her help. Isabel smiled as she put another log on the fire in Myra's chamber. William had kept his promise. Elaenor was sleeping comfortably in the adjacent room.

Isabel had made sure Angus was resting, as well. William had agreed to stay with him and was confident he would recover. Isabel was now able to turn her attention to Myra. William had found her locked in the root cellar, frightened but unharmed.

Isabel hung a kettle of water on the hook in the fireplace and turned to Myra. She was sitting on a stool beside the hearth, wrapped in a blanket and staring at the flames.

Isabel knelt beside her. "Are you sure they did not hurt you?"

Myra's eyes brimmed with tears as she wrapped the blanket tighter around her shoulders. "I heard one of those men say their master wanted me kept alive for his pleasure. Beast. I would have run their master through with the rod I use to roast pigs over the cookroom fire. 'Tis that poor boy, Brian, that is on my mind."

"Angus said he would make the arrangements for a proper burial for Brian." Isabel hugged Myra, realizing the horror the woman must have gone through wondering if her family was safe. "Please try to forget."

Myra wiped her eyes with the back of her hand. "Aye. Ye are right. I shall not dwell on it further. I am most grateful to William that both Elaenor and Angus are unharmed."

Isabel was relieved to see the spark return to Myra's eyes, and she nodded. "Yes, William fought with the strength of the legendary Irish hero Cuchulainn. I never saw anyone fight so bravely."

Her words trailed off as she realized what she had said. She had compared William to a man whose exploits were larger than life. In all the confusion, she had forgotten he was not human.

Myra patted Isabel's hand. "What is it, child?"

"It is nothing. I am just tired."

"Now, now. I know ye better than ye know yourself. Please tell me what has happened."

Isabel took a deep breath. It would feel good to share what she had learned about William. Her words flowed out as though a dam had burst. She had not realized how hard she had kept them at bay.

"After I helped William try to locate the man he searched for, we went to the artist's studio. I thought Paulette and Ossian might be able to help us. Well, when we arrived, Paulette mistook William for an artist's model. She asked him to remove his clothes in order to pose for the portrait of Poseidon I am painting."

A smile flickered over the corners of Myra's mouth. "This is not the first time a man has posed naked at the studio. Ye told me many times the artists were commissioned by the queen to re-create the Greek and Roman gods as a backdrop for the queen's costume ball. Perhaps it is different when William is the model."

"Yes—I mean, no." Isabel shook her head. "You do not understand. When William removed his shirt, I noticed the sword wounds he received a few days ago had healed without leaving any scars."

The smile disappeared from Myra's lips. Seconds crept by, and the silence dragged out into minutes. Isabel waited, knowing how difficult it must be for Myra to absorb the information. It was one thing to read about mythical beings, but quite another to know they existed.

Finally Myra took a deep breath. "Aye, lass, of course an Immortal would not have scars."

Isabel stood abruptly. "An Immortal? What are you saying?" Myra rose slowly to her feet, as though the effort took all the strength she possessed. She put her hand on Isabel's shoulder. "There are things Angus and

I should have told ye a long time ago. But I believed it was not my place. Do ye remember the stories Angus would tell ye of the legends of an Immortal race?"

Isabel paced before the hearth. "Those were myths, like the legends of Merlin, and the gods and goddesses of Olympus."

Myra shrugged. "I canna speak of them, but Immortals have been among us since the beginning. No man should have survived the wounds William sustained, yet not only did he survive but, as ye have seen for yourself, there were no scars. As a child, ye saw the proof of the existence of an Immortal race many times but chose to seek another answer."

Isabel felt as though her world was crumbling around her feet. Her life was based on lies. "What are you saying? Angus is an Immortal? That is impossible. Why did he keep it from me all these years?"

"Angus wanted to pretend, if only for a little while, that he was human. I am sorry I allowed him to deceive ye."

Isabel turned away from Myra and stared into the flames. "You should have told me. Are you an Immortal as well?"

Myra's voice was laced with tears. "No, my child. I am only human, in love with a man who will live forever."

Isabel heard the door close and knew Myra had left the chamber. Isabel's thoughts rolled in her mind like the flames over the wood in the hearth. It explained why Angus and William had become close so quickly. They shared a common bond. They were both Immortals. She shuddered. Questions without easy answers raced through her mind. What Myra told her was the stuff of legends and myths, not reality. At least, that is what she had always believed. She did not know what was true anymore. Even her growing feelings toward William hung in the balance.

Chapter 17

"Angus, what the hell were you thinking?"

William paced in front of Angus's bed, roaring mad. He'd waited until he was sure Isabel, Elaenor, and Myra were resting comfortably, and the attackers' bodies disposed of, before dealing with Angus. William felt that Angus, perhaps because he was the oldest living Immortal, had forgotten what it was like to fear death and thus had become careless with the lives around him. What other explanation could there be?

Further, if he and Isabel had not returned when they had, Elaenor would be dead, and the first phase of Bartholomew's plan would be completed.

He didn't even want to dwell too long on the ripple effects. With Elaenor—the person who would become his mother—dead, he and his brothers and sisters would cease to exist.

The thoughts scrolled through his mind, fueling his frustrations. William grabbed Angus by the shoulders and pulled him to a sitting position on the bed. "How was it possible for someone to kill your stable boy without being overheard?"

Angus frowned. "I canna answer your question. I mourn Brian's death. He was a good young man and will be missed."

William released Angus, letting him flop down. "And how could you let those men in this house?"

"They said they were your friends."

"I don't have any friends."

Angus raised an eyebrow. "And that I can understand."

William ignored the remark. "You bring up a good point. There's a reason I don't let people too close. I don't want my enemies to use them to get to me." He paused. "I hope you realize your family is no longer safe here."

Angus nodded his head slowly. "You may be right. I can understand why this Renegade would come for you, or me, for that matter, but why Elaenor? She is only a child."

William rested his hand on the hilt of his sword, thankful again that he and Isabel had arrived in time. "Elaenor is Lachlan's sister. The Renegade I hunt cannot prevent what Lachlan will do to his brother in a future time, but he can have Elaenor killed. It would be a fitting revenge."

Angus sank lower into the pillows. "I thought I was successful in keeping my family from harm."

"Really? You're always away on an adventure and no doubt made your share of enemies along the way. It's a wonder no one has tried something like this before."

William thought of Isabel, vulnerable in the midst of the Immortals at the artist's studio. His anger and frustration built once more. Instead of protecting Isabel, Angus had placed her in grave danger.

William continued. "For example, Isabel is surrounded by a ragtag assortment of Immortals. I don't trust any of them. Why do you risk her life?"

Angus appeared to age before William's eyes. He

knew it was impossible, but the man looked older, as though he carried a great weight on his shoulders.

"There is not an easy answer to your question." He took a gold chain with a key attached from around his neck and unlocked the cabinet next to the bed. He withdrew a red leather-bound book and placed it in his lap, tracing the Celtic lettering with his fingers. "Maybe this will explain my reasoning. This book is a record of many things, including the story of how I found Isabel. If anything happened to her, I wanted her to know the truth. I have tried to behave as a proper parent, but 'tis not always easy. I found her as a wee babe wailing as loud as any banshee. She was nestled in an oak tree not far from Stirling Castle and was the only survivor of a bloody battle."

William had witnessed similar scenes. There seldom were any survivors. "Seems odd that a child would be there in the first place."

"You know the Scots. Battles spring up around them as often as a sheep gives birth. Perhaps Isabel and her parents were swept up in a clan skirmish before they had an opportunity to take the child to safety."

"I'm sure you're right, but what has that to do with exposing Isabel to danger? You, above all others, know how unpredictable Immortals are."

Angus shrugged. "I suppose it began as the result of the guilt I felt for arriving too late to save her parents. Later, when Isabel, like her mother, developed a love and talent for the arts, I indulged the child, so it was difficult to find a place for her to study. The human race does not encourage their women to follow their dreams. Then one day, not too long ago, I heard Ossian was in London. He and I fought side by side under

Anthony and Cleopatra in Egypt. I knew Ossian to be a good man. It seemed the perfect solution." Angus paused and sat straighter. "Wait. How did you discover there were Immortals at the studio in the first place?" The sound of footsteps clattered toward them, interrupting their conversation. Myra burst into the room.

She glanced over at William. "Ye fool. How could ye be so careless?"

Before letting William ask what the hell she was talking about, she directed the full measure of her anger toward Angus.

"Well, I hope ye are pleased with yourself as well. I followed your advice and kept silent all these long years, believing it was for the best. And now 'tis all boiling to the surface like a kettle of soup too long over the fire."

"Calm down, love. What are you talking about?"

She shoved her hands onto her hips. "Don't ye be calling me 'love' or telling me to calm down!" She jabbed a finger in William's direction. "'Twas all his fault. I thought ye said the Protectors were intelligent creatures. I think all that is between his ears is vacant space."

Angus choked back a laugh.

William folded his hands across his chest and prayed for patience. He hadn't a clue what Myra was babbling about, but he suspected it had something to do with Isabel. Terrific, he'd upset them both.

"What have I done now?"

She turned on him. "First of all, I thank ye for saving my Elaenor and Angus, but that does not excuse your behavior. What were ye thinking when ye

179

disrobed in front of Isabel?"

Angus's voice boomed out in a deep and foreboding tone. "Disrobed? What is this I hear?"

"Ease your temper, Angus," Myra ordered. "Nothing is amiss. William removed his clothes to pose as a model for the artists. They are working to complete a commission for the queen."

Angus's eyes were hooded. He pressed out his words between clenched teeth. "The humankind's opinion and mine are as one. Women should not paint the human male form. 'Tis not proper."

Myra took a deep breath. "Well, no one is interested in your opinion. And ye are missing my point. When William removed his clothes, Isabel noticed his wounds had healed without leaving any scars."

The silence was deafening.

Both Angus and Myra leveled their gaze in William's direction. He'd assumed Isabel had known Angus was an Immortal and had made the connection regarding him as well. This was not his fault. How could she grow up in this household and not know about the Immortal race? Plus, she was working in an artist's studio surrounded by Immortals.

William glanced toward Angus and Myra again. Their expressions were the same. He guessed they considered him an idiot. He was singlehandedly setting the reputation of the Protectors back a thousand years.

No wonder Isabel had given him the silent treatment on their way home. She thought he was some sort of supernatural creature. In fact, she'd said as much, claiming he wasn't human. He just hadn't picked up on what she was trying to say.

Angus was the first to speak.

"Myra, how did you explain it to Isabel?"

She wore a smug I-told-you-so expression. "Why, love, there was only one thing to be said. The truth. I told her that ye and William are Immortals."

Angus's jaw sagged open. "We agreed Isabel should be told only in an emergency."

Myra lifted her chin. "Well, I would say what we have experienced here today would be considered such."

Angus seemed resigned. His shoulders slumped forward. "How did she take it?"

"Not well. That is why I am here. Someone has to explain it to her." She shook her head. "As though something like an Immortal race could be explained."

****

Isabel opened the door that separated Myra's chamber from Elaenor's to see if the child was still sleeping. Her thoughts drifted to the events of the last few hours. What was it that troubled her the most? The fact that there were beings that defied the laws of science, or the fact that Myra and Angus had kept the truth from her?

Before she could dwell on all the implications her questions raised, as well as William's connection to them all, she pushed open the door. Instead of sleeping, Elaenor was sitting in a chair, reading. The child gazed in Isabel's direction. In the light from the fire and candles, Elaenor's expression appeared years older than that of a child of eight. Elaenor had narrowly escaped death, yet she was as calm as though it were an everyday occurrence.

Elaenor giggled. "I could not sleep." She closed

her book, resting it in her lap. "I overheard you talking to Myra. They should never have kept the truth from you. I always disagreed with them." She tucked her legs under her. "Did Myra tell you I am an Immortal as well?"

Isabel felt as though the floor had dropped from beneath her feet.

Elaenor's eyes sparkled with mischief. "Oh, yes, there are quite a lot of us, actually. You would be surprised."

Isabel sat down on a chair by the hearth, not relying on her legs to hold her.

Elaenor sighed. "It is so hard to keep secrets. My brother, Lachlan, tells me that we must, because some might want to harm us, like they did tonight."

Isabel gripped the arms of the chair, feeling as though she had stepped into a strange dream world. "How could anyone harm you, when you are all Immortals?"

Elaenor slid down from the chair and warmed her hands by the fire. "They could cut off our heads." She turned toward Isabel. "I saw it happen once, when no one knew I was watching. There was so much blood. The head was severed from the body, but the eyes stared back at me. His mouth was open like he was trying to speak. I remembered wondering if he was still alive somehow. The memory all rushed back when the man held a knife to my throat. I really thought I was going to die."

Isabel pulled the trembling Elaenor into her arms, feeling it odd that she should be the one to comfort an Immortal. What a terrible image for so young a child to witness. She brushed the hair off Elaenor's forehead.

"You are safe now."

Elaenor tilted her head and gazed toward Isabel. "That is just what William said to me. Lachlan says the reason we are so feared is that some of us go mad and do bad things. My father did bad things." She hesitated, and her voice lowered. "I do not want to be like my father."

Isabel kissed Elaenor on the top of her head. "Do not be afraid. I am sure nothing like that could ever happen to you."

Elaenor snuggled in Isabel's arms. "My brother says that all Immortals fear growing insane. More even than their own death. There is one group that is protected. You do not have to worry about William doing bad things."

"How can you be so sure?"

"The mark of a sword that identifies William as a Protector means his blood is not bad, like my father's. You should ask Angus. He knows all about these things."

Isabel knew the mark Elaenor spoke of. Isabel had seen it on William the first day he arrived. Although William was an Immortal, he would not go insane. Was she supposed to feel comforted somehow? All she felt was confused.

"I think I shall take your advice and ask Angus. I have a feeling there is a lot more he has kept from me." Isabel paused. "Perhaps I should ask him right now. Would you like to come with me?" Isabel did not think this was a time for Elaenor to be alone.

Elaenor jumped off Isabel's lap and nodded. "Oh, yes. You will see. We are not that much different from you."

Isabel reached for Elaenor's hand and headed toward Angus's chamber. She was not sure she agreed with Elaenor, but she was willing to find out for herself. As Isabel neared Angus's chamber, she overheard Myra's comment about the difficulty of explaining the Immortal race.

With Elaenor beside her, Isabel walked into the room. "I agree, Myra. Explaining the existence of an Immortal race is indeed difficult to explain."

Isabel glanced quickly toward William. "Despite what you are, I must thank you for saving my family." Her words sounded formal, as though the two of them had just met. She realized in some ways that was true. She felt she was seeing him for the first time.

He blocked her path. "Isabel, I'm still the same man."

"You are not the same. Nothing is the same as it once was." He only nodded in response.

She walked past him and stood in front of Angus's bed. She had no delusions. He was the source of the lies. She clenched her hands at her sides. She had known no other father save Angus. He had protected and cared for her as though she were his own flesh and blood. But he had not trusted her. That omission cut deep.

"Why did you keep the truth from me?"

There was a look of torment reflected in his eyes. Angus opened his mouth to speak and then closed it again. When he did speak, the anguish caused his voice to tremble. "I wanted to pretend, if only for a while, that we were a normal family."

"Why do I think there is still more you are not telling me?"

Angus stared down at the book in his lap as Myra reached over and put her hand over Angus's. "Our child deserves the truth. And all of it."

The brief glance that passed between them chilled Isabel to the bone.

His voice was deep and distant. He held the book toward her. "Within these pages you will find the answers to many of your questions. Maybe someday you will understand why I kept the truth from you. As far as William's part in all of this, you will have to ask him. You know this much. The sooner the man he searches for is found, the sooner William will leave and our life will be as it once was."

Myra shook her head. "Angus, you are mistaken. Even if William left within the hour, nothing would be as it once was."

Chapter 18

No one lived forever.

The thought repeated through her as she pressed the book Angus had given her against her chest. She had opened the book and realized it was a record of the Immortals. Their births, deaths, and marriages. But what had that to do with her parents? She could not shake the feeling that she would not like what she discovered and was surprised she wanted to delay it for a while longer.

She wrapped the thick wool cloak around her shoulders and headed outside. A blast of ice-laced air greeted her as she stepped into the night and walked toward the river. She remembered all the times Myra and Angus had told her stories of a fabled Immortal race. The tales had been so rich in detail that it had seemed the people and their adventures were real.

Now Isabel knew the legends were true.

Even knowing it was true did not change the fact that it was difficult to grab hold of the concept. These beings did not exist under the same laws governing other living things. She reached the shore and gazed out over the water. It was on a night such as this that William had appeared. The river was devoid of ripples, frozen solid. The moon was low over the horizon. It was the between time before the night relinquished the world to the day. Light brush strokes of purple and rose spread over the horizon, heralding the dawn, and a snow-filled breeze floated in the air.

Isabel shivered and pulled the cloak tighter around her. The cold air did not bring clarity to her thoughts as she had hoped. She should go back inside. It was growing colder. As she turned to leave, she heard a cracking sound.

Water bubbled through a fissure in the frozen water as lightning crackled overhead. In the next instant, a clap of thunder vibrated through the still night air. Isabel stared at the ever-widening circle of melting ice. It was as though an underwater fire burned just below the surface. Instinctively, Isabel backed toward the manor.

Water crashed over the dock. Wave after wave flowed over the weathered boards and down the sides. The river resembled the action of the ocean during an incoming tide. The water lapped against the pilings.

Bathed in the dawn's light stood a woman.

Her waist-length hair spun around her in a silver pool. The garment she wore was a silken sheath, reflecting the shades of the ocean, from dark emerald-green to turquoise blue. The colors shifted with the breeze. The weather was brisk and cold, yet the woman stood on the dock as though it were the middle of summer. She was gazing into the shadowy depths of the river as though searching for answers.

Isabel clutched at her cloak but could not move. Time crept by on icy fingers.

The woman turned slowly to look in Isabel's direction. A smile flickered over her lips. "Hello, Isabel. Please sit and talk with me a while." Her greeting drifted over to Isabel as though on the breeze.

"You know my name?"

"I know many things."

The words she spoke were like an answer to Isabel's troubled thoughts. An otherworldly feeling wove over her. Feeling drawn to the woman, Isabel moved toward her.

In the distance, a horse's hooves clip-clopped over cobblestones, and the wheels of a cart grated as it was pulled along the street. London was starting to awaken. The sounds blended together, reminding her of red and blue and yellow paint. Separate, these vibrant colors stood out, igniting a response of either like or dislike. However, when combined, they were so obscured they lost their individuality. Isabel stood beside the woman now, and the noises seemed from another time and another place.

The woman smiled again and drew a deep breath of the frozen air. She shook her head slowly. "How easy it is in this world of yours to misstep."

The thought of turning back to the world of noise and chaos entered Isabel's thoughts, but she dismissed the notion. There was no fear, only a great calmness that washed over her.

Isabel sat down beside the creature, for that was how she began to view her. Her appearance was that of a woman, but her voice held the quality of a sea breeze. Isabel wondered if she had fallen asleep in a chair beside the hearth and was dreaming.

"I am not a dream." The woman's words should have sent shivers through Isabel. Instead she felt comforted.

The woman smiled again. "I should not have come. It is not our way to interfere. But what else was I to do?

An error was made. My error. And then I heard your thoughts and knew I must speak with you."

Isabel's head ached from the confusing and conflicting statements. She hoped the woman was wrong when she'd said it was not a dream. This encounter would be easier to explain if that were the case. After all, dreams often began in the middle, possessing neither a beginning nor an ending.

The woman had resumed talking. This time it was more to herself than Isabel. "A while ago I was summoned, and so I did what was required." Her sigh caused ripples over the liquid-smooth water. "And then I discovered the error."

The woman paused, as though expecting an answer.

"I am sorry, but I do not understand." Isabel leaned closer to the woman and realized she was no longer cold. Perhaps the same force that melted the ice was connected to the woman.

The woman laughed, the sound resembling water splashing over a stone fountain. The noise was clean and crisp. "Of course you know nothing of what I am saying. How could you? Unless William spoke of this to you."

"William? How is he connected?"

"Ah, William is at the very heart of it all." Her green eyes sparkled like gems in the queen's crown. "I will now tell you a secret these Immortals may not know. You must promise you will try to believe."

It was as though the world of fantasy and the one of reality were melding together.

"I cannot promise what I do not understand."

"Honesty. I can see why William trusts you, and

therefore so shall I." The woman laced her slender fingers together in her lap. "I am Rotan. Known as the Guardian of Time." Her voice held the musical quality of dancing water. She laughed. "The Immortals think there is only one Guardian. I am not the only one of my kind. We are many. A colony under the sea. In the Beginning Time, all on the earth knew who we were and how to ask for our help." She sighed. "Then the world changed, grew cold. It was a time of much disturbance and chaos, but it remained in the Guardians' nature to grant any request made by the People. You know them as Immortals. We taught them how to summon us, and in exchange, they vowed to make sure this formidable power would not be misused."

Isabel listened as Rotan's words turned to visions in her mind of a proud people corrupted by their own intelligence. Isabel pulled her cloak around her shoulders to ward off not the cold but the dark images.

Rotan shook her head slowly. "The knowledge that they had ultimately destroyed their world, scattering their people to the primitive lands of the earth. Thousands of years have passed, and they still have not fully succeeded in uniting all of their people. And now it might be too late."

An icy breeze rustled over the river, and whitecaps formed over the water. The ominous words hung in the air. Rotan's sigh was heavy. "And so thus it went for many generations. But there a slip in security, a relaxation, of a sort, or perhaps deliberate. It is hard to tell the true cause anymore. And then I allowed an evil being to slip into your time. This person summoned my powers, willing me to send their comrade into your century. I am young and inexperienced by the Guardians' standards and was anxious to test my skill at transporting beings through time. I neglected to determine if this person was worthy." She paused. "It could prove to be a tragic mistake. I will not return to my home until the balance is restored. Here is where I need your help. You must set aside your fears and aid William. Even if it may cost you your life."

Lightning split the sky, and a thin layer of ice was beginning to form.

Rotan stood. "I have stayed too long. The other Guardians must not discover I was here. They would not be pleased. I must go. Remember, Isabel, the words I've spoken. You and William must not fail."

Her voice trailed off in the wind like a retreating tide. Lightning once more split the sky. Isabel stood and shut her eyes against the blinding light. When she opened them, Rotan had vanished.

****

William found Isabel standing on the dock, staring out at the frozen river. Myra and Angus thought she was still in her room, but somehow he knew she'd be here. She looked as though she were lost in a trance. He guessed that discovering your view of reality had changed could unsettle even the most stable mind.

He reached her side and stood beside her.

His voice was low. He didn't want to frighten her. "There you are. I was looking for you."

She didn't move.

He wrapped another wool cloak around her shoulders. She turned in his arms. Her eyes were bright with questions, and her cheeks were chilled a soft pink from the cold breeze. There was a hesitation in the way she looked at him. But the fear he'd seen earlier was washed away.

"William, you are immortal."

It was spoken as a statement of fact, not a question. "Yes." He smiled. "But I don't howl at the moon or change into a bat. I'm just immortal."

He took a deep breath, suspecting that, in her mind, he was no different from any of the creatures he'd just mentioned.

Without commenting, she turned from him and headed up the path toward the manor. Snow covered the raised vegetable beds and dusted over a grove of apple trees. He knew that if the harsh weather continued, the trees, herbs, and flowers would not survive. The vibrant colors of dawn turned to ribbons of eggshell white. It would be another bleak day.

William followed behind her. He was gifted with all the pleasures, as well as the pain, of being human. At times, the pain far outweighed the pleasure. How could he explain that to be an Immortal meant living with the fear of becoming too attached to those who were not? He needed only to gaze into Angus's eyes when he looked at Myra to know the depth of that agony. Each day Angus would have to watch as the woman he loved died moment by moment.

And giving your heart to an Immortal woman might be the greatest risk of all. Among the humankind race it was a rare and beautiful love that could last the short span of forty or more years. How much more difficult would it be to commit to hundreds upon hundreds of lifetimes? He'd heard about the result of some of those unions. One Immortal invariably killed the other.

Isabel paused at the back entrance. Her voice held an odd quality. He had the feeling she was not really speaking to him, but to herself.

"I do not understand how it is possible that you and Angus are so different. A part of me expects to awaken. But events from my childhood continue to tumble over me as though the floodgates of my memory had opened. Angus and Myra took special pains to tell me about a unique race of Immortals they called the People. Even to go so far as to test me on aspects of their culture. As a child I did not feel it unusual. After all, along with those lessons, they placed equal importance on the gods and goddesses of Greek and Roman mythology, as well as mathematics, science, philosophy, and the arts."

He was silent. He knew she needed to reach an understanding on her own. So complete was her concentration that she appeared to ignore the bone-chilling wind that began to circle around them.

She continued in a stronger voice. "Myra said the truth was always right in front of me, but I chose to ignore it. Perhaps she was right. Something odd happened when I was about the same age as Elaenor. Angus had been out hunting and was attacked by wild boars. He was covered with blood, and his face was ashen. The servants were either screaming with hysteria or sobbing uncontrollably. Myra, however, remained calm. I remembered at the time feeling that was strange."

Isabel paused for a brief moment and then continued. "Myra ordered Angus to be taken to their chamber and forbade anyone to visit him, even me. It was the longest two days of my life. When he did emerge, he had recovered completely. Everyone said it

193

was a miracle, the result of prayer and the healing power of the herbs Myra used." Isabel paused, as though to catch her breath. "Now, I know how Angus survived. Like you, he is an Immortal."

The words that tumbled from her came to an abrupt halt. Without warning, she grabbed his right hand and turned it over. She brushed her thumb over the birthmark of a sword outlined on his wrist.

"I remember hearing about this in the stories as well, and then Elaenor mentioned it tonight." Isabel slowly lifted her gaze to his. "Elaenor claimed that because you are a Protector, you will never go insane. Is that true?"

He did not pull away. In fact, he wanted her to know it all. "Yes."

"But you are a killer."

"No. You can't think that of me. I'm not like the others." At least, he thought, not anymore. "The Protectors' reputation in the Dark centuries was unforgivable. They were merciless killers who made their own codes, their own judgments. But that's all in the past."

He wished Angus and Myra had not told Isabel that aspect of the Protectors. All he could hope for was that she would look into his soul and realize he was not capable of such acts.

Isabel withdrew her hand from his. "It was so much simpler when the only thing I was worried about was losing my heart to you."

William forgot all the training, all the codes of logic, and pulled her to him. "Isabel. You must know that my heart was yours the first moment I saw you. I would never place you in danger."

Isabel shook her head slowly. "I do not think you will have a choice."

She pushed open the door to the back entrance of the manor and rushed from him as though escaping from a burning building. He watched her retreating figure. Isabel felt the same as he did, but the knowledge was bittersweet. He sensed she believed harm would come to her because of him. Who had placed such an idea in her thoughts?

He followed her inside. The floor-to-ceiling mural on his right caught his eye. It depicted an open area of green lawns, beds of marigolds, daisies, and primroses, and trellises with climbing grapevines. On a bench beside a flowering apple tree sat a woman sketching a cat sunning itself on a rock.

It was a portrait of Isabel. As he scanned the mural, he noticed that in the bottom corner, where normally artists would sign their work, was the stylized letter I. Weaving around it were sprigs of lavender blossoms.

The attention to the smallest detail was apparent. He could almost imagine a soft spring breeze rustling through the leaves of the trees. He wanted to find her and compliment her, maybe talk about something pleasant for a change. A topic that didn't involve death. Logic intruded into his thoughts. Isabel was trying to distance herself from him, and he should respect her wishes. If he couldn't have the woman he wanted, he could at least protect her from the world Bartholomew wanted to create.

Chapter 19

There was no time for a leisurely breakfast at the manor this morning. There was too much to do. Angus informed them he would take Elaenor to Scotland very soon, but he instructed them all to behave until then as though nothing had happened. That meant Isabel, Myra, and Elaenor would continue their duties in the cookroom at Hampton Court, and Angus and William would resume their search for the man they sought.

Isabel, however, could not concentrate very long on her duties in the queen's cookroom. She had learned a great deal from the book Angus had given her. One of her parents was an Immortal. The concept was still hard to believe, but Angus had made something clear in a sprawling message beside the entry of her birth. The Immortal trait could not be passed down. There had not been time to question Angus on this strange turn of events.

Now, working to prepare a meal, Isabel's thoughts drifted once more to William. Loving someone who never aged sounded like a difficult feat. Yet, if Isabel interpreted Angus's book correctly, that was exactly what had happened in her parents' case. Her father had married an Immortal.

Maybe Elaenor was right when she said Immortals were not that much different.

An ever-present haze of smoke hung in the massive

cookroom at Hampton Court, and heat from two fireplaces, each large enough to roast an ox, added suffocating warmth. Isabel wiped the perspiration from her brow. As a child she'd enjoyed visiting Myra here, helping to tie bunches of dried marigolds, lavender, and field poppies on iron hooks to dry, but now it was just hard work.

The room bustled with activity. Both men and women chopped nuts and berries on plank tables, rolled out dough for piecrust, or braided loaves of bread. The air was thick with cinnamon, cloves, ginger, and nutmeg. This was only one of the numerous cookrooms attached to the outer walls of Hampton Court, and each one was busy. Even Elaenor had a task, the same one Isabel had had as a child: Elaenor sat beside the hearth bundling sprigs of rosemary.

Isabel blocked out the drone of chopping, pounding, and whispered conversations while she turned all her frustrations and energies to her work. She needed to get her mind off William. It would be better if she forgot him.

She dumped blanched almonds into one of a half dozen mortar bowls carved into the long oak counter and ground the nuts with a marble pestle. The plan was to immerse herself in her work so she would forget all about discovering that not only was there such a thing as creatures that were immortal but William was one of them.

She ground the almonds into a milky white powder. To think she had felt attracted to him. She pounded her thumb with the pestle by mistake. Throbbing pain shot through her as she stuffed the injured appendage in her mouth. *Blast his good-looking hide.* And to make matters worse, he behaved as though he cared what happened to her and her family.

The creak of an iron hinge drew her attention. Myra was opening the door to the bake oven. It was on the same wall as the larger of the two fireplaces. A fire had been burning all night, heating the stones in the enclosure, and now it was the right temperature for baking pies. Myra scooped out the ash while two women held a wooden platter jammed with pastries made from raisins, dried blackberries, plums, and imported apricots. When the oven was cleaned of the ash, the pies would go in, and when done, the loaves of bread would be next.

Each day was the same. It was the never-ending task of trying to feed the insatiable appetites of the nobility. The amount of food, both consumed and wasted, staggered the mind. The only change would be if dignitaries visited or they planned for a special event, like the costume ball scheduled in a few days. It was no wonder Myra encouraged her to seek other interests. Myra understood. She had turned her talents to creating new recipes and was writing them down.

She and Myra had not had time to talk since they'd arrived this morning. Isabel's questions were multiplying until her head ached with them. It did not help that the level of activity in the cookroom was escalating.

A cauldron full of water hung from a notched iron rod in the hearth. The liquid hissed and steamed as one of the men dumped cooking utensils into the boiling water to clean them. Another turned a spigot, and water from a cistern on the roof washed over one of the cutting tables, sending scraps of food into a drain in the stone floor.

Myra used a padded linen towel and unhooked a steaming kettle of wine, bringing it over to Isabel. She set it on the counter. "The queen is in a temper. Nothing seems to please her these days. She has the whole palace on edge."

Isabel shrugged. "Perhaps Her Majesty is right in her beliefs that she is with child and that is the cause of her ill health."

Myra shook her head slowly. "I wish it were true, but those close to the queen say it is impossible."

Isabel finished grinding the almonds, scooped up a handful, and dumped them in an ornate silver pitcher. She added ground ginger, honey, a pinch of crumbled saffron, and a packet of ground powder. It was one of Myra's creations and a favorite of the queen. The last ingredient was a recent addition. It was John Campbell's medicine. He demanded it be mixed in a sweet beverage, as it was bitter to the taste. In addition, Isabel was the one ordered to deliver it to the queen.

Isabel blended the ingredients. "Perhaps John Campbell's elixir will improve the queen's disposition, as well as her health. It would make it easier on us all."

Myra leaned closer as she poured the steaming wine into the pitcher. "'Tis whispered 'twould be a blessing if the queen did not recover from her illness. Her half-sister, Elizabeth, the person our Elaenor likes so much, is said to possess a strength and intelligence lacking in Mary." Myra glanced over her shoulder, as though not wanting to be overheard. "Now when ye take this to the queen, dinna forget about poor John Campbell's scars and be dropping your tray when ye see him. The stories as to how it happened are as varied as the ingredients in my quail-and-mixed-fruit recipe."

Isabel nodded and wiped the perspiration off her forehead with a cloth again. The heat in the cookroom was suffocating. "Myra, can I ask you a question?"

"Of course, child."

Isabel stirred the concoction with a wooden spoon. She had been waiting for the opportunity to talk to Myra, but she feared the answers. Not knowing, however, was far worse.

"What is it like being with someone who is an Immortal and knowing you will grow old while he will not?"

Myra sighed deeply. "I willna lie to ye. 'Tis one of the hardest things I ever faced. The more hurtful was knowing that, because of his devotion to the Immortal Codes, we could not have children. That is why ye are so precious to me. But my life would not be as rich with love without him." She paused and put her hand on Isabel's shoulder. "If the reason ye ask is due to a growing fondness for William, ye must ask yourself, will your love be strong enough to chase away all these obstacles?"

A red-faced man, whose hair stuck out of his head like straw, yelped out an order. "What are you two women gaggling about like a yard full of chickens when there is work to be done?" Without waiting for a reply, he turned to Isabel. "The physician's order was very specific. The queen must have her wine before noon, and you are to deliver it to her. Now, off with you."

Myra reached for a green-and-purple enameled tray from the shelf above the counter and placed the pitcher of almond milk on the polished surface. "The way

Finnegan carries on, 'twould think he was the queen and not Mary Tudor."

Isabel smiled as she placed an intricately carved sterling silver mug beside the pitcher.

Myra glanced over her shoulder again and then whispered, "I still dinna understand why John Campbell insisted ye be the one to give the queen her medicine. It doesna bode well. What if something should happen to her? Ye might be the one that's blamed."

Finnegan slammed an iron pot down on a nearby plank table. It rattled the pitchers and bowls, as well as Isabel's nerves. "Isabel."

"I am leaving."

She reached for the tray, hurried over to a cooling rack, and added a sugared raisin tart and a sprig of dried lavender for decoration. She whispered a thank-you to Myra and waved farewell to Elaenor as she rushed out of the cookroom.

Ice-laced air hit her in the face. She shivered. It was a stark difference from the waves of heat in the cookroom. She walked across the alleyway toward the entrance to Hampton Court. The cold was a welcome change, and her first impulse was to slow her pace, but she could not risk the wine cooling before it reached the queen.

Once inside again, she hurried down corridors where the walls were draped in rose silk, the woodwork gilded with gold leaf, and the marble floors covered by rugs imported from the Orient. The essence of Myra's words regarding William kept repeating over and over in her thoughts. "Will love be enough?"

Love?

It was an emotion she'd never thought she would

experience. Was it possible?

She stumbled over a lump in the rug. The pitcher and mug rattled on the tray as she steadied them and continued on her way. Myra insisted she was happy with Angus and reconciled with their life together, but Isabel knew there was a deep pain hidden just under the surface. Isabel had seen it in Myra's expression when Angus would go on one of his long trips. Until now, Isabel did not know its true cause. Would she share a similar fate if she stayed with William?

Isabel had to stop thinking of him. It was clouding her mind and pushing out all other rational thoughts.

The corridor widened. Isabel had almost reached her destination. The mug on the tray rattled again. This time it was not because she had tripped but because her hands were trembling. Myra had voiced Isabel's concerns regarding John Campbell and his medicine. Isabel did not fully trust him. Perhaps it was because he had not accurately diagnosed William, or perhaps because she did not know the true nature of the medicine. In either case, she felt uneasy. Isabel also shared Myra's fear that if something went wrong, it would not be John Campbell who was blamed but Isabel.

She paused at the gilt-edged doors. She had reached her destination. At this time of day, the queen could be found in the Solar, a room with high ceilings and expansive windows that let in whatever miserly light the winter months had to offer.

A guard appeared, and Isabel was shown into the room. Each time she was here her reaction did not diminish. There was a stark difference between the congestion and frantic activity of the cookroom and the tranquility of the queen's quarters.

A woman sat behind a jewel-encrusted floor harp, gently stroking the strings into a continuous melody that resembled the sound of water bubbling down a mountain stream. A wicker birdcage hung near one of the windows, and its occupant, a lark, added its voice to the music. Women in clothing as colorful as the rare peacocks strolling over the grounds clustered around the queen like bees buzzing around a hive.

The queen was playing chess with John Campbell. Isabel was glad Myra had reminded her of the physician's appearance. To say it was changed was an understatement. His head was shaved, and it looked as though someone had sliced his face and head with a jagged knife. She tore her gaze from him and concentrated on the queen. The woman wore a somber gown of burgundy silk studded with seed pearls. One bejeweled hand was curled around her dog, Snowball, while the other reached forward and hovered over the chess pieces. The queen paused, as though looking to the physician to advise her on her next move.

Isabel felt out of place and wondered why the physician had insisted she should be the one to bring the queen her medicine. It was not her place. She hoped to return to the cookroom and finish her duties in time to slip away to the artist's studio. Amongst the smell of paint and plaster was where she felt most at home.

John Campbell was the first to notice Isabel. "Ah, here you are. We were beginning to worry you had forgotten Her Majesty's medicine."

The queen's head jerked back as she whispered, "Medicine? Is it really that time already?" She withdrew her hand and stroked Snowball's fur.

Isabel kept her eyes away from the physician's face. The red welts were not as prominent as she had heard, but they gave him a cruel appearance, nonetheless. Snowball's shrill bark drew her attention. She wondered if it was her imagination, or had Snowball's newfound youth faded? The dog's eyes were glazed over and lifeless, and patches of pink skin showed through its thinning fur.

The queen turned her attention to Isabel. She held an orange stuffed with cloves to her nose. "Set the tray beside us, and then you are dismissed. The odor of smoke and soot clings to you and is offensive to us."

Isabel curtsied, set the tray down beside the queen, and retreated from the chamber. She would ask Myra if she could leave early and go to the artist's studio. It might help her take her mind off William and give her more time to think.

Isabel retraced her steps back to the cookroom and thought of William, bringing her emotions to the surface. This morning all she could think of was the fact that he was an Immortal. Now it did not seem to be so important. The only solution would be to make a mental list of all his imperfections.

That proved to be the wrong direction to take. An image of William naked came unbidden to her thoughts. She felt heat rise to her face. She quickened her pace as she neared the alleyway separating Hampton Court from the numerous cookrooms, grateful the weather was bitter cold. Maybe a stiff wind would help her forget how he looked without clothes.

She groaned. Now all she could think of was William's reaction to her the day he'd recovered from his wounds.

Chapter 20

The wind howled through the open door of the stables, and the shutters rattled against the windows. William could swear it was almost as cold in here as it was outside. It was the perfect place for a child of eight to hide.

William was supposed to be leaving with Angus for Hampton Court soon, but Elaenor had convinced him that a game of hide-and-seek would make him a better Protector. He smiled, remembering she wanted him to have more practice before they played chess.

"Elaenor. I give up. You win."

He heard sniffling and headed toward the sound. Elaenor sat perched on a high stool with her elbows on a worktable. Her face rested in the palms of her hands and her gaze was intent. Zeus lay nearby. Elaenor was staring at what looked like a small animal cage.

William walked over to her. "Is something wrong?"

She sniffled again. "Brian made this for me. He said that way I could take Zeus with me when I visited Elizabeth." She looked toward him, and her gaze tore at his heart. "Why did Brian have to die? I miss him."

William picked Elaenor up in his arms and hugged her. "I know."

She wiggled out of his embrace and sat back down, wiping her eyes with the back of her sleeve. "I do not think Brian would want me to be so sad." Her eyebrows scrunched together. It was the same expression his mother used when she was deep in thought. "I am glad I have Zeus's cage. It will always remind me of Brian." She reached over, closing and latching the door in place with a small iron padlock. It clicked shut.

Elaenor leaned down and picked up the cat. "William, what do you think of the name Luna? She was the Roman goddess of the moon." She sighed. "I wish it would stop snowing. It is hard to see the stars when the sky is so dark."

William leaned against the worktable. "Don't worry. I'm sure the weather will be back to normal soon." He hoped he could keep his promise. "Why are you asking about the name Luna?"

She whispered. "Zeus is going to have kittens. Myra told me last night. That is why he needs a new name. I am going to give my friend Elizabeth one of the kittens. I think it will cheer her. She is so sad. I saw a poem she wrote with a diamond on a glass window. '*Much suspected by me, but nothing proved can be.*' "

William couldn't tell Elaenor the details of the future, but he could ease her mind about Elizabeth's fate. William straightened. He also had an idea that would take Elaenor out of harm's way. "Elaenor, don't worry—your friend is going to be all right. In fact, how would you like to visit her?"

Elaenor's face lit up in smiles. "Oh, could I?"

"Yes. I'll tell Angus to start making the arrangements right away."

Now all he had to do was make sure he captured Bartholomew before the Renegade changed history. Minor detail.

****

Making the arrangements for Elaenor to visit Elizabeth for a few days until Angus could take her to Scotland, and convincing Myra she could survive without her, was easy compared with the chore of trying to pin down the elusive John Campbell.

William was tired of being kept waiting at Hampton Court. Angus and he had run out of words hours ago, and even a chessboard had not helped relieve the boredom.

William smiled and remembered an incident in Seattle, Washington, in the twenty-first century. It had occurred during a rare and brief period in his life when he'd been in a relationship with a woman. Jennifer had taken him to a one-man stage play entitled *Defending the Caveman.* She'd thought it would help her understand his Neanderthal behavior and also guide him toward becoming a communicative, commitment-driven humanoid.

The experiment had failed miserably. The one thing he'd taken away from the performance had been that as the male of the species, he only had a specific allotment of words to say every day, and when he'd used them up, he was done talking. He'd thought it explained his lack of communication skills, and he'd shared his newfound knowledge with Jennifer. She, however, had not been amused. Needless to say, his relationship with Jennifer hadn't lasted long after that.

Just then the door opened and they were escorted into a chamber that looked as though all the wealth in England and Scotland had been used to furnish the room. Harp music ceased as efficiently as though a switch had been turned off.

He had no problem identifying the players. Even if he hadn't known what the queen looked like from portraits, she would have been easy to spot. A crown of diamonds was perched on her head, and she looked as though she was wearing every ring and necklace she owned. Her gown was also the most elaborate.

Angus jabbed him in the ribs, reminding him to bow. When he straightened, a man who sat opposite the queen rose and was introduced as John Campbell.

The physician's mouth quivered in an attempt to smile, but the jagged scar creasing his face impeded its progress. The result more closely resembled a crack in a stone slab made by a chisel.

Angus bowed again and spoke to the physician. "I appreciate this opportunity to thank you in person for your kindness."

John Campbell arched an eyebrow.

Angus continued, "May I present my friend William? He was the one Myra and my daughter asked you to examine."

The physician only nodded in response.

The queen interrupted. "There. You have said what you came here to say. Unless there is something else, you are delaying our game of chess."

Something was not right. William focused on John Campbell. The man fit the physical description of Bartholomew, but it was hard to tell what his face really looked like, with the mass of disfiguring scars covering his skin.

William edged closer, ignoring the warning glare of Angus, and directed his attention to John Campbell. "How long have you had those scars?"

The queen paused, a silver mug halfway to her

mouth. "Well, I never. What a rude young man you are. You must leave our presence at once."

A nervous twitch circled the physician's left eye. "It is all right, Your Majesty. I do not mind answering his question." He cocked his head to the side. "I was outnumbered and viciously attacked. I heard the same happened to you not so long ago. London is a dangerous city, don't you agree?"

The queen patted the physician on the hand like a mother to her child. "My poor John. Fear not, we will find those cowards and avenge you."

Again the physician tried to smile, but his damaged facial muscles failed the task. "My only shame is that I lack the skill to heal my scars."

"There, there, we have grown used to them." The queen frowned as she turned to William. "Do not press our dear physician further." She motioned to the guard, signaling that the interview was over.

Angus and William bowed hastily as they were escorted out of the room and into the courtyard, where their horses were waiting for them.

When the guards were out of earshot, Angus was the first to break the silence. "It looks as though we can eliminate John Campbell. Those were ugly scars on his face."

William took the reins of his horse and mounted. "I wonder. I can't shake the feeling that John Campbell fits the description of the man I'm after."

Angus shook his head. "That would be impossible. Any wound an Immortal sustained would heal without leaving a scar. That man looked like his face and skull were used for sword practice."

"I know, but my instincts still say he's our man."

"And you are never wrong?"

"No."

Angus laughed and mounted his horse. "Now I know why you were sent here. You never overlook even the weakest lead. I say we pay another visit to the artist's studio. They may have heard something interesting about this John Campbell."

William followed Angus, and all the while a voice within him shouted that the coincidences between John Campbell and Bartholomew were too great. From all he'd learned so far, both had arrived in the city around the same time. But Angus had a good point.

It was inconsistent with how Immortals healed. However, the physician's injuries might be self-inflicted. William had seen worse when someone wanted to avoid detection and capture, but such behavior didn't fit the profile of the man he'd studied. Bartholomew prided himself on his appearance and his ability to attract women. It was one of the reasons the man avoided fighting: Bartholomew didn't want to risk disfigurement even if it would heal in a matter of days. William urged his horse alongside Angus's. He wanted to ask Angus to ask the artists what they knew of the physician. The scars had stopped him from taking John Campbell today, but as far as William was concerned, John Campbell and Bartholomew could be one and the same.

****

Bartholomew watched the courtyard below from the window in his chamber at Hampton Court. He had excused himself from the queen's presence and rushed to his chamber to see where William would head.

He watched William and Angus mount their horses

210

and ride toward the city. He let out a sigh of relief. The fox had tracked him to his lair, but obviously his disguise had fooled them both. Still, the Protector was too close. Something had to be done. He was also concerned about the woman Isabel. She had stared overlong at his features today, and he wondered if she guessed his wounds were self-inflicted.

His hands still trembled from the memory of being in the same room with the Protector today. His good fortune had held as the dotty queen had spoken in his defense, but he did not know how long he could have withstood William's scrutiny.

Bartholomew turned from the window and glanced at the woman asleep on his bed. A woman bought and paid for. He'd met her at the Blue Goose Inn a few days earlier. She had not bothered to hide her repulsion when she'd seen his face, but the coin he'd pressed in the palm of her hand changed the way she'd looked at him.

Last night, in the dark, she had been tolerable. However, in the glaring light of day it was he who was repulsed. Not only did her face offend him, but her body did as well. She had served his purpose, but her kind could not be trusted. Last night she had asked too many questions, in addition to sharing the secrets of her current and past clients.

It was time to end his involvement with her. The poem he wrote in tribute for her services was shorter than usual. He was not inspired. Another reason to end their acquaintance. Once the affair was completed, he would attend to the problem of William and Isabel. Bartholomew crossed the room to the oak three-drawer dresser.

On the top was a half-empty bottle of French wine

he'd discovered in one of the queen's cellars. In a palace the size of Hampton Court, he doubted it would be missed. Further, he knew the queen did not appreciate that this wine came from the Champagne province in France at the Abbey of Hautvillers. It was one of the best vineyards in all of Europe. For someone as exposed as the queen was to the best the world could offer, she was surprisingly naive to the pleasure, as well as the rewards, of her power. If the medicine worked as expected, he would have the luxury of ruling through the queen and possessing the power for himself.

He had also procured two of her finest handblown wineglasses. Bartholomew shared the beliefs of the ancient Greeks that wine drinking was a sensual experience and should involve the proper goblet.

He raised the rounded glass, admiring its contours. The shape of Helen of Troy's breasts had inspired its design—another piece of trivia he had learned in his travels. It was a benefit of being an Immortal. He could roam the earth at his leisure, enjoying what the world had to offer. Lachlan had changed all that, but soon— very soon—revenge would taste as delicious as the wine. His men had failed to kill Lachlan's sister, Elaenor, and if he knew Angus, the man was probably planning to tuck the lass away somewhere safe. There would be other chances. Until then, he would distract them, turning his attention to someone less guarded. Isabel.

Bartholomew smiled. He knew exactly how and when he would kill her.

First, however, he would have to dispense of the woman on his bed. He turned toward his red-and-blue tapestry bag, which lay on top of the dresser. Its contents had served him well over the years, and, thankfully, the waterproof lining and thick, quilted padding kept his medicines safe and dry while he journeyed back through the currents of time. It would be inconvenient if he had to replace the vials of poisons. It was always difficult to make a connection in a new city with someone who could supply you with the necessary ingredients. This time, however, it had been easier than expected. He'd found an unlikely co-conspirator who could replace his poisons if necessary.

He reached in and pulled out a small cylinder of muddy green liquid, made from the leaves of the hemlock plant. He shook his head. No, its bitter taste and mouselike odor could be detected. He chose another. Belladonna, also known as deadly nightshade. It had been good enough to poison the troops of Mark Antony during the Parthian Wars, but this solution was diluted and lacked the strength to kill. He needed something else.

The bed creaked as the woman shifted in her sleep.

Bartholomew returned the vial to its secure pocket. He plucked another and mentally listed its attributes. The poison was guaranteed to induce a long and painful death. It also left a lingering and telltale smell on the corpse.

The woman stirred again, and the covers fell away, exposing generous breasts that spilled across her chest. Bartholomew's blood warmed, remembering last night. For all the woman's faults, and there were many, she was skilled in the art of pleasure. He set the vial back in his bag to keep for another time. He might consider using the poison on William. And when he was unconscious, Bartholomew would lop off his head. He smiled, enjoying the plan.

The woman on his bed, however, had earned the right to die quickly and with pleasure. Maybe he would add more lines to the poem.

Bartholomew retrieved another poison. He caressed the vial. It was called monkshood, or wolfbane. It was perfect. Wolfbane was used as an ingredient in love potions, and the result was often not so much an increase in the ability to love as a frenzy of sexual activity often leading to death. The limited medical resources of the sixteenth century would believe she died of natural causes. And as a prostitute, exposed to countless diseases, no one would think it foul play. The plan was flawless.

He reached for the bottle of wine and poured the remaining contents into her glass, adding the wolfbane. He remembered once he had been too stingy with a poison. The miscalculation had almost cost him his life. His victim had survived and had correctly remembered what had made her ill. She'd informed her brothers. He could have stayed and fought. After all, they were only humankind, but accidents do happen. A lucky blow could have severed his head. He'd taken the only reasonable path open to him. He had run.

But that was when he was young and foolish, only a mere hundred years or so. He held the goblet up to the light, admiring the quality of the sparkling beverage. Greeks were a romantic lot and felt wine and women were a potent combination. They were correct. Again, he congratulated himself on confiscating bottles of the queen's wine. He liked his women willing and his drink of the highest quality.

The woman stretched on the bed and rubbed her

eyes. "Ah, aren't ye the handsome lad in the light of day. Ready for another ride?"

He froze in place. She had remarked on his appearance. Last night she'd said she would keep her eyes shut while they had sex. He looked toward the small tin mirror over the dresser. The scars on his face, although still visible, were fading. His decision to kill her was wise. He did not want her talking about a man whose scars could heal overnight.

He glanced over at her once again. She removed the covers and spread herself for him. He smiled as his body responded. He would indeed ride her, perhaps even to the end and beyond. The combination of ingredients he mixed would loosen her inhibitions even further. He smiled, thinking of the endless possibilities as he wondered how long it would be for the poison to take effect.

Eager to begin, Bartholomew walked slowly over to the bed. He never stayed to watch his victims die. However, the prospect excited him as he handed the glass to her.

"Drink, woman."

She reached for it and hesitated. "Name's Judith."

He sneered. "Just drink."

Chapter 21

Myra had needed her in the cookroom longer than expected, but Isabel had made good time since then. Securing her horse in the stable nearby, she walked to the back door of the studio. She was anxious to finish her portrait. She felt a renewed sense of energy as she opened the door, hoping she could transfer it to the canvas.

Without wasting a move, she went to her easel and pulled her smock over her clothes, then hesitated. It was quiet. Too quiet. She had thought there would be a buzz of activity. After all, it was only a few days before the costume ball, and not all the projects were completed.

Isabel raised her voice. "Paulette, Ossian, Jardin, Forsyth, is anyone here?"

The sound of her own voice echoed through the cavernous space. Maybe they were at Hampton Court, planning how to display the art. She shrugged off the unease she felt, removed the protecting cover from her canvas, and started to mix her paints.

She heard a loud meow and glanced toward the sound.

Puck padded toward her.

Isabel leaned down and picked him up. He was covered with red paint and had made a trail of paw prints in his wake. She smiled. "Puck, what are we to do with you? Paulette will be furious."

Puck meowed loudly and leaped from her arms, scurrying toward the shadows. He turned and sat on his haunches, staring in her direction.

"Do you want me to follow you and clean the mess you made? First, I think, we need to give you a bath. You are leaving a trail of red paint everywhere. You are just like a two-year-old, always getting into things. I hope Paulette will not decide you are too much bother. Well, let us see the damage you have done."

Isabel stepped toward Puck, but just as she reached him, he bounded forward once more, just out of reach.

"Puck. I do not have time to play."

Isabel followed the cat around a table to the back of the studio. It was Paulette's area. A finished marble statue of the goddess Athena stood as though guarding the space.

Puck sat licking his paws in front of a pool of red liquid.

Isabel's heart pounded. The consistency of the liquid was not right. It did not spread like paint. Isabel crept closer. She knelt down to touch it with the tips of her fingers. The liquid was still warm and sticky. It also looked odd. The liquid was in the shape of the letter *R*.

She bolted to her feet.

It was blood. She was sure of it.

Puck leaped into the shadows once again, turning toward her as though beckoning her to follow him once more. Her pulse racing, she followed him. As she rounded the end of the table, she saw what had caused the pool of blood.

A head, matted with hair, was severed from its body.

Paulette's head.

Isabel opened her mouth to scream, but no sound escaped, and she shuddered so violently she dropped to the floor.

The door to the studio was flung open. Startled, Isabel scrambled into the shadows, wondering if Paulette's murderer had returned. She heard male voices, and, as they drew nearer, she recognized William and Angus.

She burst from the shadows and into the safety and strength of William's embrace.

****

The world had turned upside down, and no one was safe. The words repeated themselves over and over in William's mind as he rode back to the manor. It seemed longer than just the span of a day and a half since Paulette's murder. The funeral arrangements were made, and Elaenor was safely with Elizabeth. Or as safe as anyone could be these days.

It was becoming harder and harder to keep his emotions at bay. The weather was at least cooperating. There was a reprieve from the snowfall. William didn't know if that was a good sign or merely the calm before the storm.

The downside was that he and Angus were no closer to finding Paulette's killer than they had been when they first discovered the body. All the evidence pointed in Ossian's direction. Both Jardin and Forsyth claimed that Paulette and Ossian were arguing more of late, even suggesting that Ossian had tired of Paulette. They had known each other for hundreds of years, and maybe Ossian felt death was the only way out of the relationship.

William didn't believe Ossian was capable of such

a cold-blooded act, and he had an instinct for knowing such things.

With Paulette's death, Jardin was more cooperative, reporting that a man fitting Bartholomew's description had been seen at the Blue Goose Inn. So far, no unusual deaths had been reported, and no amount of money could loosen the bartender's tongue regarding his guests.

William guided his horse toward the stables at the manor and dismounted. He wondered if Isabel had taken advantage of the momentary lull in the weather. He shook the random thoughts from his mind. He should be concentrating on finding Bartholomew, but Paulette's death had affected everyone. It reminded them of the fragility of life, even for an Immortal.

William passed through an ivy-covered arbor to the left of the stables in search of Isabel. He knew she would want to know about the funeral arrangements for Paulette.

He saw Isabel on the perimeter of an herb garden. Her shoulders were slumped forward as she brushed the snow off the tender plants. Her basket was filled with wilted bunches of parsley, mint, rosemary, and others he couldn't identify.

A soft breeze floated toward him, laced with the heady perfume of lavender. He knew that, for as long as he lived, lavender would remind him of Isabel.

A heart-wrenching sob tore through the still air. Isabel's shoulders quivered as her hands worked to remove snow from a section of the garden.

William crossed the distance separating them in a few long strides. He knelt down beside her. The troubles consuming him were forgotten as he placed his hand on her shoulder and turned her toward him.

Her eyes were red from crying. "They are all dying. Nothing I can do will save them."

He brushed the tears from her eyes. They had already begun to form ice crystals on her lashes. He took her hands in his. They were stone cold. She did not pull away from him as she had before. He hoped that was a good sign.

He lowered his voice, saying words to soothe, hoping they were true. "In the spring, when the earth is warm again, you'll have more plants than you can use."

Another sob escaped her. "Paulette was a good friend to me. Who could have killed her?"

He rubbed her icy hands to warm them. "I don't know, but I wish I did. Paulette was a gentle soul. It doesn't make any sense." He pulled Isabel to her feet. "I should get you inside."

Her chin trembled. "I overheard Angus talking to Myra just a short time ago. He told her the weather is connected to the man you seek. Do not keep the truth from me as though I were a small child. I can see for myself this is the most severe winter in memory, and it is only October. How can one man be so powerful that he can change the weather? And why would he want to do so?"

It was too late to tell her that Angus should never have told Myra that the man William hunted and the weather were connected. William was relieved this too was out in the open.

The clouds shifted across the sky and darkened. The momentary lull in the weather was over. Another storm was on its way. He rubbed her hands again, until he could feel them warm under his touch.

Isabel deserved answers. It felt good to finally tell her what was happening. He'd hated the barrier between them. "Angus is right. The weather and the man I'm after are connected. The balance between events and nature is fragile. Altering one changes them both."

"I heard Angus say you would not tell him the man's name."

William reached for her basket as they walked slowly to the manor. "The reason is complicated." He rubbed his forehead. "It involves time travel."

"Time travel?"

This was not going to be easy. Then he thought of an idea. He reached for her hand, headed back to the river, and then stopped dead in his tracks. The river was frozen solid. So much for his example of skipping a pebble across the water.

William didn't know about Isabel or Myra, but in a few short years both Elaenor and Angus would again meet Bartholomew, only he would be posing as a schoolmaster. The events of time must be guarded and allowed to play out. As Protector, part of his job was to protect this balance. He wove his arm around her waist. "The currents of time exist in a preordained pattern; when one is altered, it affects them all in an ever-widening circle, like a pebble skimming over the surface of a pond. The Immortals discovered a creature, called the Guardian, who can take us from one current of time to another."

Isabel's expression was intense. She let out her breath and stared at him for what seemed an eternity. "William. Are you from one of these other times?"

He nodded. "The future."

221

She began to laugh, softly at first, building until its joy infected him. He smiled. "What's so funny?"

"I think the gods have a sense of humor. I considered all the men I met to be unsuitable. It seems appropriate I meet someone who is not even from my world."

Her expression softened as a smile played over the contours of her mouth. It warmed him and shook him to the core. That she was beautiful was obvious for all to see. But there was more. Her eyes reflected a kind heart and a spirit that saw the good in every living being. When he looked at her, he knew beauty would always exist in the world.

She bent down and selected a stalk of lavender that had somehow escaped the severe weather. She gently squeezed the purple blooms. "It seems odd to me that as an Immortal, you are always in such a rush, when centuries lie before you. Are there not times when you long to enjoy what surrounds you?"

It occurred to him that he'd never had those thoughts until he'd met Isabel. Instead he picked a pebble from the frozen soil and rolled it around in his hand.

"It does not bother you that I am an Immortal or from the future?"

She glanced down at the sprig of lavender, holding it tenderly before her, and then she gently squeezed the lavender buds again. This time she extended her palm toward him. "Smell. The fragrance is delicious."

He did as she asked, as though there were no other option for him. William reached for her hand. Her skin was velvet to the touch. He bent toward her palm and inhaled the scent of lavender and Isabel. He lifted his head and looked toward her. Her lips were parted, her eyes a deep dark brown, the color of the earth. The color of life.

William rubbed the palm of her hand with his thumb. "Delicious."

She smiled. "I was talking about the lavender."

He leaned closer. "I know, but everything reminds me of you."

She hesitated as though the weight of the world was on her shoulders. "I do not know how I feel about you being an Immortal, but I am trying to understand. As for the other, it is the same. But as long as you promise me you will not turn into a frog, I am willing to try. Is that enough?"

His heart pounded in his ears as he lowered his voice. "Aye, it's more than enough." He gently kissed her hand.

Isabel's fingers curled around his. "I am glad."

William leaned toward her. His lips covered her mouth in a feather-soft kiss, enveloping her with warmth. His kiss deepened. He felt as though he were floating in a warm mist. William gathered her in his arms as time held its breath.

Isabel stepped back from the warmth of his embrace, confused at the extremes of emotions swirling around her. The moon was high in the night sky and shone over the blanket of snow. Crystals of ice danced and sparkled in its glow. With only William beside her, the feeling of loneliness fell away.

She spent her life surrounded by people, but it was not enough. When she was younger, she'd made herself believe it was because she never knew her real parents. She'd built a fantasy world where time was eternal and no one ever died. How ironic.

William brushed a strand of hair off her forehead. "You're a long way away."

His touch was warm and ignited a flame within her. He smiled. "I think it would be warmer in the manor. Do you want to go inside?"

She shook her head. Right now, she felt as though she had walked into one of the fireplaces in the queen's cookroom at Hampton Court. It might, however, give her time to sort out her feelings. At least, that is what she hoped. Yet there were so many questions.

He reached for her hand, but she lifted his toward her and traced the mark of the sword on his wrist. "I would like to know more about your birthmark and about the Protectors."

William smiled and kissed her hand. "It's an inherited trait that thus far holds many added gifts. The person heals more quickly than other Immortals. You already know that we are less likely to go insane, but unfortunately there is no way to predict who will bear the mark. It might skip one family only to appear several times in another. But once identified, there is only one path open for that person. They will be raised as a Protector."

"Are you saying the children are taken from their family?"

He nodded and turned away to look in the direction of the manor. "It's not that bad. We're well cared for and want for nothing."

His tone of voice told her the topic was closed. She was beginning to understand the shadows of pain she saw reflected in his eyes. Isabel always missed not knowing her parents, but Myra and Angus showered her with love. It was different for William. She suspected he had missed so much. Isabel walked beside him in silence. It felt easy and comforting and right. There did not seem to be any need for words. She had never expected to feel this way about any man, and it was unsettling. Before William arrived, she knew the path she was to take, and was content. Now, her world was turned upside down. What was even stranger, she did not mind.

They went inside together, enjoying a comfortable silence. Isabel walked through the shadow-draped corridor to the Great Hall. She lit additional candles over the mantel and watched as their light illuminated the darkness and William.

He stood near a black-and-gold lacquered table Angus had brought back with him after one of his voyages. William held an oval miniature of Myra. The portrait was in a small silver frame. Isabel remembered it was one of her first efforts. She had attempted to reflect Myra's gentle spirit in the portrait, and she had been rewarded when Angus had proclaimed it his favorite.

William held it closer to the light. "You're really very good. This is an excellent likeness."

Isabel smiled, feeling shivers of pleasure at the compliment. His opinion pleased her, for some reason.

He set the portrait down. "I'd better get a few hours of sleep. Tomorrow's going to be a long day. I plan to attend Paulette's funeral."

"Then we should go together."

A smile lifted the corners of his mouth. "I'd like that."

"You are not going to give me a list of reasons why

I should not attend?"

William tucked a strand of hair behind her ear. "I worry more about you when you're not by my side."

Isabel placed her hands against his chest, rejoicing in her boldness. She felt the definition of his muscles as they flexed beneath her touch. "I am pleased to hear you say that, as I intend to go to the studio tomorrow after the funeral. My painting is not complete, and I need you to pose again."

She was surprised to see color rise to his face.

He raked his fingers through his hair. "Can't you do the rest by memory?"

"I pride myself on my attention to detail." She arched an eyebrow. "You would not want me to misrepresent your proportions, would you?"

A broad, heart-stopping smile spread over his face. "You're talking about blackmail."

"Most definitely."

He leaned so close she could feel his warm breath over her skin. His voice vibrated through her. "If I agree, I want there to be only the two of us."

She moistened her lips with her tongue.

He winked and leaned closer to her. His mouth brushed against her lips as he whispered, "I'll take that as a yes."

She tilted her head, hands pressed against his chest. She could feel the rapid beat of his heart against her fingers as he kissed her tenderly. It was a kiss born of mutual desire and growing awareness of each other.

Her fantasies were taking a new turn. She was no longer content just to be rescued by a valiant knight. She wanted to know how it felt to press her naked body against his.

The kiss ended too soon. William stared at her for a long time before nodding a hasty goodbye.

Chapter 22

The next morning, Isabel rode beside William through the streets of London to Paulette's funeral. A feeling of gloom hung in the air. The gray, overcast day only added to the somber mood.

Angus had already left, and Myra had asked to stay behind at the manor. She was unusually quiet. Isabel suspected Paulette's death was the cause. Isabel shared Myra's grief. It was hard to understand that Paulette was gone. She was vibrant and healthy one minute and dead the next.

Isabel and William reached the river's edge. He had already told her that what she was about to witness was unusual. Isabel wanted to add that since William's arrival, everything in her life seemed strange. She did not ask, but by the whispered conversations she'd overheard between Angus and William earlier today, she had pieced together some startling facts.

Paulette was an Immortal, as was Ossian, Jardin, and Forsyth. At each new discovery of a fantastical being, Isabel wondered if being a human actually made her a minority on the planet.

Isabel shuddered, remembering how Paulette had died and the horror of the violent act. The thought still lingered in her mind as she dismounted. William reached for her hand, and they walked toward the funeral site in silence.

Angus, Jardin, and Forsyth were already there, dressed in white and silver. Their garments reminded Isabel of the style she had seen on a wood carving of Queen Hatshepsut, who ruled Egypt as pharaoh for twenty-two years.

Ossian, however, was not in attendance, which further supported most everyone's belief that he had murdered Paulette. Isabel disagreed. The fact that William shared her view only drew her closer to him. Maybe the pain Ossian felt at losing Paulette was so great he could not witness her funeral.

A drum roll, performed by Forsyth, announced that the ceremony was about to begin. Isabel watched as Paulette's body was brought to the dock on a lavishly decorated coach drawn by white horses. Paulette lay on a silver pallet, her body wrapped from head to toe in shimmering gold cloth, in much the same way as in an Egyptian burial. Angus and William placed Paulette on a wooden barge painted to a high gloss in jet black. Isabel was surprised at how slim Paulette appeared. The woman had always dressed in yards of fabric. Isabel assumed it had been to cover an ample figure, but obviously that had not been the case.

There was tension in the air as the silence deepened. The way the body was prepared, and the manner of clothes some of those in attendance wore, gave the funeral an otherworldly feel.

Over the sound of the icy wind, Angus's voice rose in a deep monotone.

"After death takes us in his embrace we will pass first through a time of light and bliss." He paused and motioned for Jardin to light a torch, and then he continued. "The next step in Paulette's journey will be spent in a time where we remember all we have experienced in life." He paused again, staring in the direction of the flickering light of the torch. His voice rose once more. "And finally we are reborn. We must always remember the words of the People:

Death in this realm is but a beginning in the next
A place where all dreams are realized
And the darkest souls are healed
For it is written that time is an illusion
And love the only reality."

Lightning flashed silently across the morning sky, and the frozen river opened up as Forsyth and Jardin shoved Paulette's body into the water and lit the barge on fire. It burst into golden flames, sending waves of heat toward Isabel. It warmed the air around her, melting the snow that covered the dock.

In the water, behind a wall of flames, Isabel saw the outline of a woman. She was pulling the barge under the surface. In the moment before it was submerged, Isabel saw this strange creature turn toward her, and she gasped. It was Rotan.

A whirlpool of swirling white water funneled downward. The churning waters quieted, and a north wind sent rippling waves toward the shore. Before Isabel's eyes, the water turned glass smooth once more and froze. The melting snow dripped from the wharf, forming icicles. Isabel smiled to herself A dream was more easily explained. The solemn respect paid to Paulette and the beauty of the ceremony brought Isabel a feeling of peace and new understanding. She had not thought a people who were immortal could so revere life that they would honor death in such a way. Rotan's presence only confirmed Isabel's observations.

Isabel turned slowly to William. "Did you see her?"

"Paulette?"

She whispered, "No, Rotan."

His eyes widened. "Who?"

Forsyth spun around, but whatever comment he wanted to make was lost as screams rent the quiet. Turning toward the sound, Isabel saw the cause.

In the distance she could see smoke and flames. From the location, it could mean only one thing.

The Blue Goose Inn was on fire.

****

William was the first to reach the inn. His horse reared back on its haunches, flailing at the smoke-choked air. A fire on the heels of Paulette's funeral was a bad omen. He watched helplessly as flames engulfed the Blue Goose Inn, curling from its windows like the tongues of the mythological dragons his ancestors had fought.

The narrow street was filled with people fleeing from the tavern and boarding house. Screams and the roar of the flames blended together as a man yelled and jumped from the roof to his death. A woman, half-clothed, followed him. Panic was everywhere. He had to take action. William jumped to the ground and tried to calm his horse. It reared again and tossed its head. Isabel, Angus, Jardin, and Forsyth were close behind him. He was relieved. It would take all their efforts to contain this blaze.

William ripped off his shirt and covered the animal's head. If his horse couldn't see the flames, he might settle down. It was one of the first things he'd learned when going into battle with a horse. William tied the animal to the hitching ring a safe distance away. He shouted orders to Angus to keep Isabel safe and prevent her from running into the inn. He recognized the fear he saw in her eyes, but he suspected it was already too late for some.

The good news, if there was any to this situation, was that the Blue Goose Inn was flanked on either side by vacant lots, no doubt the result of past fires in the city. As long as the wind did not kick up, the fire might not jump across the street.

He raced toward the inn, assessing the problem. The flames roared, consuming at will. As a firefighter, a burning building was what he knew, what he understood. To his relief, the townsfolk had begun a bucket brigade. That would help keep the fire under control long enough for him to concentrate on any rescue work. Londoners knew they had to adapt fast when a fire broke out or risk losing everything.

A man ran screaming from the tavern. William grabbed him. It was the bartender, Liam. William had to shout to be heard over the creaking of the building as the fire ate through the wood structure.

"Liam, is everyone out of the inn?"

Liam's face and clothes were covered in soot, and his arms were badly burned. He coughed and shook his head. "No, I don't think so."

William clenched his jaw. "How many are still in there?" Liam wiped his eyes with the back of his torn sleeve and shouted over the roar of the fire. "Two, maybe more. I heard a woman scream before the fire broke out. I told her to run for it, but I don't think she heard me."

"Where are they?"

"Fourth floor. All the rooms were evacuated except the last two on the end."

William nodded. "Okay, there's still time. Listen closely. I want you to get a blanket and about six men. Position them below the windows and wait for my signal. If all goes well, I want you to be ready to catch whoever jumps."

"Are you mad? Nothing can survive the blaze."

William ignored the comment as he soaked a blanket in a water trough, put it over his head, and ran toward the mouth of the inferno. Although the fire and smoke inhalation could not kill him, if badly burned, he would not be able to help others. It was a lesson he'd learned the hard way.

Heat rippled around him as he dove into the tavern and headed toward the stairs. One of the planks broke under his weight. He stumbled back and leaped over it. An overhead beam creaked. It crashed to the floor just a few feet away. Smoke billowed around him, burned his eyes, and filled his lungs. The floors were collapsing. He covered his mouth and nose with the wet blanket, trying to filter out the smoke. Although the fire was gaining ground, it was moving slowly. No doubt the snow melting on the roof had helped discourage its destructive speed.

However, if there was one thing he'd learned, it was to never underestimate the beast. Each fire had its own personality, its own set of rules. You either respected its powers or you perished. In the back of his mind, there was another thing experience had taught him. There was a strong possibility this fire had been set deliberately. But he would reason that out later when everyone was safe.

William reached the fourth floor and rounded the corner. Intense heat surrounded him. Flames licked against his bare skin, and beads of sweat formed on his forehead. He missed the protective gear of a fireman. He focused on finding survivors as he fought through the flames and headed toward the end of the corridor. He passed the room Isabel used for her private studio. It was engulfed in flames. William paused for only a split second before leaping into the room and retrieving the small portrait painted by Clarida. He tucked it in his shirt. Everything else was beyond rescue. He rushed back out into the corridor.

A woman screamed. Relief washed over him. Someone was still alive.

The sound was coming from the last door on his right. He ran in that direction and kicked open the door. The force of the vacuum created threw him back against the wall. He heard a crack and felt pain sear him. It was hard to breathe. He'd probably broken a rib or two. Gritting his teeth against the pain, he scrambled to his feet and raced into the room. A woman, clothed only in a stained and torn sheath, cowered in the corner.

William assessed the situation. She was alone, and paralyzed with fear.

He ran over to her, pulling her to her feet. His voice was calm. "You'll be safe. Come with me."

She shook her head. "No, no. I can't. He said I'd be safe only if I stay here." She turned to stare in the direction of the smoke-filled corridor.

Hysteria had set in. A few times he'd had to knock a person unconscious in order to save their life. He turned her face toward him. "What's your name?"

"Name's Zoe."

It was the woman who'd propositioned him a few days ago when he'd been looking for Isabel. "Okay, Zoe. You have to listen to me. I'm going to ease you out the window. There are men waiting to catch you."

Her eyes widened. "No, I can't."

"Yes, you can."

He picked her up in his arms, trying to contain her flailing arms and legs. She fought against him, hitting him with her clenched fists. He promised someone would catch her. He hoped that was the case. Otherwise, he would have to do this the hard way. He'd have to carry this hysterical woman down a flight of rapidly disintegrating stairs.

He gave up trying to stop her from pummeling him and slung her over his shoulder as he headed to the window and, with his free hand, opened the shutters. When he looked down, Liam and his men were waiting below. William vowed to never again underestimate the courage and resourcefulness of the people of this century.

He shouted to them, and they ran over and spread the blanket below the window. He admired their calm. They would have made fine firefighters in the twenty-first century.

He pulled the woman from his shoulder and lifted her onto the windowsill. "I need you to jump. There are men waiting for you below."

Zoe clutched at his shirt. "No. He said to stay."

There was a loud creaking sound and a crash. The shudder rocked the tavern. The building was collapsing.

William loosened Zoe's grip around his neck. He could push her over the edge, but he needed her to concentrate on the blanket. He had once seen someone jump and miss the target. He needed Zoe to focus.

"There's no more time left. Who told you to stay? Is he still here?"

She nodded frantically.

''I'll find him and convince him that jumping is his only option."

Fire leaped into the room. The thin carpet burst into flames. Zoe screamed again.

Her hand shook as she pointed to the door on the far side of the room. Her voice trembled as she spoke. "Barty's in there."

The hair on the back of his neck prickled. "Who?" He had a bad premonition.

"His real name's Bartholomew, but I called him Barty." She clutched at William's arm. "I think he's dead. Someone was in his room right before the fire broke out, and I heard screaming."

Just then the bed in her room caught on fire.

Unless there were two men by the name of Bartholomew in London fitting the Renegade's description, William's search was over. Adrenaline surged through him. He tamped it down. Like the woman, he must not lose focus. He shook her gently. "It's time to go."

She shook her head. "I'm afraid."

William lifted her chin until her gaze met his. "Zoe, I know Barty told you to stay here, but you must believe me. If you do, you'll die."

Her eyes brimmed with tears, and she swallowed. ''Are you sure someone will catch me?"

He glanced toward the street below. The men who held the makeshift rescue blanket looked strong and determined. William nodded. "Yes, I'm sure. They won't let you fall."

He turned her toward the window and directed her to sit on the ledge with her legs dangling over the edge. "I want you to take a deep breath and concentrate on landing on the blanket. Can you do that for me?"

Zoe hesitated for only a brief moment, nodded, and then pushed away from the window. Her arms and legs churned in the air as she descended downward.

A cheer rang out in the crowd as she landed in the center of the blanket. People rushed to her side.

The exhilaration he normally felt when he saved someone from the belly of a fire did not occur this time. His thoughts were on the occupant in the next room. He pulled the wet blanket over his head once more and leaped through the wall of flames. The door to the room was ajar. At least he would not have to worry about a possible vacuum created by the heat of the fire.

The room was ablaze. If Bartholomew was here, he might have been overcome with smoke inhalation. William looked around the room. In the corner, next to the window, was a body. He rushed over to the small bed and knelt beside the charred remains. William turned the body toward him.

He stumbled back. The head was missing.

It was just like what had happened to Paulette. The horror of such a death never ceased to sadden him. He bent over the body, knowing he was running out of time. The fire wouldn't wait for him. But Zoe had called this guy 'Barty,' and William had to be sure. He couldn't risk having the fire destroy evidence.

The height and weight fit Bartholomew's description, but any other distinguishing characteristics were burned beyond recognition. The word "convenient" leaped to William's thoughts. The only identifiable feature was a small glass vial attached to a metal chain. It lay in the palm of the man's hand. It looked like a container for poison. It was one of Bartholomew's trademarks.

Flames licked at William's back. The fire was growing impatient. A headless Bartholomew. William never liked it when things were tied up for him in a neat package. Only a positive DNA match would convince him this was the man he sought. There was only one option.

William found a cloak under the bed and used it to wrap the body. He didn't want to have to field questions as to why the man was decapitated.

He slung the body over his shoulder and climbed out onto the window ledge, where he shouted to Liam.

Liam waved and moved his men into place. Carrying a dead body would be awkward, but he had no other choice. The fire had destroyed all other avenues of escape. There would not be time to send the body down first and wait for Liam and his men to regroup. William and the headless Bartholomew would have to go down together. He tried to see the humor of the situation, but failed.

He positioned himself on the ledge and pushed off. He was airborne for only seconds. The added weight and the force of two bodies yanked the blanket out of the men's grip, and William landed with a thud on the hard cobblestones. Air was pushed out of his lungs, and he felt his shoulder dislocate. Damn.

A roar from the crowd went up around him. Someone clasped him on the shoulder. He winced in pain.

The inn groaned, and a large shudder shook the building as the upper floors collapsed. Dark gray smoke billowed from the remains. The Blue Goose Inn was destroyed, but Liam's men had contained the fire. The tavern's isolation from the other buildings, as well as its close proximity to the river, had prevented the flames from spreading.

William evaluated his injuries. No doubt a few broken ribs, dislocated shoulder, second-degree burns on his forearms and hands...

"William?"

He turned and saw Isabel running toward him. She jumped into his arms.

He clamped his jaw. The impact of her small frame slamming into him sent ripples of pain searing through him. But he didn't care. Isabel was in his arms. She pressed the side of her face against his cheek, and in that instant he forgot he was injured.

He put his good arm around the small of her back and pulled her closer still. He didn't know why he deserved her concern, but he wasn't about to question his good fortune.

Tears clung to her thick lashes. Her voice trembled. "I was afraid."

She hadn't asked about her paintings—she'd been concerned about him. If in fact he had found Bartholomew, William would be leaving soon. The thought hurt him more than the sum total of all his injuries put together.

Isabel's voice caught. "You could have been killed."

He didn't want to remind her that was unlikely since he was an Immortal. He wanted to bask in the glow of her concern. For the first time in his life, someone feared for his safety. He wanted this moment to go on forever.

He cupped the side of her face with the palm of his hand. "Thank you for worrying about me."

Her chin trembled under his touch. "Of course I am concerned." She reached up on her tiptoes and kissed him lightly on the mouth. "I will wait for you by the horses."

Isabel's touch was butterfly soft, melting the ice around his heart with healing warmth.

She smiled, and the gray clouds over the sun seemed to lighten as she headed toward her horse. He tore his gaze from the way her hips moved back and forth, as well as the endless possibilities her kiss had promised. Someone was calling his name.

It was Liam. "Lad, what's wrong with your shoulder? Your arm is hanging as limp as wet linen."

"Dislocated."

Before William could add, "I can do it myself," Liam held his arm in a viselike grip and wrenched it back into place.

William ground his teeth together as sharp, dull pain ripped through his shoulder. "Thanks."

Liam grinned. "Glad to help. Well, it's all gone. The fire's still smoldering, but so far we've prevented it from spreading to my warehouse. You're a brave man. I've never seen the like. Saved Zoe's life, you did. Nothing could save that man, though."

William massaged his shoulder. "You mentioned a warehouse. Do you have the means to store the body? I'll only need it for a couple of days."

Liam rubbed the stubble on his chin. "I've no

objections. If it's who I think it is, he was an odd fellow. Always paid on time, though, and insisted I keep his identity a secret."

William realized that helping to save Zoe's life had loosened Liam's tongue where money had failed.

"How long was the man here?"

"Not more than a fortnight. Never said where he was from. But I don't doubt that someone did him in. He drew the roughest sort to his side. Not a very forgiving or understanding man, or so I was told. Maybe he cheated one of them and they got even."

Zoe walked over to William, one hand on her hip. The fear was gone as she pressed against him and smiled. "Had to thank you for saving my life." She pulled the blanket over her shoulders. "Couldn't help but overhear you talking about Barty. I dinna know about the men he were acquainted with, but the women were afraid of him. A few were found dead after a night spent with him, a poem clutched in their hand. Judith is still missing. However, nothing was ever proved. An empty belly tends to chase away the fear and make a person look the other way. Yesterday was the first time I'd ever seen him. Generous with his money, though, and paid me in advance. Not many will do that ahead of time, if you get my meaning. Most want to see the goods beforehand."

What he was hearing about this guy Barty fit Bartholomew's profile. If only the body could have been positively identified. William didn't like loose ends. He should be rejoicing that Bartholomew was dead. However, he could not shake the feeling that the fire and the decapitated body fitting Bartholomew's description were too convenient.

Chapter 23

Bartholomew sat on his horse on a hill overlooking the River Thames and patted the bloody sack strapped to the pommel of his saddle. Everything had gone as planned. Actually, better than planned. He'd found a beggar on the streets about his height and weight. He'd cleaned the man up and dressed him in the finest money could buy, and then he'd arranged for him to meet the whore, Zoe. As instructed, the beggar had introduced himself to Zoe as Bartholomew.

Killing the beggar had been the easy part, and the fire had been meant to eliminate any distinguishing characteristics, but the flames had spread faster than anticipated. Bartholomew rubbed the burns on his arms.

He smiled. But then, the Protector had proved to be more fearless than expected, as well. There was never any doubt he would try to rescue the woman. The unknown factor had been whether or not she would survive long enough to identify the beggar as Bartholomew. Just in case, he'd left the vial of poison. That detail of evidence should convince the Protector he had found his man. Bartholomew was well aware of the huge file the Council of Seven had on him. He was counting on the fact the Protector knew it by heart.

Now all that was left to do was dispose of the head in the woods. He would not bother burying it. The wild animals would take care of the evidence efficiently.

Besides, he did not want to risk someone digging it up and making the connection to the body in the fire.

With any luck, the great Protector would return to his own time within the next twenty-four hours. Bartholomew laughed. The world William would return to would be unrecognizable from the one he'd left behind. By the time William realized his mistake, it would be too late to do anything about it. The future would be altered forever, a change in the balance of power from good to evil.

Bartholomew laughed again as he turned his horse to Hampton Court. Everything was progressing as planned.

****

The artist's studio was cold and deserted. Isabel shivered as she bent to add another log on the hearth while William secured the horses in the stables. She sat back on her heels and stared at the flames as the fire's warmth seeped through her. Hours before, at the Blue Goose Inn, flames had offered only death and destruction.

The loss of her paintings left an emptiness within her she doubted she would ever fill. They had represented the awakening of her talent. But as devastating as her loss was, it did not compare with the loss of life and what Liam had experienced. His establishment had burned to the ground and his livelihood along with it. If not for William, more lives would have been lost.

William.

There was a feeling of excitement that wove around her whenever she thought of him. In a short span of time he had become important to her, and now, with the man he sought dead, William would be leaving.

She shivered again and added another log to the fire, knowing full well that it was not the cold that caused her body to tremble but thoughts of William.

Isabel glanced around. The artist's studio was also doing nothing to lift her spirits. Many of the statues, as well as the large mural Jardin and Forsyth were working on, had already been moved to Hampton Court for the costume ball. The studio always pulsated with energy. Now it was an empty shell. It seemed strange and foreign to her, as though she did not belong here anymore. She could not shake the image that she was adrift on a wide sea and unsure in which direction she should set her course.

She stood and brushed the dust off her skirts and the odd notion along with it. Isabel held her hands near the flames to warm them. She was not adrift but on solid ground. She knew the knowledge she'd gained concerning her parents helped. Her journey was headed in the direction of her own choosing.

And right now, that purpose was to complete the portrait of Poseidon, commissioned by the queen as a gift for her husband. Although many would never know, including the queen, that Isabel was the artist, she wanted it to be perfect. And of greater importance, she wanted to see William.

She repeated these last thoughts as she anticipated his arrival. They had stayed behind until he'd made certain the fire was out. She wondered if he had also tried to learn why Ossian had disappeared. Restless, she glanced toward the leaded glass window.

It was midday, but the sun was well hidden behind

thick gray clouds. Its somber hues were reflected in the studio. Again the notion that she had never seen it look so barren swept over her. Perhaps more light would help. Isabel lit candles along the mantel and counters cluttered with clay jars of pigments, oil, and dried egg yolks. She smiled, remembering Paulette's patient instructions on the proper way to blend these ingredients to make paint.

Isabel's hand trembled as she lit a candle. She would miss Paulette. It was not only the lack of art that cast such a gloom over the studio but the absence of the artists, as well.

Jardin and Forsyth had accompanied the commissioned pieces to Hampton Court in order to supervise their arrangement. But even their presence would not have made the difference. It was Paulette and Ossian who had breathed life into the studio.

Isabel knew everyone suspected that Ossian had killed Paulette, but Isabel disagreed. The two might have fought openly, but there had also been laughter. Ossian's expression when he gazed toward Paulette had always been filled with love. Isabel wished he'd been present at Paulette's funeral. It could have dispelled the rumors.

William entered the studio on a blast of cold air. The candles flickered, and the fire sputtered in greeting. He hastened to close the door on the blistering wind and bolted it in place. When he turned, his smile sent tremors rippling through her. The studio took on a new life with his presence.

"Sorry it took me so long."

Her heart was hammering so hard in her chest that she found it difficult to breathe, let alone respond.

From under his cloak, he produced a basket spilling over with loaves of bread, cheese, and wine. "Liam and some of the other merchants thought we might want something to eat. There's enough for a small army. Do you want anything before we start?" He hesitated. "Or have you changed your mind about my posing for you?"

She did want something.

"I am not very hungry." Wonderful. Her voice cracked. She cleared her throat. "Maybe later. I would like to start as soon as possible."

He set the food down. "I almost forgot," he said, and reached into the folds of his shirt to withdraw a small object.

Isabel held her breath and then rushed toward him, taking the treasure from his grasp. "William, you saved the portrait. Thank you!"

He grinned. "You're welcome. All the others were already engulfed in flames."

"It doesn't matter. This is the one I prized above all the others."

He lifted her chin. "Promise me that, unlike Claricia, you will sign your name to whatever you paint."

She smiled. "You have my promise."

He raised an eyebrow. "Well, I guess we'd better get started, if you are to finish the portrait of Poseidon."

Her heart fluttered again as she watched him remove his clothes and drape them over a chair.

Isabel's hand shook as she put Claricia's painting away and tried to light additional candles, reasoning that she would need light in order to reproduce on canvas the shadows and contours of her subject. In

246

truth, she knew it was to avoid looking at William as he removed his garments.

He was standing beside her. She could feel his warmth before he spoke.

"Here, let me help you." He finished lighting the candles for her.

Isabel's face felt like it was on fire. William was naked. She looked away and turned toward the table, fumbling with a wooden bowl and a jar of pigment.

His voice carried over the sound of her efforts to mix the paint. "I'm ready."

Well, she most certainly was not. She added a touch of oil to the mixture and ground it together with a pestle. The paint would dry slowly, but she would be able to work more carefully, and the result would be a richer depth of color. She kept her eyes averted as she swirled the mixture into a thick paste. She reached for more of the pigment and hesitated. She was stalling for time. What was wrong with her?

She stole a glance over her shoulder toward William. He was stretched out on the platform, fast asleep.

A sigh escaped her lips. Awake or asleep, his power radiated toward her. His presence filled the room until all she could see or feel was William. Was this love? Or desire? The two emotions blended together like the paint she used to create vivid storm clouds.

The need to capture him on canvas overwhelmed her. It was a way for her to always have a visual reminder of him after he was gone.

Without wasting any more time, she pulled her smock over her head, tied it in place, and then picked up her brush. She was satisfied with the background of the portrait, a raging sea and a storm-fed sky. The jewel-tone colors ranged from deep sapphire, turquoise, and amethyst to emerald green. Poseidon stood in the center of the tempest, a calm presence defying the forces of nature. But she needed to complete the focal point of the portrait. The god. The man.

Isabel glanced toward William again. Paulette had been right. He was the perfect choice for Poseidon. Both William and the mythical character shared the same energy. Even asleep, there was a quiet strength that wove around him.

His body was magnificent. Hard cords of muscles flexed, even in sleep. Wide shoulders, a powerful chest and legs reminded her of the marble and bronze statues created by the ancient Greek and Roman artists.

However, William was more than a mindless warrior bent on hunting down his prey. He was a contradiction—an Immortal who behaved like a man who felt his life would end at any moment. She wished she had the time to discover the man beneath the role he played.

William yawned and stretched. Muscles rippled over his body. In one fluid movement he rose to his feet. "Sorry about that. Getting injured always makes me tired." He rubbed his arm. "It's cold in here. Do you mind if I add another log to the fire?"

Isabel shook her head. She was not cold. To the contrary, she was actually thinking the studio had caught on fire. She concentrated on the imposing figure of Poseidon on her canvas, adding layers of emotion with each brush stroke. Painting William's likeness only made her feel warmer. This ancient god probably walked around naked as well.

"Do you mind if I take a look?"

She jumped. He was standing right next to her. She turned abruptly toward him. Her brush spread a wide swath of golden paint across his bare chest.

"Oh, no!" She stumbled back against the counter. The bowl of paint she had been mixing rocked back and forth. She turned to catch it before it hit the ground, but her hand landed in the gooey mess.

He laughed. "Can I help?"

She whirled toward him, planting a handprint on his chest.

He laughed again and put his arms around her. "When you said you wanted to paint me, this was not exactly what I had in mind."

Isabel gazed up into his blue eyes, and time ceased to exist.

She was pressed against the length of him. The laughter in his voice still lingered in the air, but the expression in his eyes reflected a smoldering passion.

His hand cupped the back of her neck, sending shivers of pleasure down her spine. "I've dreamed of how your hair would feel next to my skin. It's like spun silk." Both of his hands now moved to hold the sides of her face as his mouth moved slowly toward hers. "I want you."

His words echoed the way she felt as his lips pressed against her mouth. She could feel the warm heat of him as each kiss built upon the other, feather soft and exploring, a tingling warmth that awakened the senses. The tempo changed, building with each beat of her heart. The brush dropped from her fingers as she encircled his neck, wanting more, needing more.

His hand pressed on the small of her back, pulling

her toward him as his other brushed the side of her breast.

A gasp of pleasure escaped as he caressed her through the clothes she wore.

His kiss deepened. The taste of him, the heat of him was all she knew, all she cared to know. The power of her emotions overwhelmed her.

She had never felt so on fire. She took a deep breath, placing her hand on his chest. She laughed. "I have smeared you with paint." Her words seemed far away, disconnected somehow. She reached for a cloth on a nearby table.

He smiled. "You're covered, as well." He winked. "I don't mind. I'm yours to command."

Her face inflamed as she wiped his bare skin and her fingers brushed against hard muscle.

He covered her hand with his and leaned forward. Warm breath against her skin set her shivering with desire. The cloth was forgotten as she wrapped her arms around his neck.

He drew back. "I want you, Isabel." His expression grew serious. "I'll be leaving soon. I'll understand if you…"

Isabel gazed into his eyes. They were clear, and his soul was open to her. She placed her fingers over his lips. "If you are leaving, then we must cherish the moments we have left together."

She initiated the kiss and felt him mold his body to hers. Tremors of heat rocked her as he pulled her smock over her head. The pins came loose, and her hair tumbled over his hands as she felt his warm mouth on the base of her neck.

He groaned and captured her lips once more.

Isabel felt a rumble of laughter vibrate through her. "William, what is wrong?"

He arched an eyebrow. "My body aches to feel you, but my brain hasn't a clue how to remove all the layers of clothes you wear. Can I assume you don't want me to cut them off your body?"

Isabel giggled. "Absolutely not. This is my favorite gown."

"I was afraid of that."

She draped her arms around his neck. "That first time, at the Blue Goose Inn, when you told Liam you were my husband, you gave me the impression you were a skilled and worldly lover. I would think such a man would have no problem separating a woman from her clothes."

She could not believe how bold she was, but his expression, as he gazed at her, was empowering. Her hand caressed his chest. "Did you not offer to satisfy me numerous times in one day?"

William winked. "And that is a promise I intend to keep."

He picked her up in his arms, spinning her around slowly as he walked toward the hearth. She laughed and clung to him. He paused and held her against him as he slid her down the front of his body.

He kissed her lightly on the lips and whispered, "I would gladly spend an eternity with you."

Her heart filled with the sound of his words.

His mouth lingered for a moment, and then he turned her slowly so her back was pressed against his chest. He swept her hair from the nape of her neck and kissed her, sending warm, delicious shivers racing through her.

She could feel his fingers against her back as he unlaced her gown. She took a ragged breath of air when she felt his hand slip underneath and circle around beneath her breast, his thumb brushing against a sensitive nipple. She arched against him. Her skin felt alive, responsive to his touch. She wanted more. She turned to face him, and her gown dropped from her shoulders to pool on the floor. Only her linen shift remained.

He cupped her face in his hands and kissed her until the world began to spin. She clung to him and felt him hard against her.

He paused for a moment and gazed at her. "Isabel."

She put her fingers on his mouth. She did not want words between them. Not now. Not when his touch was telling her all she needed to know.

William grabbed for his plaid, which was draped over a chair, and spread it before the fire. He reached for her and pulled her down beside him. Together they lay upon the cushion of wool as he brushed her hair gently away from her forehead. His touch sent warm shivers of pleasure racing through her. His gaze was intense, reminding her of the first time she saw him. He leaned slowly toward her and her lips parted.

His kiss breathed warmth into her heart as she molded against him in a sea of passion. His touch filled her with a sense of belonging. Her desire, passion, and need were like the flames in the hearth. They built within her. She groaned in response to his touch, aching for him, needing him.

He entered her, and the world slipped away. Only the moment was important as each wave of passion brought her closer and closer to the flame. And to love.

Chapter 24

Isabel stretched out on William's plaid. She felt as contented as a kitten that had just consumed a saucer of warm milk. His eyes were closed, and a smile flickered around his mouth. She placed a feather-soft kiss on his lips and laid her hand on his bare chest. Until now, she had been a woman who believed romance was only found in myths and legends. Unexplainable and impossible. However, she knew without a doubt that she would never love a man as she loved William. She admitted the word in her thoughts and knew it to be true.

Her fingers entwined in the soft hair on his chest, committing to memory each moment, touch, and caress that had transpired over the last few hours.

His eyes were closed, but his mouth turned in a mischievous smile. "You're giving me ideas."

Isabel snuggled closer, reveling in the touch of naked skin. She pressed closer to him and whispered, "You are still covered in paint. Shall I wash you?"

He groaned. "Okay, now it's more than just an idea." He opened his eyes and winked. "Are you sure you're not a witch?"

She laughed. "Do you suggest I have cast a spell over you?"

He traced his finger over the mounds of her breasts. Her heart fluttered in response.

William kissed her on the top of her nose. "I admit it. That's exactly what I was thinking. Too clichéd?"

She smiled. "Most definitely."

"I can't help it. I feel that the sun only shines when I'm with you."

She moved to press even closer against him. "Now, that was much better. But if there were any type of wizardry involved, it would be of your doing. After all, you are the Immortal, not I. A being that should only exist in the fantasy realm. Which reminds me. I want to learn as much as I can about your world. The book Angus gave me only recorded the deaths and births of Immortals, and the stories Angus and Myra told me as a child were not as detailed as I would like. Before, it did not matter, but everything has changed."

He kissed her on the mouth and whispered, "What are my chances of delaying the history lesson for an hour or two?"

She sat and reached for the basket of food he'd brought and set it down between them. She handed him a crusty loaf of bread. "Maybe this will take your mind off…things."

"You're asking the impossible. You're not wearing any clothes."

She warmed under his gaze. "And now you know how I felt while you posed for me. You made it very hard to concentrate."

He smiled. "I'd hoped that was your reaction." William accepted the bread and broke off a hunk. "The things I do for love."

Her heart skipped a beat at the word he'd used, and she concentrated on unwrapping and slicing the cheese. "I am dying of curiosity. Please tell me of your world."

"And I want to have you again."

She shoved a slice of cheese in his direction. "Then you must hurry."

He leaned on his elbow. "I suppose you realize this will be the ultimate test of self-control?"

She smiled, feeling very pleased as she took a bite of cheese.

He sighed dramatically and placed the cheese between two slices of bread. "Okay, here goes. I want you to first try to suspend all your belief systems, for what I am about to tell you, while true, has been dismissed as the stuff of legends and myths."

She nodded. "I will try."

He hesitated and leaned closer. "Are you sure you don't want to delay the lesson?"

"Positive."

He sighed loudly again. "If you insist. Are you familiar with Plato's legend of the lost continent of Atlantis?" He took a bite of the bread and cheese.

"Of course. Angus would read the stories to me when I was a child. As I remember, Plato claimed the story of Atlantis had been handed down to Solon, who heard it in Egypt in about 590 B.C. Angus told me it was one of the greatest legends of all time."

A smile flickered across his mouth. "You have a good memory, but Atlantis existed. Do you have any idea where it was located?"

She chose a creamy cheese rolled in oats, feeling as though she was learning about the history of a great race of people. It was exciting to realize the stories she loved were real.

"I remember something about Atlantis being located on the island of Crete or Sicily. There is also a mention of the Pillars of Hercules. In any case it was destroyed by water, the result of a cataclysmic volcanic eruption or earthquake." She took a bite, savoring the cheese's nutty flavor. "Humm, this is delicious."

He reached over and kissed the side of her mouth. "You missed a spot. You're right. It is good. Change your mind about taking a break?" His eyes gleamed with mischief and passion.

She pushed him gently back down. "I want more."

"My thoughts exactly." He finished his meal and placed his arms under his head. "You must have been a very demanding child. All right, you win. A story it is. What if I were to tell you that when Solon told Plato Atlantis was destroyed by water he was right, but not in the way he thought. Atlantis didn't sink into the ocean but was frozen over by ice that was miles thick."

She licked her fingers and was pleased when he groaned. "You are talking about a frozen continent. Where is it located?"

"You're killing me." He laced his hands together on his bare chest. "At the bottom of the world."

She scrambled back down next to him, and he draped his plaid over her shoulders. "This tale is even more intriguing than the one Angus told me. So is this where all the Immortals originated?"

William stared at the rolling flames for a long moment. He knew why Angus had retold Plato's version of what had happened. It was a way of keeping humankind from discovering the truth of the Immortals' ancestral home. He knew also the Council of Seven would not approve of his telling Isabel, but he would risk their disapproval. He needed to explain to her about his history, and that included where his people came from.

He cleared his throat. "Why don't we start with the phrase 'Once upon a time.' "

She propped her head in the crook of her arm. "Yes, please go on."

"Atlantis is located in the area known as Antarctica. Many different clans lived on the great continent. Some were governed by magic, others by logic, while still others sought a spiritual path with the gods. All differences were honored, and Atlantis flourished. Our society knew of the coming disaster hundreds of years before it occurred and knew also that Atlantis would one day become uninhabitable. Many plans were explored for trying to either live on a frozen continent or stop the inevitable advance of ice."

William stretched out and laced his fingers together on his chest. "All efforts failed. The only option left was to colonize the rest of the world. However, our elders were also well aware of the barbarian ways of those who inhabited the lands to our north. We sought a way for our people, and our way of life, to flourish. The physicians and scientists devised a plan. It took the form of an Elixir and became the medicine that would help a person recover quickly from injury or disease, enabling us to survive."

William looked over at Isabel. She was silent. He couldn't tell if she believed what he said, and it was important that she did. He hoped this story made his race seem more human.

The word lingered in his thoughts as he realized the irony. The one thing Immortals searched for was a reconnection with their humanity.

She snuggled closer. "Is there more?"

He cleared his throat. "The medicine worked better than we envisioned. It did more than restore our bodies to health—over time, it made us immortal. Eventually, this trait became hereditary."

He turned and brushed a lock of hair off her forehead. There was more, much more. He hadn't even touched on how they discovered the Guardian and the ability to travel through time. And then there were the Protectors. But he decided he'd told her enough for now. And the rest was not as pleasant. There were things about his people better left unsaid, at least for now. She didn't fear him, but she might if she learned more about his kind.

She whispered, "Thank you."

He nodded and gathered her against the length of him, kissing her. He felt a wave of emotion so strong that he recognized it at once for what it was. The gods be merciful, he was in love with Isabel de Pinze.

****

William awoke in a cold sweat.

He gasped for breath and sat bolt upright. He glanced over at Isabel. Thankfully, she was still asleep. The remnants of his dream still clung to him. Although he hadn't experienced this nightmare in a while, he knew it by heart. He also suspected his retelling of the Immortal history had brought the memory to the forefront of his mind.

The dream always began in the same place. On the day he turned thirty. The years of arduous training had ended, and the day of his initiation as a Protector began as any other. It was spring in the Highlands. White heather blanketed the rolling hills framing the rocky shores of Loch Ness.

His mind spun back at warp speed. He was in the Council chambers beneath the ruins of Urquhart Castle. No one in the outside world of humankind knew what went on inside these walls, and that was just as well. Today the entire governing board of the Immortals was in attendance. They never missed an event like this one. His uncle, Gavin, sat grave-faced behind the long table. Gavin had failed to overturn thousands of years of tradition regarding the rules that governed the Protectors, and the defeat was evident in his expression.

However, Gavin would abide by the Council's decision and show a united front. To object now would result in his dismissal from the Council. Gavin's position was hereditary, and there was no one of age who qualified as a replacement. A vacancy would result in chaos. William knew his uncle would never let that happen. The delicate balance of the world was at stake.

Gavin stood, his fists clenched at his sides. "Let's get this over with. Show the man into these chambers."

William remembered a hush fell over the group of Protector candidates. Other than himself, there were three who would be initiated today—his cousin, Alexandra Redmond, who never smiled; Artemis Finucane, who felt the world was created for his enjoyment; and Neil Mackenzie, who spent his nights mastering the game of chess and his days on the practice field. William didn't have to talk to them to know what they were thinking. What was about to happen to the man being brought before the Council was a common fear amongst the Protectors. It was a constant companion from the moment you realized the full implications of being born a Protector.

A cymbal reverberated through the room. The way

of announcing an accused into these chambers was a ritual older than the written language of the humankind race.

Two guards dressed in identical red-and-black kilts and matching swords escorted a man into the room. William recognized him at once. It was David Spencer. He was one of the guest Protectors who came now and again to help with the cadet training. But that was not why he was here today.

David had failed his last mission. A Protector only had one chance to succeed.

The guards motioned for David to kneel. It was so quiet that William imagined he could hear the water lapping against the shore through the walls of the castle.

Gavin's voice was laced with anger. William knew it was not directed at the man kneeling before him but at the judgment he must pronounce.

"David Spencer, it is within your power to decline any mission presented to you. But having accepted, there is only one result that is absolute. You must succeed. In your case, despite your being granted additional time, the result was still the same. You failed to capture and kill the butcher Daggart. He continues to roam free, killing at will. His Bloodlust has progressed to such a degree that he murdered his entire family. Another Protector will be assigned to the task of tracking down this animal."

David's shoulders slumped forward. William realized the man already accepted his fate.

The cymbal clashed again as Gavin walked from behind the long table to face David. He put his hand on the man's head. "Think carefully before you answer, for there will not be a chance to recant. You have two choices. Exile to the ice fields of Antarctica, the origins of our race...or death?"

This was what Gavin fought so hard to change. He disagreed that the penalty for failing a mission should be so harsh, and he recommended that each case be examined individually with other alternatives besides death or exile. A Protector should be allowed to step away from his duties, he argued, and given the choice of retirement or a permanent teaching position on the Protectors' campus.

These solutions were rejected. The other six members of the Council all agreed that the very nature of a Protector would prevent him from being able to mainstream into society. Protectors, they said, were reclusive and suited for one purpose, to capture or kill their prey.

The cymbal sounded again. David made his decision.

He chose death.

William rubbed his forehead, trying to block out the memory of David's senseless death as he pulled himself back to the present.

In the years since David's death, Gavin had succeeded in gaining a little ground. He was able to insist that the Protectors make an effort to mainstream into society, requiring them to have a profession outside their duties. This was the reason William was a firefighter and smoke jumper.

However, Protectors who failed a mission still had only the two options. Old ways were hard to change, and of the original four to be initiated that fateful day, William was the only one who remained. Two had chosen death, and Alexandra, exile.

Isabel stretched and smiled over at him. "Good morning."

The dark memory slipped into the chambers of his mind, out of the way, but its message not forgotten.

He smiled and kissed her on the nose. "It is now."

The door to the studio rattled, and Isabel grabbed her clothes around her. "Someone is coming."

"It's probably Liam. I told him I would help with the cleanup today."

Isabel was already on her feet as she made a dash behind a screen of unfinished paintings.

William was adept at getting ready in a hurry. He retrieved his clothes and dressed as he walked to the door. He would have preferred to spend another day with Isabel, but working to clean away debris was worthwhile. He could also check on the condition of the body he'd found in the blaze.

The coincidence and ease of finding Bartholomew still bothered him. And, as his dream so eloquently reminded him, failure was not an option. If the corpse was not Bartholomew's, William would be offered two choices on his return to the twenty-first century—death or exile. Even worse, there might not be enough time to reassign someone else to the task of tracking down the Renegade.

William paused at the door. It was not the thought of failure that was abhorrent to him: If Bartholomew was not stopped, history would be altered and a new ice age would have begun. William had not told Isabel that the reason Atlantis had turned to ice was that his ancestors had tampered with time. Thousands of years ago, only one continent in the world had been affected. This time they might not be as lucky.

He always relied on his instincts. They'd never failed him before. And what they were telling him was that Bartholomew was still out there. William just needed to flush the man out of his hole.

Chapter 25

Isabel was finished. She flipped the protective cover over the portrait of Poseidon and stretched her back. She was tired but pleased with the results. As usual, she had lost track of the hour. William had left with Liam earlier this morning to help clean up the damage caused by the fire, but he would return to ride with her to the manor. The time alone had given her the opportunity to think. She did not regret one moment with William. It was a wonderful memory she would keep with her always.

She would be like the women in legends who experience one perfect love only to lose it. Instead of feeling saddened by the knowledge, she felt relieved. She would not have to live as Myra did, growing old while the man she loved stayed the same, and wondering if he would still love her. Isabel knew the outcome beforehand. When William left, he was not coming back. However, what gave her the courage to act on her feelings for William was an entry in Angus's book. Her mother had also followed her heart.

The rear door opened, and Isabel heard the sound of a crying infant. When she turned, she was not prepared for what she saw.

Ossian stood holding a baby in the crook of one arm and a knapsack in the other. His voice was little above a whisper. "I did not expect anyone to be here."

Without waiting for an answer, he tossed the knapsack on a table near Isabel and hastened to the fireplace.

He removed one of the loose stones. "Empty. I should have known."

The infant whimpered, and Ossian rushed to the counter. With one sweep of his arm, he brushed the expensive containers of pigment and oil to the floor. They clattered and smashed onto the ground, blending together in a splash of reds, yellows, and blues.

He removed a cloth from the knapsack and changed the child's soiled linens.

Isabel moved slowly toward him. She had never heard him speak of a baby.

He smiled down at the squirming infant. "Yes, to answer your unspoken question. The child is Paulette's and mine." His voice cracked when he spoke her name.

The baby grabbed his finger in its tiny fist. Tears brimmed in Ossian's eyes as he stared at his son.

This was not making any sense. In the first place, Paulette had never mentioned that she was with child, and Isabel had never guessed. However, Paulette had gone against the fashions that cinched in a woman's waist, and so could have hidden her condition.

Isabel stood beside Ossian. It was difficult not to smile at the charming babe. He was so full of life. "Why did you keep your baby a secret? Was it because you and Paulette are Immortals?"

"Ah, so you know." He fastened the baby's linen diaper. "I am glad you know. I never liked keeping it from you." He wrapped the infant in a blanket and held him against his shoulder. "Paulette and I have been together for hundreds of years, and we finally came to the conclusion we wanted a family. Two years ago, we started making preparations. The Council gave their blessings, and after the waiting period ended, we both drank from the Elixir of Life. It removed the effect of immortality and enabled us to bear children." He smiled. "I was never so happy as when our child was born, but that was before." He paused as he choked out the words. "I did not kill Paulette."

She could see the pain reflected in his eyes and put her hand on his shoulder. "I know."

Ossian rubbed the infant's back in small circles. "I am pleased you at least do not think me capable of such a monstrous deed. And I know it sealed my fate when I was not there for Paulette's funeral." A tear escaped and traveled unchecked down his cheek.

Isabel touched the child's small, perfect hand and watched with wonder as it wound around her finger. "He is adorable. What is his name?"

"Marduk." Ossian smiled down at the child. Already a fine layer of reddish-blond hair covered the infant's head.

Ossian chuckled as the baby burped. "You know Paulette's love of the ancient gods and goddesses. She enjoyed delving into their origins and discovered the ancient Babylonians had their own names for these beings. The planet Jupiter was known as Marduk, king of the gods. It was he who slew a dragon. She liked the idea that our son would be named in honor of a Dragon Slayer."

Isabel smiled. "It is a wonderful name. But why did you keep him a secret?"

He frowned. "Did you not see the mark on his wrist? We had no choice."

"What are you talking about?"

Ossian lifted Marduk's little hand and turned it gently to the side. The shape of a sword was already visible.

Isabel touched the tiny image in surprise. "It is the mark of a Protector."

Ossian nodded slowly. "A child who bears this sign must be turned over to the Council within the first three years of his life. There are no exceptions. Paulette and I could not do it. We had little choice but to keep Marduk a secret. But somehow they found out, and when they came for him, Paulette defended our son with her life. I arrived in time to save our child, but it was too late for Paulette."

He brushed a tear from his eyes. "I have to go. Promise me you will not tell anyone."

"Your secret is safe with me, but maybe there is something William could do to help. He also thought you innocent of Paulette's murder."

"Despite that knowledge, William is the last person I could trust. He is a Protector and would feel honor bound to take my son from me. Marduk is all I have left to remind me of the only woman I have ever loved."

Isabel put her hand on Ossian's arm. "Do you know who killed her?"

"It will be safer for you if you never know."

****

Isabel was once again within the safety of the walls of the manor, and all was as it once had been, or at least that was what Angus and Myra had told her when she'd arrived with William this afternoon. The danger was over. The man William sought was dead, but Isabel was not as sure. The last words Ossian spoke to her before he left still wove through her. "It will be safer for you if you never know." Isabel disagreed. Knowledge was the only thing that kept a person safe.

She crossed to the center of the room and poured the last of the boiling water into the oversized wooden tub. The steam rose around her, inviting her into the bath. She'd been looking forward to this moment all day. She wished she knew of a way to keep the water warm for a longer span of time.

Her thoughts turned to William.

He had become important to her, and now, with the man he sought dead, William would be leaving soon. It was difficult to push the realization from her thoughts. Maybe a long soak in the bath would help her ease the tension from the long hours of painting.

She touched the linen towels lining the interior of the tub and traced the image of a rosebud that Myra had stitched in each corner. The linens were sun-bleached a brilliant white. She doubted Queen Mary had any finer.

Isabel reached for a jar of dried lavender and rose petals and sprinkled them generously over the surface of the steaming water. Her last step in preparation was to add another log to the fire and light the candles on the mantel over the hearth. The combined flames cast a warm, golden haze over the chamber. Everything was perfect.

She removed her shift, draping it over a nearby chair, and stepped into the bath. She sank into the liquid warmth and closed her eyes. The fragrant waters swirled around her as she leaned against the back of the tub and stretched out her legs.

She sank deeper and inhaled the gentle aromas. It had been a long two days. During that time she'd both finished her painting and worked alongside the townspeople to make certain the fire was extinguished. Through their efforts and William's guidance, it had not spread. She smiled as she sank deeper. But it had not been all work. That first night they had made love. She felt a warmth building inside her that had nothing to do with the water.

Her thoughts drifted to the first moment she'd seen William as he'd emerged from the River Thames. She'd thought he was unreal, a man conjured from her fantasy or a mythical being with supernatural powers. She smiled to herself, realizing she'd been closer to the truth that first night than she'd guessed. He, however, exceeded even her wildest fantasies.

She could still see William as he'd appeared framed in the window near the·top of the inn. Flames and dark gray smoke had surrounded him as he'd coaxed Zoe to jump to safety. Isabel remembered his expression. His focus had been on the woman's survival, not on the burns he'd sustained.

If she had known nothing else about him before, this dedication to the preservation of life would have earned her respect. He was passionate about saving life and living it, as well.

Only when the woman had been safely on the ground had he disappeared once more into the mouth of the flames. In that instant she'd known how she felt.

She loved him.

A knock on her chamber door broke through the solitude and her thoughts.

Startled, she sat up, and as she did, water sloshed over the edge of the tub, spilling onto the stone floor. "Who is there?"

"It's William." There was a long pause.

Her heartbeat thundered away the seconds. "Please come in."

Isabel grabbed one of the linen towels draped over the chair. She shivered as she stepped out of the tub and wrapped the cloth around her body. She needed to see him. Their ride this afternoon from the studio to the manor had been too short, and then Angus had pulled him away from her. Her pulse raced as she opened the door.

Soot covered him from head to toe, blurring the colors of his plaid, as well as the contours of his face and arms. He looked wonderful.

She smiled. "Come inside and clean yourself. You are a sight."

"Isabel." He swallowed and glanced in the direction of the tub. His words were clipped. "I shouldn't stay. I'm leaving tomorrow."

"So soon?"

Isabel found it hard to breathe as she clung to the wet towel. She should ask him to leave while her heart was still intact. But she knew it was already too late. She had spent her whole life avoiding the entanglement of a relationship. Now, more than ever, logic should win over emotion. She should let him go.

He hesitated. "I just want you to know—"

Isabel gripped the towel tighter still. "Do not leave just yet."

She pulled him into the room and shut the door. She rose on tiptoe and pressed her lips to his and whispered, "We have tonight."

He groaned and put his hand on the small of her back, pulling her against him. She could feel his fingers on her skin through the towel she wore. She wanted each touch, each caress to linger, to be savored.

She reached for his hand. "Come with me."

He arched an eyebrow but let her lead him toward the tub.

The towel she wore slid from her body and pooled at her feet. She stepped into the water. "Join me in the bath."

She laughed, watching him fumble with his belt buckle. It had taken an excruciatingly long time for him to take off his clothes when he was modeling for the portrait, but this time was different.

He growled, removed his knife, and sliced through the belt. His clothes and weapons clattered to the ground. His shoulder muscles flexed as he stood before her.

Her face warmed under his gaze. Her pulse quickened as she pulled him in opposite her. Isabel reached for a cloth, soaped it, and gently rubbed his chest. The remnants of the soot and ash dissolved under her touch. She could feel the beat of his heart under her fingertips.

He put his hand over hers. "I love you."

Her heart ached. "And I you." The words lingered like a caress in the lavender-soaked air.

She soaped the rag again and washed his arms. "The fire has burned you."

He leaned forward and kissed her gently on the lips, whispered against her mouth. "The heat from the flames is nothing compared to the heat of your touch."

She laughed again. "You have the soul of a poet."

He reached under the water, put his hands on her waist, and drew her on top of his thighs.

The tips of her breasts grazed his chest. Her skin warmed where it made contact with his. She shuddered. She could feel him beneath her. She wrapped her arms around his neck.

Her breath caught in her throat as he lowered his head and put his mouth over her nipple. Her skin tingled. His hand rested on her thigh, slowly caressing her, and she arched toward him.

His hands moved up her side and cupped her breasts. He kissed the hollow of her neck, the back of her ear. His lips lightly touched her mouth, fanning the flames within her.

She leaned toward him, pressing her breasts against him once again. He entered her, and his rhythm matched the beating of her heart. Water splashed over the sides of the tub in thick waves as she clung to him, wishing this moment would last a lifetime, maybe two.

Chapter 26

Isabel lounged on the bed in her chamber feeling content as she watched William. He was already dressed and standing at the window. She, however, felt like remaining right where she was. A new snowstorm had left its mark over the gardens below. It was wonderful to just stay in bed on a day such as this. A thought darkened her mood.

She shivered and pulled the covers around her. "With the man you hunt dead, I would think the weather should be improving."

He closed the shutters and turned toward her. "I was thinking the same thing. Maybe Mother Nature takes a few days to catch on.".

His words were not convincing. She shivered again. "I was wondering, do you know exactly how time was to be changed?"

"Simply stated, I believe the target was your queen. She's dying, and the plan might have been to keep her alive using one of our potions."

"But how would that change time?"

He smiled. "She's not a very good ruler, but the next one will be. That is, if she is crowned. Otherwise the world will be thrown off course."

She felt a shiver down her spine. She had heard something like that before. Where? Rotan. The woman she'd seen once near the shore by the manor and again

273

at Paulette's funeral. She remembered the words she'd spoken. *"You must put aside your fear and aid the Immortal William. Even if it may cost you your life."*

Isabel sat up in bed and gathered the blankets around her. "William, have you ever heard of a person named Rotan?"

He turned toward her. "I remember you mentioned her name at Paulette's funeral. She's a character in a children's story. My mother used to tell it to us. How did you learn the legend?"

Isabel curled her legs beneath her. "I have seen her."

William pushed away from the window. "That's impossible. It's just a children's story."

She smiled. "Like the lost city of Atlantis?"

William moved toward her and arched an eyebrow. He grinned. "That's different. How can Rotan be real when the only people who claim to have seen her are little children?"

She smiled. "That is not true. I saw her. Besides, you mentioned your mother told the story as well. Does that mean she believed it was true?"

He paused in front of her. "But it doesn't make any sense. This Rotan person was supposed to be from a race of people who dwelt beneath the sea. I suppose the closest way to describe them is to compare them to mermen and mermaids, only without the tails. They were said to be able to control the currents of time. It's a romantic legend. There's only one person who helps the Immortals. We call the creature the Guardian, but no one has seen it."

Isabel felt as though she was living in one of her fantasy stories as she remembered her conversation with Rotan. It was exciting. "The woman who appeared to me at the river claimed there is more than one Guardian and spoke of a colony of beings such as herself under the sea."

William leaned closer. "What else did she say?"

Isabel smiled. "I thought you said this was only a children's story?"

William eased down on the bed next to her. "You're starting to make a believer out of me."

Isabel pulled her knees against her chest. "Rotan said that she was very young and inexperienced and had allowed an evil being to slip into this century. She planned to stay here until the mistake was corrected."

He stood and began pacing in front of the fireplace. He paused and turned toward her. "Of course. That's it. We all wondered how the Renegade managed to escape through time without the Council's knowledge. The Renegade must have summoned the Guardian. It's so simple, no wonder we overlooked the possibility."

"Now I am completely lost."

William rushed over, kissed her on the mouth, and sat down beside her. "In this story about Rotan, the legend goes that she, or her people, I forget which, would grant any Immortal passage to another time. All they have to do is ask. If Rotan is real, and you've convinced me she is, so is this legend. In ancient times the original Council must not have trusted Rotan's people. They devised a set of checks and balances. Only authorized leaps through time were sanctioned." He laughed. "We thought there was only one Guardian and he, or she, was under our control."

Isabel remembered the look of confidence in Rotan's eyes. "I cannot speak about the rest of her people, but I definitely had the impression she was not the type of creature who could be controlled."

William laughed again. "This is great. If the legends about Rotan and her people are even half right, you're correct. They claim the Guardians appear, in their true form, to children and to adults they trust. I think it's this part of the legend that convinced the Council the stories were just myths—in the Council's infinite ego, they felt no being would choose children over them."

William continued. "This is priceless. I can hardly wait to tell my uncle." He hesitated. "Wait a minute. If Rotan is real, the question should be why she appeared to you. I've never heard of that happening before, unless…"

Isabel shivered as William turned toward her. "Why are you looking at me in that way?" she murmured. She did not want to tell William about Rotan's warning. Besides, the Renegade William searched for was probably dead. There was nothing to worry about.

William grew serious. "We all have been down to the river. Why wouldn't the Guardian appear to Angus, Myra, or myself?"

Isabel shook her head. She was as perplexed as William. He paused. "Why would Rotan appear to you?"

William lowered his voice and repeated the question. Isabel had the feeling he was not looking for an answer from her but was posing it to himself. He paced around the room, picking up containers of perfume, or looking at a piece of clothing. He paused near a tray of bread and cheeses. Still staring at the platter, he spoke.

"A few days ago, Angus and I were waiting to speak with the queen's physician, John Campbell. I thought he might be the Renegade I sought. Were you the one who brought the tray of food?"

"Yes. It is not part of my normal duties, but John Campbell insisted. I could not refuse."

"That sounds suspicious. What exactly did you bring? I mean, is it the same every day?"

Isabel curled her legs tighter. "It is Myra's special recipe made with almonds. It is a sweet drink used to mask the bitterness of the medicine the physician gives to the queen. Why do you ask?"

He rubbed the back of his neck, and his mood changed. He laughed. "Of course. It's the perfect plan. The Renegade uses the disguise of a physician to give the dosages of Elixir to the queen. No one would suspect. It's pure genius. A queen who is supposed to die, lives—and presto, time is changed, and no one suspects a lowly physician is responsible."

Isabel shook her head. "I do not understand."

"Isabel, this information is classified. I really shouldn't be telling you…" He cleared his throat. "Okay. I promised to answer all your questions, so here goes. I've compromised a few dozen rules already, one more won't make any difference. The potion this physician is using is called the Elixir of Life, so named because it was used in the Beginning Time to prolong life. It cheats death. Some believe if used in a controlled, consistent manner, it can turn a human into an Immortal. But so far, we've been unable to duplicate what our ancestors accomplished. The most that happens is the subject experiences a fountain of youth effect, followed on its heels by accelerated aging. But a lot of damage can be done in the process."

Her hands clenched at her sides. "And he used me to give the queen the Elixir. Now it makes sense why the queen's dog, Snowball, looked so ill the other day. Either John Campbell stopped giving the animal the Elixir, or the aging process has resumed. We never suspected the truth. Myra was concerned, though, that because I was the one giving the queen her medicine, I would be blamed along with the physician."

William nodded his head. "Myra could be right. The Renegade was hiding under my nose all the time. He figured I'd never suspect a man who was so badly scarred. The man is a master of deception, and now I can add disguise to his list. Well, John Campbell, your secret's out in the open." He kissed Isabel softly. "I plan to pay a visit to Hampton Court and see if this John Campbell is still around. If he is there, that means the body I found at the inn was a decoy."

Isabel placed her hand on William's arm, interrupting him. "The costume ball is tonight, William. There will be so many people, it might be hard to find him."

William smiled. "Don't worry. I'm not going to let him escape this time."

Despite his lighthearted words, William had the look of a man who was going into battle. She shuddered as she watched him strap on his sword and leave her chamber. Alone, she stared around the empty room, trying to absorb all she had heard. They'd solved the mystery, but she almost wished they had not.

She slid off the bed and reached for her clothes. She must not think that way. William had to succeed. It was just that she would miss him so. Isabel shook away the thoughts. She remembered she had promised to help Myra at the costume ball tonight. Afterward she and William would say their farewells. A sob escaped her. She clutched at the bedpost for support and then straightened. No, she would not think of his leaving. There would be plenty of time for tears when he was gone.

****

William raced down the stairs to the Great Hall. The knowledge that Bartholomew had been within his grasp the whole time darkened his mood, but as he rounded the corner to Angus's study, his step lightened. He had an idea, and it involved Isabel.

After he captured Bartholomew, he'd ask Isabel to return with him to his century. The costume ball would be a perfect setting.

As he turned into the study, he plowed into Angus.

Angus laughed and spun him around. "What is the hurry, lad?"

William clapped him on the shoulder. "Isabel and I believe that John Campbell is the man I'm after. The Renegade didn't die in the fire after all. I'm going to Hampton Court right now. I just wanted to let you know."

"Need any help?"

William shook his head. "No, but do you have a lock on your cellar?"

Angus nodded. "Do you really think he's going to let you take him alive?"

"I intend to at least give him the option."

"Hold on. When you ran into me, the expression on your face did not reflect that of a man ready for a fight."

William laughed and clapped Angus on the shoulder. "Right after I have the Renegade safely tucked in for the night, I'm going to ask Isabel to come with me to the twenty-first century."

Angus looked as though someone had turned off a light in his soul. "Have you lost your mind? The Council will never approve."

"I wasn't thinking of asking them."

"Take it easy, lad. You know it is against our laws, and for good reason. An Immortal can travel through time as long as they do not change anything while they are mucking about. But it is different for humankind. They are too much a part of the fabric of this world. The risk is too great."

William wanted to tell Angus that a woman had already traveled back and the world had kept spinning, but he couldn't share the information. The event would not take place until 1566.

Angus grabbed his arm. "Are you listening to me?"

William shrugged. "The Council is not infallible. If Isabel says yes, she and I will be leaving tomorrow morning." He rushed past Angus and outside into a snowstorm.

Angus had a point—the Council would be fighting mad. But he didn't care. A list of options scrolled through his mind.

Staying here in her century was not an option for him. He had to bring Bartholomew back for justice. And if he asked the Council if he could return to the sixteenth century to be with Isabel, they would say no. It seemed that was the only word they knew these days. As head of the Council, Gavin had his hands full.

The only sure bet was to take Isabel with him when he made the jump to the twenty-first century and deal with the consequences later.

His mood brightened as he opened the door leading outside and braced himself for the storm. It wouldn't matter where they lived as long as they were together.

****

Bartholomew felt like everything was falling apart. He threw aside the blankets, slipped out of his bed, and walked over to the hearth, coaxing the dying embers back to life. He'd spent a restless night. The queen was not responding to the Elixir, and he wondered what had gone wrong.

He warmed his hands over the fire. If anything, the queen's health was worse. He could understand why that miserable dog of hers had reverted back to poor health. After all, he had stopped giving the animal the medicine. He did not want to waste it. But the queen was a different matter altogether.

The only thing he could think of was that either Isabel had diluted the Elixir or she'd stopped putting it in the queen's beverage altogether. It served him right. Every time he'd relied on the miserable people in this godforsaken century, they'd failed him. He would take matters into his own hands and deal with Isabel the way he'd dealt with all the others who'd let him down.

He turned and walked over to the dresser to retrieve his knife. He paused. That meant his stay here would be extended and he would have to continue the self-torture of disfiguring his face. When this was all over, he meant to deal a special brand of revenge to the Renegade Immortal in charge of the mission, the one who'd forced him into this horror. He hated how people shunned him now because of the way he looked. He chuckled. Before coming to this century, his appearance drew women to him like a moth to a flame. They never guessed his pleasing features hid a dark and twisted soul. Now, only his money made him appealing.

Bartholomew grabbed for the knife and then looked into the tin mirror that hung on the wall above the dresser. His breath caught in his throat as he stared back at the image that greeted him. A scream caught in his throat. It threatened to choke him. He drew closer to the image of himself, and the knife slipped from his hand and clattered to the floor.

He screamed over and over until the sound of his own voice vibrated in his ears. His voice trembled. "No. This is impossible."

Bartholomew moved closer to the mirror, not trusting what he saw. Maybe he only imagined the image staring back at him. Each morning for the past week he had used the knife to disfigure his face, and by the following day the wounds were healed. It took a full two days for an Immortal to recover from a fatal injury, but only hours for cuts or bruises to heal. That was why he had to repeat the process each morning.

His hand trembled as he touched his face. Today, however, was different. The reflection was grotesque. The face was covered with red, swollen welts and pus-filled wounds. If possible, the cuts he'd made yesterday looked even worse this morning.

Bartholomew's body shook with rage. He grabbed the dresser beneath the mirror to keep from collapsing to the floor. An insidious theory crept into his mind as he remembered *The Picture of Dorian Gray.*

His laugh was shrill, and the sound seemed to

bounce off the walls. He knew that somehow his outward appearance now resembled his dark soul. He shuddered, repulsed at the man he had become.

Anger flowed through him, directed first at himself, then to the person responsible for assigning this mission, and then back again. The blame settled on the Renegade who'd made it impossible for him to do anything else. Bartholomew grabbed the mirror and threw it against the wall. It bent but did not break.

If he was doomed to spend an eternity in this form, no one was safe from his wrath. Power was what he needed. The Renegades wanted him to do all the dirty work of extending Queen Mary's miserable life long enough for them to take control of first England and then the world. They thought they could throw him a few bones as reward.

Bartholomew kicked the bent tin mirror across the room. They had misjudged him. He would not step aside and watch them reap all the glory. He would take the whole prize. The first step was ensuring the queen lasted out the year. He turned toward his wardrobe and began dressing for the costume ball.

Chapter 27

Isabel hurried toward the courtyard at Hampton Court, where the costume ball was already in progress. Myra would be in need of her help, and a part of Isabel was still anxious to see the outcome of all the artists' hard work. Before William had burst into her life, she had looked forward to this night with great anticipation, but everything since that moment in time had changed. Now all she could feel was emptiness. Although he promised to meet her here tonight, she knew William was leaving in the morning. She glanced around, hoping he was here, but he was nowhere in sight. All she could do was wait.

The air was cold and crisp, but Isabel knew nothing would deter the nobles from the festivities. Statues of the Greek and Roman gods circled a raised marble platform in the center of the garden. A pair of six-foot-high candles with the queen's crest carved into the smooth wax stood as sentries to the celebration, and a large mural depicting the Battle of Troy formed a backdrop. The guests looked as though they were covered with a fine dusting of gold, and they moved through the glittering spectacle as though enchanted. It was an example of both immense beauty and enormous extravagance.

Isabel made her way through the crush of people to the tables laden with food. Nobles wore various interpretations of the Roman toga over their thick layers of garments. Bands of gold covered their arms, and chains of the precious metal were looped around their necks. Tonight they would follow their deepest, darkest fantasy.

Bloodred wine flowed from fountains and chased away the cold, as well as their inhibitions. Isabel reached the first of a dozen long tables that were grouped on either side of a raised platform wrapped in ribbons of silver cloth. Like the varied costumes of the guests, each table had a theme of its own. One was piled high with an assortment of sugarcoated cream tarts filled with apples, figs, or grapes and laced with cinnamon, cloves, and nutmeg. Another table was stacked with almond and cherry puddings. Other tables held roast goose, duck, or pheasant, while another held salmon and mackerel.

But with all the hum of conversation, the blending of aromas and sexual tension, Isabel felt there was yet another undercurrent in the air. The feeling of anticipation wove through the crowd and the sense this might be one of the nobles' last nights of privilege.

It was obvious the queen was dying and that her reign would end without producing an heir to the throne. With a change in monarch, many here might lose all they had gained under Mary Tudor's rule. No one was really safe from such an event. Perhaps that was the real reason for such obvious displays of excess. Even if they continued in favor with England's next monarch, there was a feeling that an even more ominous threat awaited them. The unusual weather conditions spreading throughout Europe might have a profound domino effect on the economy, putting their way of life in jeopardy.

Isabel shook a sense of dark foreboding from her as she reached Myra's side. Myra, however, was too busy to do little more than nod a hasty greeting. She and the other servants all shared the same expression. Their faces were drawn with tension from both sensing a time of change and catering to the endless needs of the nobles at the costume ball.

Jardin and Forsyth seemed the only ones unaffected by the cloak of gloom. Isabel saw them standing near the queen's dais, waiting for Her Majesty's arrival. The artists basked in the glow of the guests' appreciation. Forsyth had never looked more pleased with himself and no longer worked in the cookroom. Isabel suspected that both he and Jardin felt that after tonight their talents as artists would be in demand. Isabel could not share in their excitement. It was not the same without Ossian and Paulette. The tragedy of Paulette's murder, in addition to knowing Ossian must hide to save their son, dulled Isabel's excitement at seeing the artists' works on display.

She felt disconnected from the event. Acknowledgment was no longer important to her. She had finished the portrait of Poseidon and considered it her best work, but it was no longer enough. Isabel realized what Paulette had tried to tell her the night William arrived in London—Life was its own reward.

Trumpets sounded, announcing the arrival of the jewel-bedecked queen. She was not dressed as the other nobles but wore a deep purple-and-gold velvet gown with diamonds sewn into the fabric. The contrast made her stand out from the crowd. Isabel guessed that had been the queen's intent all along.

The Trojan horse was next and was wheeled into position. It was drawn not by horses but by six men dressed as gladiators. The crowd roared with laughter and wild cheers. All knew what was to happen next. The horse was filled with scantily clad women dressed as vestal virgins. Lewd shouts and cheers wove through the crowd, encouraging the women to show themselves. This was the signal that the celebrations were in full force. The height of decadence played out for the fulfillment of all present.

Minstrels, dressed in a less ostentatious display, wove through the press of costumes, playing hand-held harps or reed instruments. The high-pitched notes floated on the icy breeze and added to the air of anticipation.

Isabel glanced over at the queen. She did not look well, and the gown she wore was not flattering. It only emphasized her bloated body and hollow eyes. Death seemed to be knocking at the queen's door.

The music rose to a fever pitch until the air vibrated. Suddenly a cymbal clanged, and a hush fell over the gardens. The cymbal sounded again, and the vestal virgins emerged from the belly of the Trojan horse to a cheering crowd.

The applause exploded as the music rose to a fever pitch. The tempo increased. Isabel felt bodies press in around her. She needed to escape. She searched the crowd for William. The only place she wanted to be was in his arms.

Out of the corner of her eye Isabel saw a flash of red. It seemed out of place in a sea of white and gold. Her pulse quickened. It was John Campbell, and he was moving in the direction of the queen. He held a silver tray that contained a glass pitcher and goblet. Steam rose from the pitcher. No doubt it was the almond milk used to mask the bitter taste of his medicine. He was here to carry out his plan.

An icy shiver ran up her spine. William planned to come to Hampton Court in order to find this man. She wanted to believe William was still all right and had just not found the physician as yet, but there was no way to be certain. Then she remembered Paulette and the letter *R* etched in blood beside the body.

Isabel glanced quickly toward the crowd. There was still no sign of William, and everyone was preoccupied with watching the vestal virgins dance through the crowd. Cold and fear raced through her. She blew on her hands to warm them. Just as Rotan had predicted, it would be up to her to stop the physician.

Isabel turned and found Myra arranging tarts on a platter. Isabel kissed her on the cheek in a silent farewell.

Despite the cold, perspiration formed on Myra's forehead. She wiped her brow with the back of her hand. "Where are you going, child? There is much to do."

"If you see William, just tell him I know where to find John Campbell."

Myra reached for Isabel and held her arm. "What are you saying? I do not trust the man. You should stay away from him."

Before Myra could say more, she was pulled away when it was discovered the queen's favorite dessert was in ruins. It gave Isabel the opportunity to disappear into the crowd.

Isabel paused and saw a glimpse of John Campbell.

He was heading toward the back of the dais, an area draped in shadows. She withdrew her knife and followed him.

The images of the brightly dressed nobles blurred as she focused her attention on the physician. No one stopped her. Either the guards were so engrossed in the celebrations, or they felt she was of little import. After all, she was only a servant.

The physician hesitated, as though waiting for the right moment to ascend the dais. It gave Isabel the chance she needed while everyone's focus was on the dancers. She edged closer to him. John Campbell was so intent on his target that he seemed unaware of her presence. Until it was too late. Isabel stepped in front of him and blocked his path to the queen.

His eyes widened, and he growled under his breath, "Get out of my way."

She bit down on her lip to keep it from trembling. His appearance was more frightening than she remembered. Hatred for all living things appeared to be mirrored in his gaze. But too much was at stake for her to be overcome with fear. She swallowed the bile that rose to her throat and lifted her chin in renewed defiance.

"William told me who you are and your intentions. You are the Renegade that killed Paulette and intend to change time."

The physician sneered. "I claim responsibility for many deaths, but Paulette's is not one of them. However, I will be happy to add you to the list if you do not step aside and let me finish what I came here to do."

Isabel tightened her grip on her knife, hiding it in the folds of her gown. There was something in the tone of his voice that made her believe he had not been the Renegade who'd killed Paulette. That meant there were more. Isabel must prevent the physician from reaching the queen, and then she must warn William.

She held the knife toward him. "I will not allow you to reach the queen."

The expression that crossed his features caused Isabel to shudder. It was the look of death. Hers. This was what Rotan had asked of her. The evil this man possessed must be stopped at any cost. He was only one, and to release hundreds more of his kind would indeed reduce the world to a living hell.

The first step would be to prevent him from giving his Elixir to the queen. Isabel reached out and knocked the tray out of his grasp. The contents spilled to the ground. The sound of clanging metal and breaking glass was muffled by the laughter of the celebrations. The event went unnoticed.

John Campbell reached toward her, but she managed to sidestep out of his grasp. In the next instant, she plunged the knife into his chest.

He staggered back and clutched at his wound. Blood seeped through his fingers. The physician roared in anger and withdrew his sword, advancing toward her. Out of the corner of her eyes Isabel saw Jardin coming toward her. Isabel could almost taste the relief she felt.

"Jardin. I am so glad to see you. This was the man who killed Paulette."

Jardin's lip curled up in a smile. "Really? How interesting." Jardin raised her blade toward John Campbell and pointed it at his throat. "How careless. You are such a fool. No wonder you have failed."

Isabel felt a shiver race up her spine. Jardin's

response was not what she expected. Something was terribly wrong. She had the strange feeling they knew each other.

Without warning, Jardin turned toward Isabel and flicked the knife out of her hand, shoving her toward John Campbell. She narrowed her gaze toward the physician. "This mission has failed. We have missed our opportunity in this century, but we will have another chance in the future." She laughed. "As Immortals, time is always on our side. Now dispose of her quickly. It is the least you can do."

****

William had failed to locate Bartholomew, and Isabel seemed to have vanished as well. William didn't like the coincidence. Bartholomew had slipped out of his grasp every time he'd come close. He'd found his quarters, only to discover Bartholomew had gone to one of the cookrooms. That had proved to be a dead end as well, until William had been told the physician was at the costume ball. So, here he was, standing on the perimeter of the largest display of decadence he'd ever seen in his life.

Just as he was about to leave and search another part of Hampton Court, a woman's scream rose above the celebrations—and was ignored.

He instinctively knew it was Isabel. He tightened his grip around the hilt of his sword and ran toward the sound. It was coming from an alcove around the side of the gardens.

He raced forward, and his heart seemed to stop when he saw Bartholomew holding a knife to Isabel's throat. Her expression was set in stone. Whatever fear she was experiencing, she had successfully blocked.

William approached cautiously. He could not lose her.

She raised her chin in defiance. "I am not afraid to die."

Bartholomew laughed. "I must commend you on selecting such a brave woman. If we had more time, I would ask you how you do it. The women I pick are all simpering fools that deserve death. Isabel was so bold as to knock the Elixir out of my grasp before I could give it to the queen."

William forced a calmness he didn't feel and moved forward slowly. To rush Bartholomew now would mean certain death for Isabel. He must wait for the right opportunity. He visualized Bartholomew's head on a pike.

William glanced quickly toward Isabel. A smile flickered across her lips as she mouthed the words, "I love you."

He held her gaze, trying to infuse all the love he felt for her in one glance. He could not let her die.

He clenched his jaw and leveled his gaze toward Bartholomew. "Release her. She's not involved in this."

Bartholomew cackled. "Ah, what is that I see in your eyes? Concern for a humankind woman? Or something more? Most interesting. Yes, most interesting indeed, but you are wrong. She is involved. She knows too much and prevented me from fulfilling my mission."

"Let her go, and I promise to spare your life."

"But you would take me back to spend an eternity rotting in a dungeon?"

William said his words slowly. "It would be better than death."

Bartholomew sneered. "I wonder." He chuckled. "I

have a better plan. Leave now, and you will not watch your woman die. But if you make one more move toward me, I promise you that the image of her death will haunt your nightmares."

Bartholomew held William's world in his grasp.

The knife glinted in the candlelight as Bartholomew pressed it against Isabel's throat. The blade cut through her flesh, and rivulets of blood formed on the blade. Isabel clenched her hands at her sides. It was the only indication she gave that she was in pain.

William's focus centered on his enemy as he fought the impulse to rush forward and wrench Isabel free. If he failed, Isabel would die as Bartholomew pledged.

William gathered his resolve. One of his strengths was outwaiting those he sought. His steadfastness unnerved them, and when they made a mistake, William was there to move in for the kill.

All he would have to do was keep Bartholomew talking.

Screams rose above the cheers and laughter of the celebrations. Bartholomew, distracted by the sound, loosened his grip on Isabel. She seized the opportunity and pushed against him to free herself, but Bartholomew held onto her. William's instincts screamed in protest against her sudden actions. He knew they were the wrong thing to attempt with Bartholomew, but there was no turning back. William tasted fear as he lunged forward.

He was too late.

As though William was seeing it all in slow motion, Bartholomew raised his dagger and plunged the blade into Isabel's heart.

Her eyes widened as shock and pain washed over her, and her face drained of color.

William pushed Bartholomew to the ground as Isabel crumpled into his arms. He pressed his hand against her wound to try and stop the flow of blood. Wave after wave of the thick, sticky liquid flowed through his fingers, taking her life force with it.

A spasm of pain racked through her. She clutched at his shirt. "William, I have to tell you."

Tears blinded him. "Save your strength. I'll get someone here to help you."

Her voice trembled. "Ossian did not kill Paulette." She gulped for air. "They had a son. Marduk." She reached toward William and whispered, "John Campbell is not the only Renegade."

"Isabel, I know. They are many in my century, but it's no longer my concern. Save your strength. It doesn't matter anymore. You're all that matters. Hold on."

A shadow of a smile flickered over her pale lips. "William, kiss me goodbye."

His throat constricted with tears as he leaned toward her. He had seen death too often not to recognize the signs. He knew she was slipping from him. "Isabel, I will love you until the day I die."

He kissed her gently and felt the warmth of her lips fade. He drew back.

Her eyes widened again, and the haunting shadow of death passed over them.

William shouted for her to come back to him, but he knew she could no longer hear him. She was gone. His world was taken from him. Tears stung his eyes as he bent down and lightly kissed her mouth. Her lips were as cold as the depths of Loch Ness.

Hot fury replaced his sorrow and banked his anger until all he could see was the red glow of revenge. Isabel had been filled with kindness that had warmed everyone in its path. Bartholomew had extinguished the flame.

William raised his head and turned to her murderer. The fool stood as though staked to the ground. Well, William would make that a reality.

He rose slowly. "That was a mistake. Prepare to die."

Bartholomew unsheathed his sword. His eyes darted from William to Isabel and then back again. "Despite my orders, it was not my intent to kill her, at least not yet. She caught me by surprise, and I reacted without—"

"Enough!" William roared. He raised his sword and ran toward Bartholomew.

Steel on steel echoed over the walls of Hampton Court. William drove Bartholomew back toward the river. He forced his grief aside and replaced it with revenge.

Bartholomew fought through William's defenses, cutting him on the arm. White-hot pain seared his flesh. William welcomed the reality. Isabel had felt the same pain. One difference separated them—William was still alive. Anger once more burst through him like the power of a storm at sea. Molten rage poured through his blood as he pressed the attack.

William arched his sword over his head, and with one powerful stroke he sliced through Bartholomew's neck. William noted that his victim's eyes widened and then glazed over as the head toppled from the body. Blood gushed and splattered over the ground, turning gray stones to crimson. William stared at Bartholomew, expecting the self-inflicted scars covering the man's face to heal, as though in death the Immortal might be forgiven his sins. But the scars remained. It would be left to a higher power to decide Bartholomew's fate.

William's breathing slowed. His hold on his sword loosened as the blade slipped from his hand and clattered to the ground. His heart felt heavy, and its beat quieted in his chest. A heart that now beat without purpose. William turned slowly toward Isabel's lifeless body.

Tears welled unchecked in his eyes as he walked over to her. He sank to his knees beside her and brushed the hair off her forehead. Her eyes were closed, and her expression was peaceful. His heart swelled anew with the weight of his love and his loss. He would see to her burial. He now understood what had motivated the man who'd built the Taj Mahal in his wife's memory. It was a living monument that spoke of eternal love. He gathered Isabel in his arms and stood.

William heard another wave of screams from the crowd and saw Angus running toward him. The man came to an abrupt halt. A look of anguish crossed Angus's face as he focused his gaze on Isabel. Like William, Angus had seen too much death not to recognize it.

Angus cried out as though the pain he felt were a physical blow. He asked the question nonetheless. "Is she dead?"

William tried to push back the sorrow closing in on him. "Yes. Isabel is dead. I killed the Renegade who took her from us."

Angus nodded slowly, blinking back his tears. "I do not know how I will tell Myra. It will break her heart." He straightened. "We must take Isabel from here at once. I do not want strangers staring at my daughter. The queen has collapsed and is said to be dying. Soon this area will be surrounded. 'Tis a dangerous time. Myra is already on her way to the manor."

Chapter 28

William kicked in the front door to the manor and rushed inside, laying Isabel on a cushioned bench beside the hearth. There wasn't time to dispose of Bartholomew's body, and he was past caring if it would be discovered. Angus was right behind him, shouting for Myra. When he heard her answer him, he went directly to her.

Within a matter of seconds William heard a heart-wrenching scream pierce the silence. Moments later Myra rushed toward him.

Myra threw her arms around Isabel and sobbed, tears flowing in a steady stream down her cheeks. William wished he could release his grief the way she did, but he felt dead inside.

Angus walked past him and crossed to the fire to warm his hands. His back was to them as he spoke in a monotone. His voice was devoid of emotion. "The queen's guards are everywhere. Her Majesty is on her deathbed. What I did not tell you before was that I heard there is talk of blaming Isabel. Someone in the cookroom claims Isabel was adding a mysterious ingredient to the queen's almond milk drink. They suggested it was poison."

Myra stood, her hands clenched at her sides. "What should it matter now? They should let our daughter rest in peace." Her words trailed off in a sob.

A strange calmness drifted over Angus's expression. His voice rose in volume. "Perhaps all is not lost. A thought has crossed my mind. Maybe Isabel is not dead."

Myra brushed her tears away quickly. "Angus, what are ye saying? Do not give me false hope."

William interrupted, feeling a shift in their emotions, thinking they'd all lost their minds. "What's going on?"

Angus put his arm around Myra's shoulder. "Isabel always healed faster than other humans, but that still did not prove she might favor her mother's heritage. And there was no way to test the theory, until now."

William narrowed his gaze, feeling like an outsider. "You're not making any sense. What're you talking about?"

"Sit down, lad. Myra, could you bring us some tea?"

Myra was surprisingly calm, but William's own emotions were swinging from one extreme to the other like a pendulum out of control. He could not shake the feeling that Angus was throwing him a slim thread of hope. He grabbed for it.

"I don't want any tea."

Myra kissed Angus on the cheek. "I think 'tis best if I leave the two of you alone."

"Aye. But we still canna be certain. Perhaps we should not hope."

Myra smiled. "Sometimes hope is all we have." She left the room with a lightness in her step, convincing William that everyone was stark raving mad.

William roared, releasing his pent-up frustration.

"Would someone please tell me what's going on?"

Angus cleared his throat. "Isabel's mother was an Immortal."

The statement knocked the wind out of William's lungs. He backed toward the hearth and ignored the impulse to strangle Angus for keeping the knowledge from him. The good news was that Isabel would not die. A weight lifted off his heart.

William regained his composure. "Then all we have to do is wait."

"'Tis not that simple."

"But you just said that Isabel's mother was an Immortal."

Angus scratched his beard. "Aye, but her father was not. In my memory, a union between an Immortal and an individual from the humankind race, that resulted in a child, was never recorded. We do not know if the Immortal trait will be transferred to the child or not. What is more, if it is, will it possess the same strength or be diluted? 'Tis this uncertainty that is the reason the Council forbids such a union in the first place."

"I don't give a damn about genetics, or the rules of the Council. You just told me there's a chance Isabel will live. That's all I need to know."

"'Tis a slim chance at best, lad. Isabel was a healthy babe, but she also bears a scar she received from falling off her horse when she was just a child."

William felt deflated. "So she's like her father?"

"Perhaps, but there is only one test that matters. It was the one I could never risk."

William said what he knew they were both thinking. "You couldn't put a knife through her heart with the slim hope the Healing Sleep would restore her to life."

Angus nodded slowly.

The thread of hope that William was holding onto slipped from his fingers. He mentally grasped it tighter. "Then, we will wait."

"Aye, lad, that is what should be done, but we cannot. 'Tis too dangerous. By now, John Campbell's body will have been discovered, and news spread that Isabel is missing. As I said before, it is rumored Isabel poisoned the queen. With Mary ill and Elizabeth's people vying for control, blood will flow. No one is safe, especially anyone who had direct contact with Mary Tudor. I will take Myra and Elaenor a long way from here. However, you must bring Isabel to your century. That is the only place she will be safe."

William stared toward Isabel. "Are you crazy? My intention was to ask Isabel to come with me, but a jump through time is risky even in the best of circumstances. No one has ever tried it while locked in the Healing Sleep."

Angus shook his head. "We do not have a choice. Isabel cannot remain here. She is too well known. Even if Isabel were not blamed for the queen's illness, there is always the possibility someone witnessed her attack. Knowledge she survived a fatal injury would only place her in grave danger. There would be talk of witchcraft. Nay, her only hope is with you."

William glanced toward Isabel again. He hated it when Angus was right. William could try to take her out of London, perhaps France or Germany, but how far would he get traveling with someone who appeared dead? The journey would be one obstacle after another.

It would be simpler if he took one smooth path. The one that led to the twenty-first century.

****

It was almost dawn. Once the decision to leave with Isabel was made, it took longer than William liked to say his farewells. The snow had begun to melt and the river to thaw—a good sign the plan to change history had failed, but it also reminded William of Isabel's last words. She believed there were more Renegades. At the time, he'd been too concerned for her welfare to focus on what she'd been trying to tell him. Was it possible she'd wanted to warn him that Bartholomew had had an accomplice in this century?

It was information Gavin would need to know and all the more reason to return to the twenty-first century as soon as possible. The network of Renegades was more widespread than they had once suspected.

William gently gathered Isabel in his arms and headed toward the water. This next step was always one that intrigued him. In the Beginning Time, the Immortals went through elaborate ceremonies to summon the Guardian. Animals, as well as wines and exotic foods, were sacrificed to any body of water that fed into an ocean. Then, over a period of centuries, it was determined that a drop of the Elixir in a river or ocean would accomplish the same goal. In the twenty-first century, the Immortals discovered another breakthrough. All they had to do was think about traveling through time and, with any luck, the Guardian would appear.

William liked the old methods better. It seemed more exact somehow, less guesswork. He paused by the river's edge. Elaenor had kissed Isabel goodbye, and

Myra had cleaned and bandaged her wound. The only thing consoling Myra over the knowledge she would never see her daughter again was the belief that Isabel might live. William knew Angus was not as certain by the way he'd held on to Isabel's hand.

Still holding Isabel in his arms, William knelt down and dipped his hand in the water. "Okay, Rotan, it's time you appeared and jumped us to the twenty-first century."

He'd used the name Isabel had claimed was the name of the Guardian. It made the creature seem more real, more human somehow. It also made him feel closer to Isabel. He searched the river for any ripples or sign Rotan was near. There was none.

The back door to the manor banged open. Angus was shouting, but William couldn't distinguish the words. It must be a warning the queen's guards were approaching the manor. He'd better not waste any more time. He lifted Isabel in his arms and strode into the numbing water. It was now or never. He hoped this Rotan person was reliable, or it could mean the end for both him and Isabel.

Then he felt warm currents swirl around him, a sign the Guardian was near.

No matter how many times he jumped through time, the process still amazed him. Einstein talked about it, and later Stephen Hawking expressed his views on what the People had discovered thousands of years before: The laws of physics support the possibility of time travel. The faster you travel through space, the slower time passes.

William could feel the vibrations just beneath the surface. The currents churned and increased in velocity as William and Isabel were pulled beneath the water. A sound like waves crashing against a jagged cliff echoed in his ears. Air was forced out of his lungs, and an eternity passed by in a matter of seconds.

****

William broke the surface of the water and filled his lungs with the fragrant air of the Highlands. Rotan had brought him back to the place of his birth—Inverness, Scotland. What was more important, Isabel was still in his arms.

The currents that had helped transport him from the sixteenth to the twenty-first century pushed him toward the rocky shores of Loch Ness. In the predawn light, the ruins of Urquhart Castle loomed slate gray. But the stronghold was not his destination. As his feet touched solid ground, he heard voices and footsteps coming toward him.

William laid Isabel down gently, hiding her behind an outcropping of boulders and a clump of white heather. He drew his sword and gripped it with both hands. His fingers were still numb from the cold waters, but he could already feel adrenaline pumping through his veins and warming his blood. He was thankful a Protector recovered from his injuries even faster than other Immortals.

The voices grew louder, and he heard someone shout his name over the drone of conversation. He couldn't distinguish any other words, but it was evident from the tone that there was an argument in full swing. Just because someone knew he was here didn't mean they were allies. Bartholomew had died without disclosing the name of the leader of the Renegades who'd orchestrated the plan to change history.

William risked a glance around the shore. His own escape was blocked. If the men who approached were part of a Renegade band, William had two options— stay and fight or swim to the opposite shore. Swimming with Isabel was out of the question.

He edged closer to her. In the shadows she resembled someone sleeping. It was only on closer examination that the chilling reality closed in. She was not breathing. Her skin was ice cold to the touch, perhaps even more than would be normal after the bone-chilling experience of time travel. He could not risk additional exposure, especially in Loch Ness. It was thirty-two degrees in the spring and summer months, and this was the dead of winter.

Someone slipped on the loose rocks and swore. William edged into the shadows and gripped the hilt of his sword. They might know he was here, but they wouldn't be prepared for an ambush. They were behaving like men who didn't care that their approach might be overheard. They either expected to find him exhausted on the shore, or, at least, not suspicious they might be Renegades.

The men reached the clearing. Each carried a flashlight. The beams were aimed in the direction of the shore, not where William was hiding. The bright light illuminated the area directly in front of them, keeping their faces obscured in shadows.

One of the men walked to William, scratching his bald head.

William seized his advantage and raised his blade. "State our name and purpose."

The man chuckled. It wasn't the response William expected.

"'Tis Angus, lad." He shouted to the others. "I told you I should have come alone. The lad has not survived this long by being the trusting sort." He turned and grabbed William in a bear hug.

William smiled in relief. The last time he'd seen Angus in this century, the man had still had hair. Now, in addition to being bald, he was also sporting an eye patch. William laughed. "What happened to your hair?"

Angus rubbed his hand over the top of his head. "I have a need to change my appearance from time to time if I'm to remain in Scotland." He winked. "And the eye patch draws the ladies to me like moths to a flame. The only problem is I keep forgetting which eye I am to cover."

William noted that he was the only one who saw the humor in Angus's joke. The other men must not have a sense of humor. They gathered around him, stone-faced. The only one William recognized was Forsyth. The man hadn't changed in appearance, and even his clothes had the same look as they'd had in the sixteenth century. They were oversized and mismatched. Forsyth fit the stereotype of an artist who cared more for perfection on canvas than in his appearance.

The other two had the look of Protectors in training. They fired questions that ranged from what it was like to travel back in time to the skill level of those William had fought. Their faces were expressionless, their gazes intense. William knew it was an attitude they'd spent their childhood perfecting. After all, he'd done it as well.

Meeting Protectors was always the same: Their purpose was to strike fear into those they encountered.

William realized the mask they wore was not just for the benefit of those they met; it was for themselves as well. It was the fear of failure that pushed the joy of life out of their souls.

The exchange ended, and everyone stared at him in anticipation. William knew what was on their minds. Each time he returned from a mission it was the same surface chatter, followed by silence while they waited to learn the answer to the question they would never voice: Did you succeed?

William didn't want to drag it out any more than he had to. There was something more important on his mind. Isabel.

He interrupted the silence. "Bartholomew's dead. His plan to change time failed."

A collective sigh of relief gusted through all four men.

William omitted his suspicions that Bartholomew might have had an accomplice in the sixteenth century. That was information he was not about to share with Forsyth and the two Protectors.

Forsyth's voice cracked and sputtered as though from lack of use. "I was wondering. You don't have to answer, that is to say, you might not know. Strange though. So, I thought I'd ask." Forsyth paused as though regrouping to gather his thoughts.

William noticed Angus's expression harden as he moved his head almost imperceptibly from side to side. The meaning was clear—whatever question Forsyth asked, William was to answer no.

Like a child's windup toy, Forsyth began to speak. His words came out in a flurry. "So much happened the night of the costume ball. First the queen became ill, next the physician disappeared, and then Isabel…" His voice trailed off, only to pick up momentum. "Do you know what might have happened to her?"

William was thankful he'd hidden Isabel from view, and he lied. "No, I haven't a clue."

Angus slapped Forsyth on the back so hard the man's eyeballs bulged. "Hey, old man, I'm as sad about Isabel as you, more, if truth be told. She was like a daughter. But let her rest in peace. Remember, I helped you search for her, but there was so much chaos in those weeks following the queen's death that anything could have happened." He motioned to the two Protectors. "Payan. Macintyre."

At the mention of their names, they straightened as though saluting in a parade, and flanked Forsyth.

Angus turned to the artist. "Forsyth, why don't you let these men take you back to Lachlan's home. There's nothing more to be done here."

Forsyth muttered incoherently, jerked his chin down in what passed as a nod, and did as Angus ordered.

As the three men blended into the shadows, Angus held his hand toward William in a sign to keep silent. When the sound of the men's footsteps faded over the gravel path, Angus whispered, "I never did trust Forsyth, and now I am convinced he has something to do with all this. After you left with Isabel, I went back to Hampton Court to see what I could find out about the physician. The place where he died was scrubbed clean, and not a word about a body. It was all very odd. He had to have had an accomplice."

"I think that was what Isabel was trying to tell me after Bartholomew's attack."

Angus sucked in his breath. "Isabel." Worry lines crinkled around his eyes. "The coast is clear. Where is she? Did she survive the jump?"

William stepped aside and guided Angus to the outcropping of rocks.

Angus's eyes flowed over with tears as he silently knelt down and stared at Isabel. He touched her cheek. "I cannot believe it. I never thought I would see her again. You did well, lad. You kept her safe during the jump." He looked toward William. "She doesn't look dead, just asleep. Or is that just wishful thinking on my part?"

William put his hand on Angus's shoulder. "No, I agree. I think there's a chance, but I want to get her inside. Her body temperature dropped dangerously when we time-traveled."

Angus wiped his eyes with the heel of his hand. "You did well, lad. You saved my daughter. The rest is in the hands of the gods."

William said a silent prayer. He hoped the gods were listening. He gathered Isabel in his arms and headed toward the pathway. "What's Forsyth doing here, anyway?"

"Lachlan and Amber are expecting a baby. Everyone's here."

"Hey, that's great."

Angus arched an eyebrow. "Caused quite a stir with the Council, but no one tells Lachlan what to do. You should see your uncle Gavin. He's as pleased as they come. He's almost like the Gavin I used to know."

Angus paused again. "It's unfortunate the occasion gave people like Forsyth an excuse to come to Inverness. There's something odd about that one. When he was at the artist's studio, I never gave him a second thought. But right after the costume ball, when it was discovered Isabel was missing, he came to life. He became obsessed with finding her. I had the impression he thought Isabel knew something about Paulette's murder."

William wondered if Forsyth was Bartholomew's accomplice. He didn't seem the type to be giving orders, rather the one who followed them. But looks were often deceiving. After all, Bartholomew had disfigured his face in order to carry out the plan.

William shrugged. "Isabel was with the artists for a while. Maybe Forsyth was just grief-stricken because she was missing."

Angus rubbed his eye under the patch. "I thought that at first. As time passed, I forgot about Forsyth. Then he appeared on Lachlan's doorstep, insisting he come with me to greet you when you arrived. Gavin and I thought it was suspicious that he even knew about the jump. That is the reason I invited Macintyre and Payatt along. They'll be initiated as Protectors soon, and I knew they could be trusted to be overzealous and loud. As predicted, they leaped at the chance to see the return of a Protector and played their roles perfectly. They argued over who should be the one to pull you from the water. I wanted to make as much noise as possible to give you a chance to hide Isabel."

William smiled. "You're as crafty as ever."

Angus laughed. "I only get better with age. Now, let's smuggle Isabel into the house. Amber has prepared a room for her. We want to keep Isabel a secret as long as possible."

Chapter 29

Lachlan MacAlpin's home in Scotland was better described as a compound. The main building overlooked Loch Ness and Urquhart Castle, and from its top floors the town of Inverness was visible.

William carried Isabel in the back entrance and followed Angus down a long corridor. It was lined with ancestral portraits. He knew the identity of everyone by heart. It was one of the first lessons you learned as a child. Every Immortal had a portrait commissioned in the year of their thirty-fifth birthday. It was believed that it was not until you reached the age of thirty-five that the true nature of your character showed on your face and in your heart. It was also the age at which an Immortal's body stopped the aging process.

He smiled and cradled Isabel close to him. She wouldn't be as interested in who these people were as in the artists who painted the portraits.

The Immortals in the portraits were clothed in fashions that spanned centuries, as well as countries. William passed a man in a suit of gleaming armor and a woman clad in chain mail, wielding a sword, her head covered by a helmet. These were Lachlan's father and mother. Farther along the corridor was a portrait of a man, dressed in the clothes of a Roman soldier, who rode in a chariot pulled by a team of four white horses. In another portrait, a woman in a full suit of armor fought a Bengal tiger. It was a pictorial history of his race.

The corridor ended and Angus opened the door to the spacious room prepared for Isabel. William entered and glanced toward the mahogany four-poster bed. To a casual observer, the figures carved into the headboard and bedposts were only decorative. Only an Immortal would recognize their symbolism. William felt it a fitting place for Isabel. Although she was only half Immortal, he hoped the DNA from her mother would prove to be the stronger of the two.

William laid Isabel gently down on the bed. He wouldn't think about what his life would be like if she didn't survive. He'd brought her safely back to his century. The really difficult task lay ahead. He would have to wait.

****

Time passed slowly. It was four days since William's return. To him, it seemed like a hundred. He'd traded in his kilt for jeans and a wool sweater, and he spent the entire time looking after her. William only agreed to venture out of Isabel's room when Gavin requested his presence for a meeting with the Council in the Chamber of Knowledge.

The world had not changed, proof positive his mission had been a success, but they wanted the details of the mission. Right now, the last thing William wanted to do was meet with the Council of Seven. However, here he was in the damp rooms under the ruins of Urquhart Castle, doing just that.

The Chamber had not changed during the passage of the centuries. The castle above was a shadow of its former glory, but below the water line, time ceased to exist. Torches were still the only source of light and illuminated a vestibule and then a larger room beyond. Separating the two was a pair of stone dividers. Cut into their six-inch-thick surface were Celtic designs.

The Council asked if William knew who the leader of the Renegades might be. He told them he hadn't a clue. Their informant was found beheaded a few days ago, so they were running out of leads.

William, however, was not the only topic on their agenda. The newly initiated Protectors would be sworn in today. Jardin, who was elevated to the position of Historian, droned on about the purpose of each seat on the Council.

Only three positions had changed since his uncle Lachlan was leader. Lachlan had stepped down when he'd taken the Elixir of Life in order to marry Amber. An ancient law stipulated that in order for an Immortal to serve on the Council, their blood must be pure and unchanged. Marcail, Lachlan's cousin, had also left the Council to marry. Jinga Mbandi, a Warrior Queen from Angola, had taken Marcail's place.

The next position vacated had been the one held by Hsi Wang Mu. She'd always felt responsible for not killing the monster Subedei when she'd had the chance. Lachlan said she'd told him her nightmares were filled with the ghosts of those Subedei had butchered. She'd been in Paris during the French Revolution amid the era of the guillotine and had switched places with one of the nobles slated for execution. She'd died in the woman's place. Jardin claimed she'd tried to save Hsi Wang Mu's life but had arrived too late. As reward, the Council had appointed Jardin to take Hsi Wang Mu's position.

Those who still remained were the twins Artemis and Theseus. They were explorers and acted as one voice on all matters. It was a constant source of frustration to Gavin. Next to them sat Kuan Yin, wrapped in her trademark gown of gossamer blue silk. She was a living legend in China and was revered for her boundless compassion and lovingkindness. Sitting beside her was Zambodo, a great African warrior. He'd lost his hand in a battle against Subedei's forces. The ancients had failed to discover a way to rejuvenate an appendage once it was severed, so Zambodo was leading the research to find a solution.

Gavin now held Lachlan's position and was vocal in his support of setting limits for the amount of time an Immortal could serve on the Council. He believed this concept would bring new energy and new ideas which were essential elements if their race was to survive in an ever-changing world.

William scanned the room. The Council of Seven sat in silence as they studied his report. He turned his attention to Jardin. She was reviewing the meaning of each position on the board for the young Protector initiates. This familiar litany kept his mind from dwelling on Isabel, who lay as still as death. He shook the dark image from his mind as he looked over the Council seats.

Jardin droned on as she reviewed what each one should already know by heart. "Each seat on the Council corresponds to the planets deemed most important by the People during the Beginning Time. The first is the Sun and is the only position on the board that is hereditary. Gavin MacAlpin holds this position. This person acts as judge, maintaining the balance of right and wrong. The second represents the planet Jupiter. This person's role is to enforce our codes. The next is Mercury, who is charged with keeping records and recording history. Mars guards the Elixirs and supervises in medical research. Saturn supervises the wealth and property of the Immortals. Venus advises on battles or wars. The last is the Moon, who guards the secrets of the magical elements of our race, as well as overseeing marriage requests."

William looked again at Jardin. She had not changed in over five hundred years, but then, she was an Immortal. He'd not had a chance to talk with her since his arrival.

Suddenly Gavin glanced in William's direction, dismissing him. Gavin looked tired and beaten down. He was under pressure to find the Renegades, but so far, all their efforts had resulted in a dead end.

William was glad to be out of the damp chambers as he made his way to the surface. He didn't like being away from Isabel this long, and the atmosphere in the Council chamber was oppressive.

Jardin stopped him on the way up to the surface. "I want to congratulate you on your success. We have also learned that you brought the artist Isabel de Pinze back with you. Most unusual, but I suppose the nephew of the great Lachlan MacAlpin is allowed to bend a few rules."

William kept his composure. If she'd bothered to read his file, she would have known following rules was never his thing. It bothered him that she'd learned about Isabel, but keeping a secret when the compound was crawling with people was difficult, at best.

Jardin didn't wait for him to answer. "As a member

of the Council, I am aware that Isabel's mother was Immortal. Angus confessed his part in keeping it a secret and awaits our decision as to his punishment. Has Isabel recovered?"

"No."

The hair on the nape of his neck prickled. That was never a good sign. He hadn't remembered Jardin as being the talkative type, but maybe people changed over time. He knew he had. He brushed sticky cobwebs out of his way as he continued up the stairs. The Council insisted on keeping Urquhart Castle in disrepair so it appeared to be a fit habitat for only spiders and bats. The Council felt it would keep the curious tourists away. It worked.

Jardin was talking as though he'd encouraged her to say more. She followed behind him. "Perhaps Isabel will not awaken. After all, her blood is not pure."

That was blunt. William was determined not to let it bother him and decided to change the subject. For some reason Isabel felt that not only was Ossian innocent of Paulette's murder but there was another Renegade involved with Bartholomew. Maybe as a member of the Council Jardin had heard what had happened to Ossian after he'd left London. Ossian might have a clue as to the identity of Bartholomew's accomplice.

"I was wondering—did anyone ever find Ossian?"

Jardin's expression darkened. "Ah, now there's a name I haven't heard in a long time. No, after he killed Paulette, he disappeared. He was never heard from again. I am sure he is dead, and good riddance."

William heard the venom in Jardin's voice. He wondered what had caused it. He also didn't like things tied up in neat packages, but he decided not to share his opinion with Jardin. He didn't trust her. Perhaps it was because all of a sudden she was talking to him nonstop, and in the sixteenth century she wouldn't give him the time of day. It was as though she was fishing for information. Well, she wouldn't get it from him.

"I suppose you're right."

Jardin shrugged. "I heard Ossian and Paulette were together for hundreds and hundreds of years. Maybe the monotony of a hundred more undermined their relationship." She laughed. "I find I need the space and freedom to be with whomever I wish whenever the notion takes me. I cannot think of a worse fate than the prospect of an eternity with the same person."

William remembered a time when he'd felt the same. He no longer agreed with Jardin.

Jardin was talking again. "Despite my warnings, Ossian and Paulette married, and a year later received permission to drink the Elixir of Life. It was shortly after that the trouble started. Ossian may have also tired of Paulette and regretted his decision."

William remembered the story of Thia and Morag. They'd agreed to take the Elixir. Thia had held to her bargain, but when it had been Morag's turn, he'd run. Although many had offered to take his place, Thia had refused them, demanding what was her right: Death for Morag. It had taken over a hundred years for a Protector to track down and capture Morag and bring him to justice at Urquhart Castle. By that time Thia had been crumbling with age and insanity.

Lachlan said that when Angus had performed the execution and chopped off Morag's head, Thia had danced and laughed with glee around the Chamber of

Knowledge. The woman had finally been taken from the room, and she'd died several days later. But the situation with Ossian and Paulette was different. Children were the ultimate gift, and according to Isabel, they'd been blessed with a son.

He turned to speak to her over his shoulder. "I still can't believe Ossian would kill Paulette. They loved each other, and, according to you, he'd already taken the Elixir."

Jardin looked around as if afraid of being overheard. "The trouble began after the child was born. Paulette named him Marduk. I was there as a witness to the birth. Being a Protector, I am sure you will understand what happened next and realize why Ossian killed Paulette. The child bore the mark of the Protector, and Paulette refused to allow the boy to be raised as was his destiny."

William felt his blood run cold. Part of his training was to know the name and background of every Protector who'd ever lived. "I've never heard of him."

Jardin smiled. 'Tm sure you have not. I believe Ossian killed her because of it. I never knew what became of their son. Perhaps Ossian went insane and killed Marduk and then himself."

William shuddered as he reached the top of the stairs. The grass spread out like a thick carpet toward the house Lachlan had named Eternal. He'd built it for Amber and the family they hoped to have.

An Immortal parent killing a child or mate was rare but not unknown in a race where Bloodlust was the norm. Lachlan's father had killed his eldest son, Fearghus, while on a battlefield in northern Scotland. The father had been so consumed by Bloodlust that he'd been incapable of distinguishing friend from foe.

But the birthmark of a Protector—that set them apart and also guaranteed them immunity from the disease. He would never fall prey to the insanity of Bloodlust, but he was robbed of the right to choose his own destiny. Perhaps it was this fact that had prompted Paulette to deny her son his birthright.

He could not fault a mother for wanting to spare her child from such a life. His sister, Marion, had told him their mother had been heartsick when she'd discovered his birthmark and had known she must allow him to be taken from her. He often wondered what he would do in a similar circumstance.

A crowd gathered on the wraparound deck of Lachlan's home overlooking Loch Ness. He saw Forsyth flittering amongst the group like an indecisive bee in a field of wildflowers. The man kept popping into his line of vision. It was odd that he was here. Forsyth didn't have any close connections to the MacAlpin clan.

"Jardin, have you kept in contact with Forsyth over the years? Weren't you and he close at one time?"

Jardin paused for half a heartbeat and then laughed. "Close?" She pointed a slender finger toward Forsyth. "With that? He's a talented artist, for that much I'll give him credit, but we were never 'close.' When Elizabeth took the throne, she wanted nothing to do with anyone connected with her half-sister, Mary. Forsyth and I parted ways. I would hear from him from time to time. He studied in Italy, Germany, and then France. Why do you ask?"

"No reason, really. I think I'd better get back. I want to check in on Isabel."

"We didn't have a chance to talk about her. Perhaps I could see her."

"Maybe later."

William stuffed his hands in his pockets as he headed inside, toward Isabel's room. Amber was watching over her while he met with the Council. So far, he'd succeeded in limiting visitors. He wanted to keep it that way. He passed by the crush of people who called his name, ignoring them. The advantage of being a Protector was that everyone expected you to be rude.

Jardin's explanation of why she thought Ossian had killed Paulette didn't ring true. From just the short time he'd talked with Ossian, the man didn't strike him as a killer. And William had an instinct for such things. It kept him alive. The only time William had heard of a man killing the mother of his child was when he was in the grip of the Bloodlust insanity. Again, this profile didn't fit Ossian. He'd never thought about Jardin, one way or another. But today she'd just put herself on his radar screen. He decided he would make some inquiries about the talkative Jardin.

****

William combed his fingers through his hair and glanced toward the bed. Isabel lay as she had for the last four days, her dark hair fanned out across the satin pillows, her skin as white as the snow that blanketed London in the sixteenth century. However, her lips were not ruby red, like Snow White's or Sleeping Beauty's, but pale pink.

There were no outward signs of death. Rather, she resembled a person locked in a deep sleep. He only wished that, like the enchanted women of fairy tales, she could be awakened with a kiss. He smiled, realizing he must be more tired than he thought to be thinking about fairy tales.

This morning he thought he'd seen her eyelids flutter. He knew that could mean she was locked in a dream, which announced the end to the Healing Sleep. But now her lids were as motionless as granite. Every once in a while, he thought he saw cobalt blue lines encircling her wrists—the "magic bracelet" that signified that an Immortal was in the Healing Sleep—but he would look closer and the marks would fade. He noticed the sprigs of lavender Amber had picked for Isabel's room. It was a thoughtful touch, and William remembered to thank her for the gesture.

He went over to the stone fireplace. Lachlan's compound was equipped with all the modern conveniences. William felt, however, that the fire would make Isabel feel more at home as she made the transition from the sixteenth century to the twenty-first. His gaze blurred as he stared at the flames. If she recovered, that is.

Isabel must not die. He no longer wanted to be alone. The thought clutched at his heart. He touched his chest as though a weight had lodged there. From the moment he'd brought Isabel to his time, he'd never given up hope. He glanced toward the four-poster bed where she lay as still as though she were carved from a single block of stone.

He walked over to her and stared down, willing her to awaken. He brushed the hair from her forehead. She'd done the same for him when he'd first dropped into her world. It seemed so long ago. It seemed like yesterday.

The fairy tales he'd thought of a short time ago

swirled in his mind. They promised true love and happier-ever-after endings.

"It couldn't hurt." William leaned down and kissed Isabel lightly on the mouth. "Awaken, my love," he whispered.

A dog's bark startled him. He turned toward the sound. "Misfit? What're you doing here?"

The dog bounded into William's outstretched arms, wagging his tail and slathering William's face with his tongue.

Angus stood in the doorway holding a long cardboard tube under his arm. "Gavin insisted the mongrel be brought here from Montana in his private jet. I'm sure we broke a dozen or more international rules along the way by smuggling Misfit into Scotland."

William laughed and scratched Misfit behind the ear. "I thought my uncle didn't like dogs."

"I was as surprised as you. I guess he's trying to change. Hey, I also discovered you didn't open the birthday present I sent you." Angus shoved the long tube toward him.

William stood and took it from Angus. He removed the rolled canvas. "It's a painting."

Angus winked. "Not just any painting. Take a closer look."

"Holy…"

"Exactly."

William felt like he'd been hit by a thunderbolt. It was the portrait of Poseidon Isabel had painted in the sixteenth century. "Angus, the Council wouldn't have approved if they'd known you'd given this to me."

Angus grinned. "I didn't care. I thought it was time I started breaking a few rules." He squared his shoulders. "I should be going."

"Wait. What's wrong?"

Angus's shoulders seemed to cave in on themselves. "I'm a fool. A damn fool. Not a day goes by that I don't think of Myra."

William could feel Angus's pain. It looked as though it was consuming him. "She knew how you felt. You loved her."

Angus's eyes narrowed, and anger laced his words. "Did I? Not enough to challenge the Council and give up my Immortality. I used to think it was the most important thing in my life. What an idiot. In the end, I was as much responsible for Myra's death as the ravages of time. I broke her heart. I was on an assignment when I heard she was dying. I went back to be with her." A sob choked him. "She refused to see me. I never had a chance to say goodbye."

"Angus, don't do this to yourself."

Angus pulled away. "I'm fine. I'll survive." Anger wove through his words. "I always do. Just promise me you'll not make the same mistake I did. There's nothing as important as love. 'Tis the only reality. Lachlan understood, and when I finally did, it was too late." He turned. "I have to go, but Amber said she would be glad to watch over Isabel again so you could get out in the fresh air."

"I was outside just this morning."

He laughed. "She said you'd say that, but a visit to the crumbling ruins of Urquhart doesn't count. You'd better do as the lady requests. She always gets her way in the end."

As the door closed behind Angus and clicked in place, William examined the portrait he held. He expected to see Isabel's stylized letter I. Instead, he saw the name Isabel de Pinze. Pride swelled within him. Isabel had found the courage to sign her name in strong, clean brush strokes.

He set the portrait on the table and walked over to the bed, staring down at the woman he loved. Isabel had so much to offer the world. He reached for her hand and once more thought about fairy tales. It had taken a hundred years for Sleeping Beauty to awaken with a kiss. Isabel was worth the wait.

Chapter 30

"William, what are you planning to do? Hasten your own death? I know Amber recommended you get outside, but you've taken it to the extreme."

William downed a container of water before speaking. He'd run to Inverness and back, a total of sixteen miles, round trip. It had been a good workout. It had gotten his heart pumping and had controlled the stress, or at least that had been the plan. But all he had done was think of Isabel. At least his body felt rejuvenated after four days of inactivity.

He stretched his muscles. Sweat clung to his body as he glanced over at the loch.

Angus was beside him in an instant. "I know what you're thinking, and it's out of the question. The water's too cold."

William smiled. "For you, maybe."

Angus folded his arms across his chest and frowned. "I may act older than any living Immortal, but this body is as fit as yours. Instead of throwing down a challenge, why don't we talk about what has you as skittish as oil on a griddle? You are training like you intend to compete in the Boston Marathon."

"Not a bad idea."

"William. Talk to me."

William paced back and forth. His adrenaline rush from the run had almost worn off. He raked his fingers through his damp hair. "I don't know what I'm going to do if Isabel doesn't survive."

Angus stuffed his hands in the pockets of his jeans. "You will go on."

"Like you?"

"Don't compare us. We are not the same in that regard. You were never given the opportunity to choose between Immortality and life with Isabel. I failed the test. This is something you have to work out on your own. I'm finished with the lecture. Besides, I have problems of my own. I'm on my way to meet with Jardin. Gavin says I have to endure a reprimand for keeping Isabel's parents a secret. Almost forgot. Lachlan wants to meet with you in his study. He said it was urgent."

William watched Angus head down the path leading to Urquhart Castle. Then, turning toward the house, he entered the side door and walked down a long corridor that led to Lachlan's study. When he reached the room, William paused. The carved double doors were already open.

Lachlan's study was a reflection of its owner. Floor-to-ceiling built-in shelves hugged the walls and were stuffed with books. Before Lachlan and Amber wed, he was a medieval history professor at the University of Edinburgh. Lachlan was the author of many of the books on those shelves. The furniture was mahogany leather and seemed to blend in with the dark wood floors. A crystal vase filled with a bouquet of heather and wildflowers sat on Lachlan's desk. William suspected this last touch was Amber's influence.

A fireplace as large as any William had seen in the castles in Europe dominated the far wall. A fire blazed, and flames rolled around the logs in the hearth. A pair of Claymore swords were crossed and hung over the mantel. He'd heard that sometime in the eighteenth century Lachlan had set aside his weapons, never to pick them up again. It was rumored that while fighting on a battlefield in France he'd almost killed Gavin.

William heard laughter. Gavin and Lachlan were in the far corner of the study, engaged in a game of chess.

"That makes five games out of five." Lachlan laughed.

"Admit it, little brother, you are not the man you used to be."

It was difficult for William to imagine that before Lachlan met Amber, he was considered as cold and emotionless as the steel of his sword.

Gavin's laughter was as hearty as Lachlan's. "It's all part of my strategy to wear you down with overconfidence. Let's make the outcome more interesting. The winner of the next round takes over as leader of the Council."

"That is your position. I would not deprive you of the pleasure. Besides, I cannot rule, remember. I have taken the Elixir and am no longer Immortal."

Gavin raised an eyebrow. "That rule is only one of the many I plan to change."

Lachlan noticed William. "'Tis good to see you, lad. Why don't you close the door." When it clicked into place, Lachlan stood and motioned for William to join him. "You are just in time. Come, you can help ease some of Gavin's concerns."

Gavin stood as well, as though unable to sit still. All humor was gone from his face. "That's not true. I have moved past concern and am now onto a case of white-hot fear. I don't know who to trust on the Council. Zambodo and Queen Jinga's loyalty are without question. And I believe Kuan Yin is at least open to change. But the rest of them oppose me openly. At first I thought the Renegades were just a band of disorganized Immortals that found it difficult to conform. But when Bartholomew's escape was orchestrated, Lachlan and I began to feel it was something more. We believe there's a Renegade on the Council. Maybe two."

William stuffed his hands in the pocket of his jeans. "What do you think of Jardin?"

"Interesting you should ask. She's our prime suspect. Jardin and I fought together in both world wars. She's a good soldier to have on your side, but don't cross her. She respects only one position—her own."

Lachlan put his hand on Gavin's shoulder. "The time to act is upon us. We don't know for certain who we can trust on the Council, so we will not seek their aid or advice." He turned to William. "I have read your report but do not share the Council's opinion that the Renegades will crawl back into their holes. They risked much to send Bartholomew through time. Just as we seek to find those responsible, so too will they seek to eliminate anyone they feel might expose them."

William folded his arms across his chest. "What do you have in mind?"

Lachlan shook his head. "There seems to be a more than normal interest in Isabel. I think there are those who fear she will recover. Perhaps they believe she knows who helped Bartholomew. I believe they will try to kill her."

William had a bad feeling. 'Tm not going to like your plan, am I." It was not a question.

Gavin was the first to speak. "No, I don't think you'll like it at all."

William raised his voice. "I won't put Isabel in danger."

Gavin moved toward him. "I can't know what you're feeling, but my brother is right. We have to force their hand. The formal announcement of Lachlan and Amber's child tonight is the perfect opportunity. It's either that or wait for them to kill us one at a time."

William rubbed his forehead. "Do you really think that will happen?"

Lachlan nodded and sat down again. "Aye, there's little doubt." He picked up the pawn. "William, join me in a game of chess, and we can sort out the details. My instincts tell me you are very good at this game."

****

As William opened the door to Isabel's room, all was the same. He also realized one thing more. Lachlan and Gavin were right. He hated their plan, but he also agreed that they didn't have much choice. William glanced toward the bed. Isabel looked as though she were asleep.

A wave of disappointment crashed against him.

He pushed it away as he saw Amber set down a book and get up from a wingback chair. She was watching over Isabel while he was away. He was a little in awe of Amber. She'd managed where many had failed. Her faith that Lachlan could overcome the Bloodlust that had consumed both his mother and father had succeeded where others had failed.

A calico cat jumped down from the window seat

and scampered by her side. It alternated between darting ahead and weaving in and out of her legs as she walked toward William.

Her face and hair glowed in the light spilling through the window. He'd heard it said that women expecting a child shone with an inner glow. Well, it was certainly true of Amber.

She nodded, expecting to pass him on her way out the door. They'd never spoken more than a half dozen words in the past, and he figured she didn't expect anything would be different now. However, William needed to talk to her.

"Thank you for watching over Isabel, and for the bouquet of lavender."

She seemed startled he had spoken but quickly regained her composure. "You're welcome."

The seconds ticked by. He felt the cat rub against his legs and bent to pick her up, rubbing the cat behind her ear. "Amber, there's something I'd like to ask you."

She smiled. "You can ask me anything you like." She patted her stomach. "I am feeling rather generous of late."

"First of all, congratulations. When's your baby due?"

"July fourth." She laughed. "I told Lachlan it was a fitting date for our child, since I was born in the United States. It proves we should spend more time there."

The cat purred contentedly in the crook of William's arm. He smiled, enjoying how easy it was to talk to Amber. "What did my uncle have to say about traveling to America?"

She smiled. "Oh, you know Lachlan. He did his share of grumbling. I think he even stated that the only civilized place to live was Scotland. I told him I liked it as well, but a place with more sunshine, now and again, might be worth exploring."

William knew Lachlan might complain, but he would drain the loch if Amber asked him to. "So when do you leave?"

She laughed. "Gavin asked us the same thing. I told Lachlan that spending the baby's first Christmas in Arizona would be ideal, and he has already chartered a plane." She paused. "You have a wonderful way with animals. Una doesn't like most people."

William looked down at the cat, remembering Elaenor's patient instruction on how to hold animals. Una was purring contentedly in his arms. "Well, I'll be darned. My mother would never believe it."

"Oh, yes, she would. Lachlan said his sister often talked about you with fondness. She said you had a good heart, despite your belief that a Protector didn't need one. You only needed to fall in love with the right person." Amber smiled again. "Well, now that you are here, I should probably be going. Lachlan will be on the verge of sending out a patrol." She chuckled. "I swear that man would wrap me in cotton until the child was born, if I let him."

She silently walked around William and headed toward the door. He didn't want to miss this opportunity.

"Amber."

She turned, expectantly. "Yes?"

"Can I ask you a question? And you don't have to answer if you don't want to."

"Humm. I'll tell you what I'll do. You ask your question and I'll let you know. Agreed?"

He nodded slowly. "How did you decide to stay with Lachlan, even knowing he was an Immortal? It's a question I wanted to ask Myra but never had the chance."

She laced her fingers together. "Is that really your question, or is it something else?"

"What do you mean?"

"Aren't you really asking if Isabel will stay with you?"

"Thank you for not saying 'if she recovers.' "

Amber reached over and squeezed his hand. "If you only know one thing about me, it's that I like to dwell only on the positive. The negative takes too much energy. To get back to your question, Isabel is half Immortal, so that should ease some of your questions."

"She may still grow old at a faster rate than I."

"Yes, that's true. I struggled for a long time with the question until I realized the depth of my love for Lachlan, and then it no longer mattered. Now my question to you is, do you love her because of her youth and beauty, or is there more? A woman senses such things. If she believes in the power and strength of your love, nothing else will matter."

Amber took the cat out of William's arms. "Come, Una, it's time for your meal. I'm sure Lachlan is waiting for us both with a pitcher of warm milk and shortbread cookies. Although I hope mine are dipped in chocolate." She smiled at William. "I think Lachlan has purchased enough food to feed the population of Inverness. Fortunately, Forsyth has offered to help us. He is a strange man. I'm not sure what sort of artist he is, but he's a wizard in the kitchen. Will you be coming to the celebrations tonight?"

He remembered Lachlan's plan. William had little choice.

"I wouldn't miss them."

Chapter 31

It was a cloudless night. The full moon illuminated Loch Ness and shone as bright as the floodlights lining the patio and walkways leading down to the water. The lyrical sound of bagpipes set the mood, and the tempo of the music reflected the spirit of celebration. The announcement that an Immortal was to have a child was their most important event. Particularly now, William thought, when their numbers approached extinction.

The amount and variety of food reminded him of the lavish display at the costume ball, except this banquet had a decidedly Scottish theme. Myra would have enjoyed the attention to detail. There was everything from haggis to shortbread, with generous servings of salmon and smoked haddock. In the center of each table was an ice sculpture depicting the MacAlpin crest. The image of a claymore and an oak tree, symbolizing long life, was clearly visible. The theme was carried through on gold-green-and-black banners hanging from the upper balconies. Waiters, dressed in kilts, wove through the crowd offering warm appetizers for those too engrossed in conversation to make it over to the tables. Everywhere there was a crush of people gobbling up food as though it was their last meal.

Except William. He wasn't hungry. He was too concerned for Isabel's safety.

William recognized some of the faces, but he was in no mood for small talk. It was a skill he'd never learned. He pushed through the crowd and headed toward the perimeter of the lawn that overlooked Loch Ness. Lachlan's plan kept spinning around in his head. They had let it be known that William would only leave Isabel's side if Amber could watch over her. Since the celebrations were in honor of Amber and Lachlan's child, however, Amber would not in fact be available to stay with Isabel.

With William attending the celebrations as well, it would look as though Isabel was alone. But that would not be the case. Gavin had told the Council he would be in the Chamber of Knowledge and did not want to be disturbed. The plan was for Gavin to slip away and guard Isabel.

Nothing should go wrong. Maybe that was what had William on edge. There was no such thing as a perfect plan.

The air bristled with energy. William hoped it was excitement over the birth of an Immortal child and not something else. The celebrations were in full swing. The fireworks display sparkled over Loch Ness. They reflected like stars in the calm waters, and with each new explosion of color he heard a sigh of appreciation. It rivaled the Fourth of July displays William had witnessed in the States.

However, William didn't feel like celebrating. He'd just checked in on Isabel, and her condition was the same. The only thing preventing the Council from declaring her dead was Gavin's influence, but that would not last indefinitely.

He saw Angus sitting on a bench looking toward

the fireworks display. William knew Angus was aware of Lachlan's plan to appear to leave Isabel unguarded. The man looked calm. It made William feel confident. Maybe they were all worrying for nothing.

A new kaleidoscope of color burst over the loch and crackled in the sky as William approached Angus. He noticed Angus was holding the small framed picture of Myra that Isabel had painted for him. William admitted that until he'd fallen in love with Isabel, he'd never even come close to understanding how sharp the pain could be when you lost the person you loved.

He put his hand on Angus's shoulder and concentrated on keeping his voice light. "Great celebration."

Angus stiffened and tucked the picture of Myra into an inside coat pocket. He blinked. "Aye, that it is, lad." He cleared his throat. "A special time." He reached for a plate of food on the bench beside him and took a bite of steak pie. "But I feel naked without my sword. Blast the Council's order that we check our weapons out of respect for the occasion. It's not right." He spoke between mouthfuls. "By the way, how's Isabel?"

"The same."

Angus glanced back toward the display of lights. "Don't give up hope. She's a strong one. If anyone will survive, it's Isabel. I don't care what Jardin or some of the other Council members have to say on the matter."

William heard warning bells going off in his head. "What did she say?"

Angus harrumphed. "I know Jardin's supposed to be the best woman warrior since Boadicea, but sometimes I think it would be better if she kept her opinions to herself. In addition, on tonight of all nights, she's going around saying that because Amber is humankind her chances of bringing her babe to term are slim to none."

William sat down beside him. He was stunned by the cruelty of Jardin's remarks. "Why would she say that?"

"She insists a union between an Immortal and humankind was forbidden for a reason. To prove her point, she insists she knew Isabel's parents. I was stunned. You'd think she would have said something to me about that when Isabel was painting at the studio."

"I agree. That is odd."

William gazed at the calm waters. They mirrored the fiery explosions of light and were as much a mystery to him as Isabel's life. Her parents were the biggest question of all.

"While we're on the subject, why don't you tell me about Isabel's parents?"

Angus sighed. "I know only bits and pieces, not the whole. I'd known Isabel's mother, Marguerite de Pinze, for a long time. If I'd been a betting man, I would have wagered she would be the last Immortal to drink from the Elixir of Life. Her family, like Lachlan's, had their share of Bloodlust. Marguerite survived its curse but vowed never to have children." Angus smiled. "That was, of course, before she met the pirate Paul Tuitean."

Angus reached down, picked up a pebble, and threw it toward the center of the loch. They were too far away to see if it hit its mark. Angus didn't seem to care and settled back down.

"Damn waste. I heard there was a battle and thought I'd join in the fray. By the time I arrived, the meadow was stained with blood and littered with the dead. I found Marguerite's body and, a short distance away, Paul's. It was then I heard a baby cry. It was evident one of the child's parents had placed her in a basket and lodged it between two limbs in an ancient oak tree. The child's name was pinned to her clothes. I believed Isabel's parents had been caught up in a clan war, but now I'm not so sure. I don't know why I didn't think of this sooner. Marguerite was beheaded, while Paul was not. Whoever killed them knew who they were."

William felt a shiver up his spine. "Isabel was fortunate you came along when you did."

"Aye, and it was a double blessing. Myra yearned for the child I could not give her."

Angus's emotions were closed off again as he spoke Myra's name. He seemed to retreat farther and farther into himself His words droned on. "Jardin claimed Isabel was not their first child. Marguerite had two miscarriages before Isabel was born."

"So that's the reason Jardin told Amber she might not carry her baby to term?"

"Aye."

William clenched his fists together, remembering how happy Amber had looked and sounded earlier today. "I'm surprised Lachlan didn't kill Jardin."

Angus arched his eyebrow. "Oh, he still may. Except right now, he's with Amber, trying to ease her fears. He told me he was taking her to Inverness, but not to let anyone know. I guess he figured with so many people here, no one would notice their absence. I believe the real reason is that he doesn't trust himself to remain calm if he sees Jardin." Angus finished his meat pie. "Gavin has already asked that she be voted off the Council. She's been a thorn in his side and has blocked change since the moment she was appointed. This was just the last straw. I heard Gavin's disapproval of her didn't go down well. It will be interesting to see how things work out. She has a lot of supporters."

Angus wiped his fingers on a napkin. "Lachlan's spared no expense. I think this is the finest birth announcement celebration I've ever attended. And Forsyth's cooking is food fit for the gods. Who could have guessed that pale shadow of a man was a talented chef as well as painter? There's enough food here to feed the whole town of Inverness. Good thing, too, as there are a number of people I don't recognize."

William felt uneasy. "Really? I would have thought you'd know everyone here."

"Surprised me as well. The only one I'm concerned about, however, is that sullen mountain of a man with blond hair." Angus cocked his head in the direction of a door that led inside the house.

The man in question leaned against the red brick wall near the entrance. He wore a traditional kilt in colors William didn't recognize. His arms were folded across his chest as he surveyed the crowd. The guy reminded William of how a hawk looked when he was searching for its prey. There was also something about him that was familiar.

William rubbed his neck. "Do you know his name?"

"No, and when I tried to talk to him, he just walked off as though I was talking to the wind." Angus held his stomach. "Hell. I think I ate too much." He straightened and burped. "Ah, that's a little better. Where were we?

Oh, yes, the stranger. Maybe you can get him to come around. I think I'm going to find something cool to drink. It might help put out the fire in my gut."

"No problem. I'll see what I can find out."

Angus stood. His shoulders slumped forward. He made his way to the side of the house, where a long table was brimming over with iced soft drinks.

William turned to where the stranger had stood moments before. The man had vanished.

Curious. It was probably nothing. The fact Angus didn't know him couldn't be that unusual, nor was the fact that the man was unwilling to tell Angus his name. There was probably a logical explanation.

Like hell.

William decided to go on a little hunting expedition of his own. He passed the tables of assorted beverages and desserts. They were unusually devoid of people. And there was something else. The bagpipes had stopped playing. Maybe, like Angus, the guests were finally finished eating. Maybe the celebrations were winding down. He glanced at his watch. It was only eight p.m., too early for party-loving Scots to call it a night.

Then he heard it. Or rather, the silence hit him louder than a sonic boom. Where was everyone? It was as though they'd all gone home and neglected to tell him. Even the constant sound of fireworks had ceased.

The word "odd" didn't come close to describing the unease he felt coiling around his stomach.

He turned the corner and nearly tripped over a body. The man's eyes were glazed over, and foam oozed from his mouth.

"What the…"

William looked around. In the shadows, bodies were littered around the side patio like confetti after New Year's Eve. Men and women looked as though they'd tried to make it to the beverage table, as if they'd been searching for water in the desert.

Some people lay sprawled on the ground, while others were slumped over chairs. He found Angus face down in a flowerbed. William knelt down and turned Angus on his back. Angus's eyes held the same glazed look as the man William had almost tripped over.

A list of possible explanations rapidly clicked through his mind. Poison gas. A gun with a silencer. And then another possibility surfaced. The last time he saw Angus, he was complaining that his stomach was bothering him. Since William hadn't eaten anything tonight, the list narrowed.

Food poisoning.

William stood slowly. This scenario fit Bartholomew's preferred method of killing. But the man was dead. There was no doubt on that point. However, they hadn't yet found the person who'd orchestrated Bartholomew's escape into the sixteenth century. Maybe they shared a preferred method of murder.

Lachlan and Gavin were right. The Renegades were making their move, but it wasn't just Isabel they were after tonight—they wanted to eliminate the whole MacAlpin clan.

Then he heard an unmistakable sound. It turned his blood to ice. It was the sound a sword makes as it slices through flesh and bone.

Instinct took over as William reached for his blade. It was gone. William remembered Angus's frustration that weapons would not be allowed during the celebrations.

Isabel.

She was in danger. He could feel it.

William eased silently into the shadows and hugged the wall. He needed time to think. What he really needed was a weapon. He had no idea how many Renegades there were to deal with. He suspected their plan was to poison everyone, and then chop off their heads at their leisure. It was the mark of a coward and someone with access to the kitchen. He tried to speculate on who fit the profile. It had to be someone who was Bartholomew's contact in both the twenty-first century and the sixteenth. Forsyth.

Amber had mentioned that Forsyth was involved in tonight's preparations. No doubt he'd poisoned the food, but William was convinced he hadn't acted alone.

William heard the sound of laughter as a sword cut through flesh again. He could rush out and try to overpower the assailant, but without a weapon or knowing how many there were, it would be suicide.

William heard movement behind him and turned. It was the stranger Angus had pointed out to him earlier. The man was moving toward him as quietly as a cat. He stepped over a body and crept toward William. There was a sword in each hand.

William ducked farther into the shadows, and when the man drew near, William noticed the weapons he held were clean. Either the man had a cleanliness fetish and wiped blood off his weapon each time he made a kill, or he was not involved. If that were the situation, William now had an ally. If not, he would just relieve the stranger of his weapons.

Another swipe of the sword broke the silence. The stranger straightened and looked toward the sound. As he turned, William sprang into action.

He gripped the man from behind and put his arm around his neck. "Who are you?"

"The Avenging Angel."

William tightened his grip on the man's neck. "Try again."

The stranger choked. "Name's Marduk. But we're wasting time. They'll all die if we don't hurry."

It was Ossian and Paulette's son. William wanted to ask him where the hell he'd been for over five hundred years, but Marduk was right. This wasn't any time for pleasantries.

William loosened his hold a fraction. "I'm listening."

"I brought you a weapon."

William took a chance. He released Marduk and caught the sword he tossed to him. William tested the weight of the blade, arcing it through the air. "How do I know I can trust you?"

"You don't. But what choice do you have?"

William liked the man's logic and recognized the blades. "The swords belong to Lachlan."

Marduk shrugged and grinned. "It was either these or his letter opener."

"Good choice."

"I thought so." Marduk glanced over the deathlike quiet of the grounds. "Any idea what happened here?"

"I figure someone poisoned the food, and now they intend to finish the job without a fight."

Marduk swung his sword, testing its weight. "That sounds about right. It must be some kind of power play." He leveled his gaze. "I say we kill anyone still standing and ask questions later."

"Sounds good to me. I'm going to work my way into the house. I think they plan to murder Isabel as well."

"The woman who time-traveled back with you from the sixteenth century?"

William nodded. Marduk seemed to know a lot for a man who appeared to have dropped out of nowhere. Well, if they survived this night, there'd be plenty of opportunity to fill in the blanks.

Marduk pointed his sword toward the rear of the house. "I'll clear you a path."

William gripped his sword. "Let's go."

They rounded the corner and saw Artemis, one of the members of the Council. He stood over the unconscious body of a newly initiated Protector, Macintyre. Artemis arced his sword over his head, preparing to administer a killing blow. Before Artemis could accomplish his goal and sever Macintyre's head, Marduk sprang into action. He blocked Artemis's attack with his blade.

Marduk shouted, "I can take care of this one, you go on."

William didn't know where Marduk had been all these years, but if he were ever to take on a partner, this guy would be his first choice. He caught a glint of steel farther ahead and ran toward it. He heard the clash of metal on metal behind him as he surged forward. Instinct told him Marduk had matters well in hand.

In the artificial glow of a gas lantern, Theseus stood over a body. His eyes gleamed in an unnatural glow as he held the severed head by its hair, as though displaying a trophy. It was eerie, reminding William of executions in the Middle Ages. It chilled him to the bone.

William saw Theseus's eyes widen as the man realized he wasn't alone. As though in slow motion, Theseus set the head down and slowly turned toward him. "Why aren't you dead?"

"I was just about to ask you the same question, but I'm prepared to remedy that situation."

"Funny, I was thinking the same thing." Theseus roared and charged.

William sidestepped, turned, and struck the man's blade. The blow vibrated through him. He struck again, driving his assailant back as the coward fought for survival. He ducked as Theseus swung his blade wildly. William drove his blade into the man's chest and grabbed him before he fell.

William ground out his words. "Tell me who's behind this and why, and I'll spare your life."

Theseus coughed up blood as he clutched at the gaping hole in his chest. His laugh sounded hollow. "The why is no secret." He coughed again. "Gavin's too soft. He wants to change our way of life."

Theseus's voice trailed off as his eyes rolled and his head lolled back. The man drifted into unconsciousness before he could say anything else.

William released his hold and let the body slump to the ground. "Damn."

Marduk appeared and glanced in Theseus's direction. "Well done. Did he tell you anything?"

"Only that we were right. It's some kind of takeover. The idiot fainted before he could give me a name. How about you? Any luck?"

"No, nothing. Could be they don't even know who they're working for."

"My thoughts exactly. You go around to the front. I'm going to check the house."

Marduk nodded as he disappeared into the shadows.

One thought sounded over and over in William's mind—He had to reach Isabel before it was too late.

Chapter 32

Isabel remembered the pain first. It seared through her, disappearing as quickly as it occurred. Memories scrolled out of sequence through her mind. The look of passion in William's eyes as they made love. Myra comforting her after she burned her finger trying to pick up an iron pot. Her father's look of fear as he hid her between the limbs of a tree. Her father? How could she remember his face? Before she could dwell longer on the image, another took its place.

Angus teaching her how to ride a horse. She saw William again, and this time despair was reflected in his expression as he held her close.

Somewhere in the recesses of her mind she knew she was dreaming. And as realization took hold, the images faded from her mind like slow-dissolving morning mist on a spring day. Her eyes still closed, she stretched, trying to hold onto the memories. But it was like trying to grasp a cloud. Her bed felt different somehow. More firm, the covering softer. She snuggled deeper into the warmth and wondered how long she had been abed.

Then she remembered it all.

John Campbell had stabbed her during the costume ball. Myra was no doubt letting her sleep away the day in order to regain her strength.

Her stomach rumbled. She was hungry. That must

be a good sign. She stretched again and opened her eyes.

Isabel bolted to a sitting position. Where was she?

She did not recognize this chamber. It was as large as those at Hampton Court. The walls were paneled in oak, and rugs like those Angus brought Myra from the Orient covered the wood floor. Tables and chairs of a style she did not recognize were arranged in groupings around the large room. A fire danced cheerily in the stone fireplace.

She sucked in her breath. Over the mantel was the picture of Poseidon. How did it come to be here? It was to be a present for the queen.

Isabel threw back her covers and slipped to the ground. Odd. The floor was warm against her bare feet. What was more, the nightgown she wore was not hers. It fell around her ankles in shimmering folds of rose pink. She felt the cloth between her fingers. It was made from the finest silk.

She searched her memory but could not remember anything after being stabbed. She crossed to the fire to examine the portrait more closely, as though hoping it could offer an answer. Two overstuffed chairs faced the hearth. As she drew near, she saw the remnants of a plate of food scattered on the floor. Walking around toward the front of the chair, she sucked in her breath and covered her mouth to stifle a scream.

A man was slumped over the arm of the chair. He appeared to be dead.

The door banged open.

She sighed with relief as she saw a familiar face. "Forsyth, I am so glad to see you. I awoke and have no idea where I am." She pointed to the unconscious man in the chair. "Do you know who he is? And please tell me where I can find Myra. I am sure she will be pleased I am awake."

He drew his sword. "Myra is dead." He sneered. "Long dead."

Isabel staggered toward the fireplace until she could feel its heat on the back of her legs. "Dead. That's not possible. The last time I saw her, she was full of life."

Forsyth laughed. "This is priceless. You don't know, do you?"

He was changed somehow. She knew him as a quiet man who seemed to blend into the pictures he painted. Not only was there an edge to his voice now, but he also brandished a sword. Isabel was not aware he knew how to use one.

She had the uncomfortable urge to defend herself against a man she once felt was her friend. She wished she had her dagger. The only thing she could see that might be used as a weapon was a long iron poker resting against the fireplace.

Forsyth walked to the far side of the room and closed the window hangings. She seized the opportunity to edge closer to the poker. Her fingers gripped it as she hid it behind her back.

He strode toward her in a few easy steps. "It's too bad you are awake. I was hoping to do this without your knowledge. But it cannot be helped. You are a passable artist, so I will make this easy for you. Your death will be swift. I can promise you that much."

Her fingers curled around the thick metal rod. "Passable? What do you mean I am only a 'passable artist'? My portrait of Poseidon is so lifelike, the character all but jumps off the canvas."

He gazed quietly at the painting over the mantel. "You are right. Your skill has improved, but the fact remains that women have no place in the field of art. Please understand I do not want to kill you. It is for a greater cause." Forsyth arced his sword over his head.

Isabel had no intention of waiting for death. She swung her poker around and blocked the attack. His blade glanced off her weapon. Isabel swung again and hit him on the side of the head. Blood poured from the wound.

"Forsyth, I see you are no match for Isabel." Forsyth whirled toward the sound of his name.

William stood framed in the doorway. The expression on his face matched that of the god Poseidon. Isabel almost expected William to pull a lightning bolt from the sky and hurl it at Forsyth. William did the next best thing.

He lunged toward the startled Forsyth, knocked the sword out of his hand, and punched him in the face.

Forsyth crumpled to the ground like a doll without its stuffing.

Then the room filled with strangers.

William was beside her and said the obvious. "You're awake."

Someone hauled Forsyth over his shoulders and left the room. A man with a bald head, who looked suspiciously like Angus, walked toward her.

"Lass, I knew you would awaken." His smile spread over his face, and tears glinted in his eyes.

She clung to William, half afraid she was still dreaming.

"Angus, where is your hair?"

He laughed and rubbed his head. "I'll have William fill in the blanks."

William put his arm protectively around Isabel's waist. "Looks like the poison was only temporary."

Angus grinned. "Aye. Those who are awake are fighting mad at what happened." He shook his head as a shadow erased his smile. "Queen Jinga and Kuan Yin were not as lucky. But if not for you and Marduk, it would've been a massacre."

The man in the chair moaned and held his head.

Isabel turned toward William. "I feel as though I have been asleep for days and missed something of grave importance."

Angus helped the man in the chair to his feet. "William will tell you everything, lass. I think it best if I leave the two of you alone."

As the door closed, William pulled her against him. "What was the last thing you remember?"

"John Campbell stabbed me. I thought I was dying."

He brushed a kiss on her forehead. "You did."

"What?"

He nodded. "Aye, my love. You're like your mother. You're an Immortal."

She pulled back. "It's not possible."

He drew her once more against him. "Do you trust me?"

"Of course."

He took a deep breath. "Then prepare yourself for a story that's as rich as any legend you've ever heard, complete with a happily-ever-after ending."

****

A week had passed since the night of the

Renegades' attack. William stretched out on the bed. Morning sunlight streamed into the room. It only added to his good mood. He couldn't stop smiling. Isabel had recovered and was enjoying all she could learn about her new world. He heard the shower turn on again. It was Isabel's third today. Fourth, if you counted the one they'd shared this morning. She was in awe of all the wonders of his century, especially being able to control the temperature of the water in her shower.

Everything was back to normal. Or as normal as life as an Immortal could be. Forsyth, Artemis, and Theseus were imprisoned, awaiting judgment, and Amber's doctor predicted a normal pregnancy and birth. Lachlan was talking about having another celebration—this time, however, without food. The only thing clouding the victory was the fact that Jardin was missing.

He heard a soft knock on the door and grabbed for his jeans. He pulled them on as he walked over to see who it was.

"Angus. This is not a good time."

Angus jabbed him in the ribs. "I know, lad, but I just came to say goodbye. The Council asked my help in selecting a trainer for Marduk. He might be a Protector, but he's spent the last five hundred years wandering the globe on his own. He's undisciplined and has a chip on his shoulder a foot thick."

"Sounds like this would be a perfect job for you."

"I am only a mentor. Marduk's going to be fighting mad when he finds out that a woman is assigned as his instructor." Angus rubbed his bald head. "I'm getting too old for this."

William heard Isabel turn off the shower. "I should

probably get back inside."

"Only one more thing, lad. The Council wants to meet with you. Another assignment is the rumor. I think it has something to do with Jardin."

"Tell them I'll let them know."

Angus grabbed William in a bear hug. "Take care of Isabel. Don't make the same mistake I did."

"I won't."

As the door shut behind Angus, William heard Isabel come into the room.

She stood beside the bed. A towel was draped around her body, and her hair hung long and wet over her shoulders. She looked delicious.

A smile curled the edges of her mouth. "Did I hear Angus's voice?"

William joined her. "Yes. He just came by to say he would be leaving on another assignment." He took a strand of hair between his fingers. "I think the Council will offer me another mission."

"That is impressive."

He winked. "Well, what can I say? I'm the best."

"And modest, as well." She kissed him, and a familiar warmth enveloped him. She smiled against his lips. "I was thinking. Maybe I could go with you. Why should you have all the fun?"

William looked at her. "It's too dangerous. I can't risk it." She tugged at the hair on his chest. "But you said it yourself, you are the best. You could show me what to do. I love you and have no intention of letting you out of my sight. When do we have to let the Council know about our decision?"

"Our decision? Maybe I should retire as a Protector and just be a fireman or a smoke jumper."

She sat down on the bed and drew him to her. "I love you, William, but you must be mad. I saw how you reacted in the fire at the inn. You are reckless with your own life and take unnecessary chances."

"That's all part of being a fireman."

"Exactly the point I wish to make. I have given this much thought. Firefighting is much too dangerous a profession for you. I have the perfect solution."

"Am I going to like your idea?"

She leaned closer. "You will think it the best plan ever devised. I will gather the information, and you will capture the villains. You need me."

"You're one hundred percent right on that score."

Isabel kissed him and whispered, "Now that we have that settled, answer my question. How long before we meet with the Council?"

"A few hours."

Her eyes twinkled with mischief. "Well, I suppose that will just have to do, for what I have in mind."

William cupped the side of her face in the palm of his hand. "Isabel, I'd do anything you asked of me. Nothing in my life is as important to me as you. I love you."

She brushed a soft kiss across his mouth. "I think I knew you loved me the first moment we kissed. It just took me a while to realize that I love you, as well."

A word about the author...

Pam Binder is a *New York Times*, *USA Today*, and Amazon bestselling author. She loves Irish and Scottish myths and legends, travel, and most of all her family.

Pam is the president of the Pacific Northwest Writers Association and writes historical and contemporary fiction, romance, young adult and fantasy.